A MAGICAL KISS

Vivian's skin was silky, her hair shimmery. Dex let his fingers linger on her neck a moment longer than they needed to before his hand dropped.

"There," he said.

Vivian turned to face him. "Thank you."

He smiled. "My pleasure."

It was his pleasure. She was his pleasure. He ran his forefinger along her cheekbone and she leaned into his touch. She was enjoying this as much as he was. He could feel her longing mingling with his own.

He cupped her cheek with his hand, and then leaned in, hesitating for a moment in case she wanted to back away. She didn't. Her gaze met his and then her eyes closed as their lips touched.

For a moment, his lips rested against hers, then their mouths opened together and they explored each other. She tasted good. She felt good.

He cupped her other cheek, holding her gently. His eyes were closed too, but he couldn't remember when he closed them. Maybe when she had. They seemed to be in tune on everything else.

He felt himself disappear into her, and knew, for the first time in his life, that he had found the person he had been looking for—even though he hadn't realized he'd been searching.

It felt as if he'd come home. . . .

Books by Kristine Grayson

UTTERLY CHARMING

THOROUGHLY KISSED

COMPLETELY SMITTEN

SIMPLY IRRESISTIBLE

Published by Zebra Books

SIMPLY
IRRESISTIBLE

Kristine Grayson

ZEBRA BOOKS
KENSINGTON PUBLISHING CORP.
http://www.kensingtonbooks.com

For Julius Schwartz,
with love

Acknowledgments

Many thanks to John Scognamiglio for all his work on these books, and to Merrilee Heifetz for believing in them. And to my husband Dean, whose adventurous life informs these books more than he realizes.

One

"Why do all superheroes have to look like Superman?" Vivian Kineally asked as she studied the interior of her nephew's comic book. She was sitting on the stoop outside her apartment building, her eleven-year-old nephew Kyle beside her.

The sun cast its warm rays on the concrete steps and illuminated Kyle's latest hand-drawn effort. In the week that Vivian had lived in Portland, the sun had been out every day. She had no idea how the city had gotten its rainy, gloomy reputation.

"He doesn't look like Superman," Kyle said, craning his neck over the double-page spread that rested on Vivian's knees.

"Yes he does." Vivian traced the hero's chin, feeling the pen marks beneath her finger. "See? He's got the same lantern jaw that Siegel and Shuster gave the original in Nineteen-thirty-eight. He's even got the dimple in his chin."

She loved that dimple. She had always thought— and never admitted aloud—that the Siegel and Shuster Superman, the original, was the handsomest man she had ever seen. Even if he was only a creation of paper and pen.

"Superman doesn't have a dimple," Kyle said.

"Sure he does." Vivian smiled at her nephew. Kyle was thin and bookish, his round glasses sliding to the bottom of his nose. His fingers were stained with ink, and the fleshy side of his palm had traces of the red he'd used to color the book. "Take a look, especially in the first thirty years or so, before he got associated with Christopher Reeve."

"I didn't want my character to look like Superman," Kyle said. "Spider-man doesn't look like Superman."

Kyle wrapped his arms around his waist and leaned forward, extending his Nike-covered feet down three steps. Vivian's brother, Travers, kept Kyle dressed like the athlete he would never be. Vivian wondered how Kyle would do now that she had relocated here.

"Actually," Vivian said, "they all look like Superman. They have to. They need the muscles and the strong chin. Could you imagine wearing one of those costumes if you have a weak chin? You'd look like—"

"Michael Keaton in *Batman,*" Kyle said before she could. She'd made that argument before.

"You said you wanted to know what I thought," she said.

"*After* you've read it," Kyle said. "I think this one is really different."

Vivian smiled at him. Kyle's greatest dream was to become a comic book writer. Travers said that was her fault. Vivian had the most extensive comic book collection of anyone she knew—and she knew a lot of comic book fans.

When she was a kid, comic books had been her

escape. In them, she found people with secret identities and super powers, mutants who decided to fight on the side of all that was good and right. She had a super power too, although she had never thought of it as that, at least not when she was growing up. Then it had simply been something else that marked her as different.

She hated being different so much. She was teased by her peers. She used to look at the superheroes and daydream that someday she would meet one, and he would sweep her off her feet.

She could even imagine the panel art: an entire page with Superman or Batman or some other square-jawed (and dimple-chinned) superhero with a cape, carrying her in his arms, her head draped back, her arm loosely wrapped around his neck.

Vivian slid her own round glasses up her nose and stared at Kyle's art. He was spectacular for someone his age. There was a confidence to his work that most young artists lacked. His stories were still derivative, but she knew that originality took time—and Kyle had plenty of time.

She raised her head, seeing if she got a sense of her brother Travers. She was psychic, and there were some people she was particularly attuned to. Her brother Travers was one of them. So was her younger sister Megan. Until a few weeks ago, Vivian had been attuned to her Aunt Eugenia too.

"You okay, Aunt Viv?" Kyle asked.

The family question. Everyone was always worried whether Vivian was all right. It had started before she could even remember. She would say things or get a funny look, and everyone would panic. At thirteen, she'd started to black out, and her parents had taken her to specialist after specialist to see if there was some physical cause.

Then her Aunt Eugenia had come to visit. Mysterious, wealthy Aunt Eugenia, whose age no one knew and whose exact relationship to Vivian's mother was unclear as well. Vivian's grandmother once said that Eugenia wasn't a blood relation at all, but a close, close friend who had wormed her way into the family's hearts through deeds of goodness.

With family members who talked like that, was it any wonder that Vivian had fallen in love with comic books?

She smiled.

"Aunt Vivian?" Kyle was peering at her, his face owlish in the bright light.

"I'm all right," she said, the words so familiar she didn't have to think about them.

Aunt Eugenia had told the family that Vivian's blackouts were normal, that her power was growing stronger. Vivian's mother had gotten upset over the use of the word *power* until Aunt Eugenia made Vivian's mother admit what she had always feared about her daughter—that Vivian had an amazing psychic talent, a talent that seemed to be growing worse (or better, depending on one's perspective).

The blackouts faded once Vivian hit high school, but by then she was the weird kid. She wore glasses, she had been too skinny, and she had passed out all through middle school. Sometimes she blurted out things that other kids had only been thinking, and eventually they all stayed away from her.

Vivian put her arm around Kyle. He was going to face that same horrible world in a few years. There was nothing worse than middle school, especially for a sensitive kid.

"Dad's coming, isn't he?" Kyle asked, looking down the street. This was a side street downtown, with a great view of the mountains, rivers, and bridges, and the added benefit of very little traffic.

"I don't sense him yet," Vivian said.

Travers had taken the car into the local Jiffy Lube to make certain it was ready for the long drive home. When he returned, he expected Kyle to be ready to leave.

Travers wanted to stay with Vivian—and Kyle had argued for it—but they had other obligations. School was starting next week, and Travers had enrolled Kyle in some expensive gifted and talented program that no one had even imagined yet in Oregon. Kyle was heading home, and Vivian didn't argue with the decision.

She had a sense, just a sense—and she wasn't even sure if it was accurate because her senses about herself often were not—that staying in Portland would be dangerous.

"You're going to mail me your next comic, right?" Vivian asked.

Kyle's gaze returned to hers. His eyes were a pale blue like his father's. He would be reedy and handsome someday, just like his father. The relationship showed.

Of course Kyle's relationship to Vivian didn't show. Vivian, like her brother and sister, had been adopted. All three looked very different. Vivian was small, skinny, and dark. Travers was tall, slender, and blond, and Megan was a green-eyed redhead who, at twenty-five, still hadn't lost her baby fat.

"Mail?" Kyle made that sound as if Vivian were talking about communicating by Pony Express. "I was planning to scan it and email it to you."

She ran her hand gently over the comic he'd

just given her. "I like the way this feels. I can see the work you've done, watch the paper curl—"

"And my original can get lost in the snail mail. C'mon, Aunt Viv. Let's move into the twenty-first century."

It was an old tease and an accurate one. It had taken Vivian years to get a computer. She had refused to buy a VCR, and now VCRs were almost obsolete. When she moved here, Travers had given her a DVD player as a housewarming gift, and Kyle had made certain she knew how to use it before they left.

They were both afraid she'd be lonely. They were right. She'd never lived so far from her family before.

But it wasn't just her family she would miss. She had no friends here. All her friends in L.A. thought she was moving for a man. But there was no man either. There never had been.

That loneliness seemed permanent.

Then, for no particular reason, she thought of Travers, his hands on the steering wheel of his S.U.V., the radio playing Clint Black's "No Time to Kill." Travers was thinking about the words, worrying about Vivian, and trying to figure out a way to get her to come back to L.A.

"He's almost here," Vivian said to Kyle.

"Can't we just stay here with you?" Kyle asked. "I'm scared for you, Aunt Viv. Dad told Aunt Megan that the old lady was murdered. What if that same person comes after you?"

"Aunt Eugenia wasn't an old lady," Vivian said. At least, she never seemed like an old lady, although she had to be at least eighty. She had looked the same all of Vivian's life—and, apparently, all of Vivian's mother's life as well.

One of Vivian's many tasks would be to track down a birth certificate—if that was possible. Aunt

Eugenia's mansion had burned down the morning after the police found her body.

"But what if, Aunt Viv?"

Travers had turned onto Burnside, which wasn't very far away. He had the radio blaring in his S.U.V., and now the station was playing Alan Jackson. Vivian wanted to put her hand over her ears but knew that wouldn't solve the problem. Somehow Travers's environment was leaking into her own.

"Aunt Viv?"

"Sorry," Vivian said. "Your dad's listening to country again."

"Yech." Kyle wrinkled his nose. "I'm not going to listen to that going home."

"Good luck," Vivian said.

"You're not going to answer me, are you?" Kyle said. "Are you scared, Aunt Viv?"

"Scared?" She turned toward him. She was scared, but not of dying. Of living in a strange town for several months. Of testing new skills with her psychic powers. And trying to figure out all the clues Aunt Eugenia had sent her the week before she died.

Oh, and visiting the attorney who had contacted her about Aunt Eugenia's will—the one that dated from the day Vivian was adopted. Apparently, Eugenia had left her entire estate—worth several million dollars—to Vivian.

Vivian couldn't believe that Eugenia hadn't updated the will after Travers's and Megan's adoptions. There had to be another version somewhere. She just had to find it.

"I'm not scared," she said to Kyle. "Not of being murdered, anyway. They think she was just in the wrong place at the wrong time."

"I don't," Kyle whispered. "I think she knew something."

That dramatic comic book imagination of his.

Vivian would have to quell this right away. "Why do you think that?"

But as she asked the question, Travers's S.U.V. turned onto her street and sped past the parked cars in front of the other apartment buildings. He drove twice as fast as anyone in Oregon, and Vivian was afraid he'd get pulled over.

Oregon cops wouldn't be lenient on Travers. He had California plates and a California driver's license. She'd learned, in her short week in Portland, that the only people Oregonians consistently discriminated against were Californians.

"That's Dad!" Kyle said, standing and waving as if Travers had forgotten where Vivian lived during the hour he'd been gone.

The moment passed. Vivian clutched the comic book, careful not to crease its pages, and followed her nephew down the stairs. Travers stopped right in front of the building. The booming bass from his S.U.V.'s speakers blended with the sounds in her mind.

When he shut off the ignition, Vivian heaved a sigh of relief.

Kyle stopped at the bottom of the stairs, waiting on the edge of the cracked concrete sidewalk. When Vivian stopped beside him, he whispered without turning his head, "I don't want to go."

"I don't want you to either," she said. "But there's no point in staying. I might be home in a month."

Although she doubted it. Eugenia's estate was a mess. The fire created even more problems, and the murder—well, there were things about the murder that Vivian hadn't told anyone. Things she had seen, things she had felt, while Aunt Eugenia had been dying.

In spite of herself, Vivian shivered.

"You won't be home in a month," Kyle said. "I don't think you're coming back to L.A. at all."

Vivian peered at him. Her glasses had slid down her nose again and she saw a dual image of him— the young eleven-year-old crisply outlined against the backdrop of his father's black S.U.V., and a fuzzy, larger version, the man Kyle might become.

Vivian shoved her glasses back into place, pushing so hard she poked a fingernail into the soft skin on the bridge of her nose.

"You don't know that, Kyle," she said as she watched her brother get out of his car. He looked sleek, put-together, and expensive, something she always wondered how he managed to do on his accountant's salary. "None of us know that."

"You're psychic," he whispered.

"Yeah, but I'm not able to see the future. Just the present." And sometimes that was more than enough.

"I thought psychics see the future," he whispered.

"I wish I did," Vivian said. "Sometimes I think it would make life a whole lot easier."

"I don't think it does," Kyle said, and for the first time in Vivian's recollection, he sounded a lot older than eleven.

She looked at him, feeling an odd sensation, as if she were missing something. But he was already running down the sidewalk to greet his father, as if they'd been separated for years instead of hours.

Vivian followed, sighing. For the first time, she realized just how difficult life was going to be here. She wouldn't have Travers's common sense to rely on, or Kyle's jokes to give her joy.

But she didn't want them facing the same thing Aunt Eugenia had faced. Vivian could take care of herself, but she couldn't handle it if something happened to her family.

Her sixth sense had been working overtime—and she knew Kyle and Travers were leaving none too soon.

TWO

Dexter Grant looked inside the filthy box sitting on top of his pristine countertop. Five mewling kittens nosed the crumpled newspaper as if it held the secrets of the universe. They were tiny, five weeks old at best. They hadn't lost their downy fur yet and their eyes were barely open.

"I don't take animals," he said to the woman who stood across the counter from him. She was meticulously dressed, wearing a silk suit that shone in the light from the hundred working aquariums that lined the walls.

"You're a pet store, aren't you?" she snapped.

He nearly corrected her—*he* wasn't the pet store; he *owned* the pet store—but he knew that it would gain him nothing. And he already had a heck of a battle on his hands, one that was becoming all too familiar these days.

So he thought he'd try a different tack. "These kittens are too young to be away from their mother."

"She's dead," the woman said flatly.

Her son, who had been eyeing the exotic fish in the saltwater tanks, started. The boy had been Dex's clue that something was wrong here from the start. Even though the woman was painstakingly put together, the boy was a mess—his hair uncombed, his skin dirty, and his shirt ripped. He was old enough to take care of himself—maybe thirteen at most—and old enough to rebel against an obsessed parent.

"How'd she die?" Dex asked. Nursing mother cats rarely left their broods. It was unusual for one to die when she had kittens this young.

"Squashed," the woman said, moving her hand in dismissal. Bracelets jangled as she did.

"Squashed?" Dex asked.

The boy was watching closely now, as if he couldn't believe what he was hearing.

"And the kittens were unharmed?" Dex asked.

"Miracles do happen," the woman said without a trace of irony. "So how much are you going to pay me for them?"

"Pay you?" Dex choked. That part was new.

"They're stock, and you're a store. You should pay your suppliers," the woman said.

"They're mammals, and I specialize in fish," Dex said. "Besides, they haven't been weaned yet."

"So wean them," the woman said.

As if he could snap his fingers and wean the kittens. Then he shook his head. He *could* do that—he had all sorts of magic powers—but he wouldn't. The less he tampered with the natural order of things, the better.

Still, this had already gone farther than he liked. He couldn't very well give the kittens back to this woman. She would take them to every pet store in Portland and, when she discovered that stores didn't pay for strays, she'd probably dump them beside the road.

He truly despised people like her, but he couldn't do much about her—at least through regular legal means. And the things he wanted to do would get him in trouble with the Fates. He'd spent the last few decades watching his back so that the Fates had nothing to hold against him.

There were a few other things he could do, things on the borderline between legal and not, things that would at least prevent her from coming into contact with vulnerable creatures again.

"Ma'am," Dex said, "kittens this young need more than I can give them. You need to—"

"I don't need to do anything," she said. "They're your responsibility now. Come along, Harold."

Harold. Poor kid. Dex had known quite a few Harolds in his hundred years, but most had been born at the turn of the twentieth century. Kids who would make it in the twenty-first would see the name Harold as something to overcome.

The woman headed to the door. The kid followed, as if he were a prisoner being led by an invisible chain.

"I'm sorry," the kid whispered as he passed Dex. And that was what decided him.

Dex did snap his fingers—that was one of the many ways he could do magic—freezing time around him: the woman, the boy, the fish, and the poor, mewling kittens. The woman's manicured fingers just brushed the door handle and the kid was in front of the counter, the embarrassed and worried look still on his acne-covered face.

The kittens appeared even younger than they had a moment before. Dex revised their ages downward another week. Their eyes had probably just opened.

It was up to him. Look at what he'd become. Dexter Grant: Kitten Superhero. It wasn't a title he minded, although it did lack the glamour of his past.

Still, he stepped into the role. With a delicate movement of his fingers, he opened a rip in reality, searching for the kittens' mother. He found her in the woods outside an expensive house on Portland's west side, plaintively meowing for her missing children.

How did he know that was what he was going to find? This cruel woman had taken the kittens away from their mother, seeing dollar signs. The cat didn't even have a collar, and her coat was rough. She was probably a stray who'd ventured into the wrong yard.

Then Dex glanced at the boy. Or maybe she had become a companion to a lonely child.

He sighed. Maybe he wasn't just a kitten superhero. Maybe he still had some weaknesses for human beings. Now he had to do more spells, just because this horrible woman had walked into his store.

He did the spells in rapid succession. First, he clapped his hands together, bringing the mother cat to her babies. She landed inside the box—and he had to do an emergency spell before she thought her frozen offspring were dead.

The kittens started mewling, and the mother cat heaved a sigh of relief. She didn't even look confused about her sudden change of venue. She just seemed happy that she had found her brood.

She lay down and the kittens nuzzled at her teats. Dex smiled, relieved that this one would turn out all right. Then he spelled the boy, adding a memory. The boy would think he had managed to defy his mother and had brought the mother cat in on his own.

Then Dex did one last spell. He put a hex on the woman herself, making her seem poisonous to any domesticated animal that came to her for help. That, at least, would prevent this from happening again.

The kid wouldn't be able to have pets while he was growing up, but given the mother's insensitivity, that would probably be a good thing. No sense in teaching Harold how to mistreat animals. With his subtle rebellious nature and his tender heart, he might grow up to be one of those people who adopted animals instead of harming them, so long as he didn't have his mother's example.

The mother cat was purring. She looked up at him with warm, adoring eyes. "We'll take care of you," Dex said, wishing it would be as easy as those last few spells had been. He'd have to dig into his meager coffers to fix the cat and vaccinate her, and he'd have to do the same with the kittens.

Then he'd have to figure out how to give them away. He already had way too many animals at his house. He didn't want to sell the kittens at the store, but he might have no choice. He'd have to use more magic in that case. He wasn't about to let a kitten go home with someone he didn't know.

Dex snapped his fingers and the "freeze" spell ended. The woman continued her way out the door. But Dex touched the kid's arm as he passed.

"You did the right thing, bringing the mother and her kittens here," Dex said.

The kid turned toward him, stopped, and touched the box. He peered in like a hungry man being denied food. "I wanted to take them to the shelter, but she wouldn't. She said that was too far and they were just cats."

And you couldn't make a profit at the shelter.

"You know her attitude about animals is wrong,"

Dex said, treading lightly. No matter how awful a parent, a child often refused to see it.

"How come you don't have pets in a pet store?" Harold blurted out, as if he'd been bottling in the question.

Dex smiled at him. "I can't bear to part with the animals."

Harold nodded. His fingers dipped into the box and lightly touched the mother cat's back. She closed her eyes and continued purring. Dex shouldn't have worried about Harold; the cat was letting him know the boy was all right.

"I always wanted a cat," Harold said.

"You'll be able to have one," Dex said, "just as soon as you move out."

Harold's smile left. "You noticed that too, huh?"

"It wasn't hard to miss. You know, you could always volunteer at the shelter. They need extra help, particularly in the winter."

The shop door opened. A bell tinkled above. The woman stuck her face back inside. "Harold!"

Her tone made Dex jump.

"Coming, Mom," Harold said. Then he whispered, "Thanks," as he hurried out the door.

Dex watched the boy and his mother through the shop window. They crossed the parking lot, the mother berating the boy. Dex had the magic to spell that relationship too, maybe even fix it, but such intervention in mortal lives wasn't allowed. The Fates had already given him a warning, telling him that he was violating the rules made centuries before he was born.

He wouldn't get another warning. They would zap him away from whatever he was doing—even if he was saving a life—and then they'd try him, and probably send him away for a millennium.

If he'd been a slightly different man, he would have continued intervening—after all, what was the point of magic powers if you couldn't use them for all that was good and right?—but he couldn't stand the thought of the Fates' punishment.

He'd heard about some of the sentences the Fates had dealt out, like forcing master musician Apollo to listen to Wagner's *Ring Cycle* for three hundred years, which would have been bad enough even if the singers hadn't been nearly a half step flat. The last thing Dex wanted to do was be sent to some Fate-imagined hell, probably (for him) a place without any animals at all, just because he had done something he believed to be right.

So he'd had to rely on his own instincts, pushing where he could push and being subtle everywhere else. He'd done both here. If he had to defend his spells to the Fates, he'd tell them the truth—he'd hexed the mother so that no other animals would cross her path. And he'd tell the Fates that the only reason he'd spelled the boy was to make certain the kid wouldn't notice anything wrong when Dex had to bring the mother cat to her kittens.

All the things he had to do to pretend he wasn't using his magic. He resented it. And he missed the days when he saw trouble and responded, using the gift he'd been given.

Dex leaned over the box of kittens just like Harold had. The kittens were still nursing, and the mother cat was still purring. Everything looked fine, but Dex had a lot of work to do if he was going to care for these cats—and he would be the one to care for them. The local shelter was overstocked with strays and kittens, and he didn't want to throw more into the mix.

Someday he wished he could find someone else who cared as much about animals as he did. Someone who wasn't a vet or a pet store owner, someone who had a warm heart and a good soul.

Someone female.

He smiled at himself. In a hundred years, he hadn't met a woman who interested him. Even though his personal prophecy from the Fates said he would have a great love, he didn't believe it.

No woman had ever interested him beyond a passing fancy. He was beginning to think he'd never meet the right one.

He picked up the phone and dialed his vet's number from memory. As the ringing sounded in his ear, he swiveled toward the cash register. He started punching in the prices for a cat bed, a litter box, and some Science Diet cat food. He was becoming his own best customer.

"Heart's too soft, Grant," he muttered to himself as the vet's tech put him on hold. But he'd always known that was his problem.

He also knew that he really wasn't interested in a solution.

Her name was not Erika O'Connell, but that was the name she had been using for the past twenty years. Her time with that name was almost up: When you were in the public eye as long as she had been, people tended to notice when you didn't age. She figured she had another ten years before she had to fake a spectacular death or disappear on a trip to a remote outpost.

Unfortunately, there weren't that many remote outposts left, not like it had been when she was a child—four thousand years ago—when everything, it seemed, was remote.

Erika O'Connell—whose real name, Eris, was not something she had shared with anyone—sat behind the desk in her Los Angeles office. She had her shoes off. They lay on the tasteful white carpet, the heel of one inside the other.

Hard-copy files rested on all the leather furniture—only a custom-built wooden desk chair had escaped the clutter. Even her plants were messy because she preferred them that way—overgrown, trailing down the sides of tables and onto the floor.

She was talking on her cell phone, listening to a meeting on speaker phone, watching CNN, KAHS, FOX News, and CNBC on the double split-screen television that sat on one corner of her desk. In the center of her desk, her state-of-the-art IBM with more bells, whistles, and other unnecessary items, remained on AOL, pinging whenever she received e-mail. In one corner of that screen, stock quotes ran in real time, and in the other corner, ESPN shared the tiny television monitor with C-SPAN.

And on the far corner of her desk, her handy-dandy laptop was synchronizing that day's schedule with her Palm.

Who needed magic in the twenty-first century? Technology did everything for her.

The intercom on her desk buzzed, and she tapped it lightly. "In a meeting," she said to the secretary, whose name she had never bothered to learn.

Eris rarely used the Los Angeles office—she preferred the New York headquarters because no one could predict what was going to happen on any given day in the Big Apple—and she viewed being here as a great inconvenience. But she had had to meet some stockholders the night before, and once in a while she had to go to them.

Besides, her A-team was here, covering yet another entertainment scandal, and she was looking for a way to pry them loose. Her network, KAHS, had risen to the top tier of the cable news shows in two short years, but she still had a long way to go to become number one.

She didn't want to do it by imitating this week's rival. Instead, she had to establish her own voice. And doing that required more than covering the latest Hollywood divorce. She wanted to cover stories that would change the world—not all at once, but one little layer at a time.

She had just hung up from the conference call when her son—who was, dangerously, calling himself Stri these days—appeared before her. At 3800 and something, he wasn't even close to young, but he liked to pretend at it. This time, he had a shaved head, a jacket that was more chain than fabric, and more tattoos than she had ever seen on a human being.

"Busy," she said as she was about to dial another conference call.

"Yeah," Stri said, "but I got news you can't cover in any part of your multimedia empire."

She flicked the cell phone shut without saying good-bye and pulled a red-tipped fingernail away from the speaker phone. "What?"

He grinned. He had blacked out or discarded half of his teeth. It didn't look menacing. In fact, it made him look like a peasant during the Russian Revolution—even with the ridiculous clothes. Or maybe she only thought that because she could remember the Russian Revolution.

"Well?" she asked when he didn't answer.

Her door opened and the nameless secretary—a mouse of a mortal, brown skin, brown hair, brown clothes (weren't people in Los Angeles supposed to be prettier than average? What went wrong here?)—crept into the room to throw more paper on one of the chairs.

"I'm having a meeting," Eris snapped, furious that her son hadn't come in by normal channels.

"Just more numbers from overseas, ma'am," the secretary said. "I thought you might want to see them immediately."

"Fine," Eris said. "Next time, e-mail them to me. I'll see them quicker."

"Yes, ma'am." And the secretary backed out.

Stri didn't even turn around, nor did he wait for the door to close to start telling his news. He always created trouble. That was one of the things Eris loved about him—most of the time.

"The kids have taken the oath and are now exploring their new office," he said.

Eris forgot her irritation with him. "When?"

"Just a few minutes ago," he said. "Saw them get flown into Mount Olympus and was their first customer when they got out. They have a lot to learn."

Eris laughed. "Wonderful. And the Fates?"

He shrugged. "On their own, I guess."

"Even better," she said. "Put some kind of trace on them. Let me know if they get anywhere close to the mortal realm."

Stri grinned. "Will do, Mommy Dearest. You gonna hunt them down? Or are you going for more finesse than that?"

She raised a single eyebrow at him, giving him the stare she had used when she was a twenty-two-year-old mother with no magical powers at all. He cringed. Of all the tricks in her bag, that one was the most effective—at least with Stri.

"Guess you're going for finesse," he said.

"Have I ever done anything else?" she asked, and he looked away.

"I'll trace them," he said. "But there are rumors they're heading into Faery, and I'm not going in there again."

Last time he did, he ate some of the food and

lost a hundred years before Eris even noticed he was missing.

"Just trace the Fates," she said.

"Why can't you do it?"

"Because if I do," she said, flipping open her cell phone again, "they'll think I'm up to something. If you do it, they'll think you're just creating trouble."

"I'm not someone who should be ignored." He crossed his arms, and the tattoos bulged.

"No, darling, you're not," she said, glancing at the divided television screen. "You're something to be tolerated, and you should be proud of that. Now go away and let Mommy take over the world."

He peered at the television too. "I still think you should put me on the air."

"Busy," she said, just like she had when he came in.

"Jeez, Mom, I'm doing you a favor."

"No, dear," she said, picking up a pencil to dial with so that she wouldn't break a nail. "You're doing me a job. Now get out before I stop cleaning up after you and you'll be in trouble with the Powers That Be."

"If the Fates are really gone, that won't matter," he said.

"We'll see." Eris dialed, but stopped before the last number. " 'Bye."

Stri frowned, his pout looking perfectly natural on his tattooed and pierced face. He waited just long enough for her to catch the full impact of the look and then he vanished, leaving a cloud of red smoke that smelled of cherry bombs.

With a wave of a hand, Eris made the smoke disappear. She wished she could make everything else that bothered her disappear as quickly, but that would be obvious, and she hated nothing more than the obvious.

She smiled. Everything was going well. She was

even ahead of schedule. With the Fates gone, her life would get a whole lot easier.

She might even abandon some of her finesse and reveal a tiny corner of herself.

The last time she had done that, the world had taken notice.

It would take notice again.

Three

Vivian was dreaming of a world filled with homeless kittens, kittens that people kept dumping on her doorstep, expecting her to take care of them. They were little and they seemed to be multiplying asexually. Every time she touched one, there would suddenly be two, but she couldn't stop herself from picking them up.

Then the kittens started pounding in unison, as if they all wanted to join the cast of *Stomp*, and she kept telling them to stop, but they wouldn't. It took her a few minutes to realize that the pounding really existed.

She sat up and rubbed a hand over her face before glancing at the fancy CD alarm clock that Travers insisted she buy. 6:45 A.M. Light was coming in through the sides of the linen shade, but the bedroom was still dark.

Her heart was pounding and her eyes were made of glue. She hadn't had much sleep. She'd stayed up, reading and rereading Kyle's comic book, missing her family already.

It felt like she was in a hotel. She'd only been living here for a week and everything was unfamiliar. Even though it was her nightstand against her bed, her blue sheets and pillow cases surrounding her, her specially built comic book shelves holding all the boxes of her collections, the arrangement was different than the one she'd had in L.A. And she wasn't used to the sounds of the building yet.

Somehow she hadn't thought the walls were this thin.

The pounding continued. She flopped back on the mattress and pulled a pillow over her face, wishing her neighbor would answer the damn door. Who pounded at someone's door this early in the morning anyway?

"Vivian!" a female voice shouted. "Vivian, please. We know you're in there. Please let us in!"

The voice sounded panicked. In fact, it sounded so panicked that it kept changing tone. Soprano, alto, mezzo-soprano. How weird was that?

Then Vivian pulled the pillow off her face. No one knew her here. No one except her landlord, and she had gotten the impression he hadn't paid much attention to her application, only to her check.

She hadn't gone to the police yet to see their file on Eugenia, and she hadn't gone to the lawyer. Vivian was waiting until Travers left, which had taken him five days longer than he had promised.

That mezzo-soprano/alto/soprano voice wasn't his. And that was the only thing she could be sure of.

She got out of bed, grabbed her robe, and shoved her feet into her bunny slippers. She opened the bedroom door and stepped into the combination living room/dining area. The floor-to-ceiling windows sent a cold draft across the hardwood floor.

Sunlight poured in, making her glass-topped dining room table sparkle.

Vivian braced one hand on a chair as she made her way to the door. The pounding grew louder the closer she got.

"Vivian!"

Maybe this was some kind of scam to get someone to open her door in the middle of the night. Or the earliest part of the morning, as the case may be.

"Let us in!"

Vivian peered through the peephole. Three women were crowded on the landing. Three gorgeous women, all the same height, with movie-star good looks.

"Please!" cried the blonde closest to the door.

The other two were looking over their shoulders down the stairs as if they were afraid of something outside.

Vivian made sure the chain was on, then pulled the door open until the chain caught.

"Do I know you?" she asked, peering into the hallway. The women looked in her direction. They had bright eyes and matching expressions—sort of a combination between exasperation and panic.

"Of course you know us," the redhead snapped. "Let us in."

"I don't remember meeting you," Vivian said.

"Please!" The brunette sounded terrified.

Vivian was a sucker for terror. When she was a kid, she used to pretend that she would rescue people who were terrified and save them with her psychic powers.

As if that would ever happen.

But the fantasy was real enough to get her to consider unlatching the chain. "This isn't some kind of scam, is it?"

"Scam?" the blonde asked.

"No, it's not," the redhead said.

"Please!" the brunette said again, in that exact same terrified tone.

Vivian gave up. If they were going to mug her, they were going to mug her. Their frightened act was convincing. She closed the door to unlatch the chain—and heard squeals of dismay from the hallway. Then she undid the chain and pulled the door open again.

She was nearly bowled over as the three women ran inside.

"Oh, thank you!" the blonde said.

"You'd better spell the door," said the redhead.

"Or maybe the entire building," the brunette said.

Vivian frowned. She was probably still dreaming. That was the only explanation. But her feet were cold despite the bunny slippers, and she had that woozy feeling she usually got when she woke up badly. To her recollection, she'd never had that feeling in a dream before.

"What is going on?" Vivian asked. "Who are you?"

All three women gaped at her. Even though they looked very different—the blonde was blue-eyed and delicate; the redhead green-eyed and zaftig; the brunette brown-eyed and model-thin—they had the same expression on their faces.

"What do you mean, who are we?" the blonde asked.

"You know who we are," the redhead said.

"No," Vivian said. "I'm sorry. I don't."

"Oh, no," the brunette said.

"Are you telling me that Eugenia told you nothing?" the blonde asked.

"About what?" Vivian asked.

The women were very close to the door, huddled against it in fact, and it took Vivian a moment to realize that she was preventing them from moving deeper into the apartment.

Downstairs something banged. She hoped it was only a door.

"I'm Atropos," the brunette said.

"And I'm Clotho," the blonde said.

"And I'm Lachesis," said the redhead.

Then they all stared at her as if she should recognize their admittedly odd names.

"I'm sorry," Vivian said. "I've never heard of you."

"We're the Fates!" they said in unison, and that was when she knew she was dreaming. Kyle's comic book was coming back to haunt her. Either that, or Aunt Eugenia had been involved in something even stranger than usual.

"Are you a rock group?" Vivian asked, deciding to play into the dream rather than fight it.

"A what?" Atropos asked.

"A rock group," Clotho said quietly. "You know, like in those beach party movies."

"Annette Funicello?" Lachesis asked, and then shuddered.

"We're not that shallow," Atropos said.

"No, no, no," Clotho said. "We're the Fates."

"You know," Lachesis said, just in case Vivian missed it. "The Fates."

Vivian was apparently staring at them blankly because Atropos said in exasperation, "Shouldn't we have fallen into human mythology by now?"

"I thought we had," Clotho said. "The Greeks referred to us properly."

"And then the Norse," said Lachesis.

"Who got it wrong," Atropos added as an aside, "calling us the Norn."

"The Weird Sisters," they said in unison.

"As if we're sisters at all," said Clotho.

Vivian's head was spinning. She was beginning to suspect something was seriously wrong here—she was awake and this still wasn't making sense.

"And that Wagner," Lachesis said, "dressing us the way he did."

"No sane woman would wear those clothes," said Atropos.

"I don't think that was him," Clotho said. "I think it was the director."

"I still didn't like it," Lachesis said. "I'd rather be a Valkyrie—"

"Stop!" Vivian put a hand to her head. The spinning continued. "One at a time, tell me what's going on."

The women stared at her as if she'd made an improper request. Another door banged downstairs—or was that a car backfiring outside? Vivian couldn't tell.

"I think the last time we spoke one at a time," Atropos said.

"Completing an entire thought on our own," said Clotho.

"Had to be three thousand years ago," said Lachesis.

They all looked confused. Or crazy. Or maybe Vivian was the crazy one.

"I don't care," Vivian said. "Just tell me what's happening."

"Oh, dear," Atropos said. "This will be difficult if you have no idea who we are."

"Can you spell the building first?" Clotho asked.

"I can't spell anything," Vivian snapped, and then she paused. "You don't mean spell-spell, do you? As in spelling bee?"

The women stared at each other, looking even more confused.

"I suppose not," Vivian said. "That would be too simple."

She marched across her floor and headed into the kitchen, pushing open the swinging door. The kitchen had been remodeled just before she moved in and still had that new plastic smell appliances sometimes had. Her large blue teakettle, shaped like the Tick with his little antennae serving as a handle, looked out of place on the black stove.

She grabbed the kettle, turned on the cold water, and shoved the kettle beneath it. Breakfast. She needed breakfast. And time to think.

These women had mentioned Aunt Eugenia. So they were connected to Vivian somehow, and they thought Aunt Eugenia had told her something.

Maybe Aunt Eugenia had. She had sent Vivian a box full of papers the week before she died. Vivian had scanned them to look for a new version of the will and had found nothing except hand-written notes, books, and newspaper clippings from the previous century. She planned to go through it all when she had more time.

Cold water splashed on her hand. She shut off the faucet, dried off the teakettle, and set it on the stove. Then she slid out her toaster and put an English muffin inside.

The women would be able to smell the food. Vivian sighed. She hated being impolite, even to strangers—and was there a better word for these women? *strange–ers?*—so she supposed to ease her own mind she'd have to offer them something.

Vivian pushed open the swinging door and held it in place. The strange women were still standing in her entry, huddled together and talking quietly.

"I'm going to have breakfast," Vivian said. "Would you like something to eat?"

"Food!" Lachesis said with relief.

"Oh, yes," Atropos said. "We haven't had food in hours."

Clotho clapped her hands together. "How about some chocolate crepes, followed by one of those egg-cheese things—"

"An omelet," Lachesis said.

"Three omelets," Atropos said.

"And perhaps some freshly ripened grapes," Clotho said. "You know the type. At the very peak—"

"I have English muffins or Pop Tarts," Vivian said, wishing she'd never made the offer. "And if you want the muffins, you get a choice of peanut butter, margarine, strawberry jelly, or cream cheese."

The toaster popped. She went back into the kitchen and slathered peanut butter on her English muffins. She didn't care what the women wanted.

"And," Vivian shouted so that they could hear her, "you make them yourself."

Her remark was greeted with silence. She poured orange juice into a McDonalds' promotional glass from the third Batman movie, and carried it through the swinging door to the glass-topped table.

The three women had gathered around her table in anticipation of food, and now that she had refused to give them what they wanted, they stared at her.

Vivian set her glass down as if nothing were wrong. But something was wrong, and she just realized what it was.

She had no sense of these women. She always had a sense of people—whether they were good or bad, whether they meant to harm her or not, whether they were self-involved or saintly.

That was why she'd had no idea they were at her door—why she had assumed they were at someone else's. And that was what bothered her the most about them. It wasn't their odd way of talking or their appearance. It was that they made no impact on her psyche. As if they weren't there at all.

She almost touched one, then realized that would be a mistake. They were here, and present. They had moved her chairs, and they brought with them the faint scent of summer sunshine, not to mention all the noise.

There had been only one other person in the whole world Vivian could never sense, and that had been Aunt Eugenia. Aunt Eugenia, whom these women claimed to know.

"You really have no idea who we are, do you?" Lachesis asked.

Vivian looked up from her contemplation of her orange juice glass. "No, I don't."

Atropos licked her lips nervously. "Do you have any chocolate? We'll eat anything chocolate for breakfast."

The teakettle whistled. Vivian sighed. She did have some chocolate truffles that Kyle had bought her the day before, and she hadn't been planning on eating them. They looked too rich for her.

She went back into the kitchen, took the teakettle off the burner, and shut it off. Then she made some Earl Gray, put the teapot, her muffin, the truffles, and some X-Men mugs on a tray, and carried the whole thing back to the dining room.

"All right," she said as she set the tray down near her orange juice glass. "Sit down. Tell me what's going on, and convince me not to call the police."

"Well, for one thing, your police can't help," Clotho said.

"They lack the power." Atropos reached for a truffle.

Lachesis slapped her hand. "We haven't been invited yet."

"Yes, you have," Vivian said. "The chocolate is for you."

"Thank you," the three women said in unison, and it was as if she had given them the world. They each took a truffle, bit into it at the same time, and got the identical expression of joy on their faces.

Vivian ate her muffin, the peanut butter making her tongue stick to the roof of her mouth. She drank some orange juice to dislodge it. "You do owe me an explanation."

Clotho nodded. "We're trying to think of the best way to tell you."

"What did Eugenia tell you about the magical world?" Lachesis asked.

"The magical world?" Vivian repeated. "Eugenia told my parents I'm psychic."

"And?" Atropos asked.

"And to tolerate what happened to me, saying that it was pretty normal for someone with my abilities," Vivian said.

"And?" Clotho asked.

"And that Eugenia had been psychic when she was a kid, so she understood what was going on." Vivian frowned.

Eugenia had said *had been*, as if being psychic was something someone outgrew. She never exhibited any psychic powers around Vivian that she could remember, but maybe Eugenia had had different talents. Maybe she could foresee the future. Maybe that was why she had sent Vivian that box the week before her death.

Maybe that was what Eugenia had meant when she used to invite Vivian to Portland, claiming they were running out of time. *I'm not young anymore,* Eugenia would say during their phone calls.

Nonsense, Vivian used to say, *you're going to live forever, Aunt.*

"And?" Lachesis asked.

"And what?" Vivian said.

"What else did she tell you?"

Vivian shrugged. "Bits and pieces here and there. So I wouldn't feel like a freak. Even though I did. Because I was. Am. You know. You do know that I'm psychic, right?"

"We know everything about you, child," Atropos said, and Vivian started. She'd never had anyone her own age call her *child* before.

"Or we used to," Clotho said.

"And we will again," Lachesis said, her voice rising the way people's voices did when they were trying to cheer other people up.

"How old are you?" Atropos asked.

"I thought you knew everything about me," Vivian said.

Clotho waved a hand in dismissal. "We're never great with details."

"I'm twenty-six," Vivian said.

"Twenty-six," Lachesis said to the other two. "That's old enough. In fact, that's too old. Eugenia should have started the training long before that."

"Training?" Vivian asked.

"She did tell you that she was your mentor, right?" Atropos said.

"Well, it was obvious," Vivian said. "No one else I ever met could have been my mentor."

"For your magical training," Clotho said.

"My what?" Vivian asked.

"Your training, you know, how to control your powers," Lachesis said.

"My what?" Vivian asked again.

"Your powers, you know, the ones you'll come into after menopause," Atropos said.

"What are you talking about?" Vivian asked. "Are you saying I'll be Super Hot-flash Woman?"

"Your magical powers," Clotho said.

"I can't believe Eugenia didn't tell you," Lachesis said.

"She's always so responsible," Atropos said.

"Except lately," Clotho said.

"She could have told us about losing the house," Lachesis said.

"And her change of address," Atropos said. "If she had planned better, we wouldn't be here now."

She addressed that last to Vivian. Vivian, who felt like she was only getting half of this conversation anyway, set her English muffin down.

"Um," she said cautiously, "you do know that Eugenia died at the beginning of the month."

"She what?" All three women spoke in unison.

"Impossible," said Clotho.

"We would have known," said Lachesis at the same time.

"We *should* have known," said Atropos a second later.

"I'm sorry to tell you this way," Vivian said. "She was murdered."

The three women didn't respond to that. Instead they looked at each other, and for the first time, Vivian got a sense of them. The sense was fleeting and odd, as if they were communicating with each other telepathically.

They were frightened. That much she could tell, even without her gifts.

A car alarm went off in the street. All three women jumped. So did Vivian, but she pretended that she hadn't. To cover her own nervousness, she poured tea into all four mugs.

"You were going to explain things to me," Vivian

said, her hand shaking. She set the teapot down. She was more on edge than she had thought.

"We were," Clotho said.

"But first," Lachesis said.

"Explain why you weren't studying with Eugenia," Atropos said.

"I didn't know I was supposed to," Vivian said.

"Surely she invited you up here," Clotho said.

"She wanted me to spend some time with her, yes," Vivian said. "But I had a business to run, and she wouldn't come to L.A."

"A business?" Lachesis said. "You mean that psychic hotline?"

"You thought that was more important than your training?" Atropos asked.

Vivian felt her cheeks flush. If she had known Eugenia was going to die so soon, she would have made a point of coming here. But she hadn't known. That wasn't how her gifts manifested themselves.

"I think I did some good with that hotline." Vivian's voice sounded small.

It had seemed like a good idea at the time—a psychic hotline with real psychics, not people who traced your phone number or used your credit reports (gleaned from your credit card number) to give them their "special" knowledge.

And it had worked. Her hotline got to be known as the hotline to call. But she had to shut it down. There weren't that many real psychics walking around Los Angeles, and most of the real ones didn't want anything to do with her little idea.

Eventually, there were too many calls for her to handle. Even though she was minting money, she had to close the doors—and then she slept for what seemed like two months straight.

That was just before Eugenia died.

"Some good?" Clotho said.

"You would have done more good if you had had training," Lachesis said.

"Training in what?" Vivian asked again.

"Magic," Atropos said.

"But Aunt Eugenia wasn't a magician," Vivian said.

"No," Clotho said. "She was a mage, just like you will be someday."

"A mage," Vivian said, trying to wrap her mind around the difference between *mage* and *magician*, besides the spelling and the number of syllables.

Another car alarm went off, and then another. The three women clutched each other's hands.

"He's getting close," Lachesis said.

"This was a stupid idea," Atropos said.

"We agreed on it," Clotho said.

"We were forced into it," Lachesis said.

"It's too late," Atropos said. "We made the choice."

Vivian glanced out the window. Three cars in front of the building across the street were blaring, their headlights blinking on and off. She had no idea what could have set them off.

"All right." Clotho's delicate mouth was covered in chocolate. She didn't seem to notice. "We'll do our best to explain, but since your mentor failed on the job, you probably won't believe this."

Lachesis handed Clotho a napkin, then said, "Before we do this, perhaps we should ask her about Blackstone."

"Blackstone? The magician?" Vivian asked.

"Yes!" they said in pleased unison.

"Do you know him?" Atropos asked.

"I know of him," Vivian said, wondering how she could know a man who had been dead for a very long time.

"Good." Clotho looked relieved. "Then you go to his restaurant."

"What?" Vivian asked. That spinning feeling had returned.

"What's it called?" Làchesis looked at her companions. "Quixote?"

"Quixotic?" Vivian asked. "It's next door."

The women smiled at her as if she'd won a prize.

"I've been there. What does it have to do with Blackstone?"

"He owns it," Atropos said. "Or he did. It wasn't open this morning. Do you know why?"

Vivian shrugged. "It doesn't serve breakfast. I'm sure it won't open until eleven or so."

A dog started barking nearby, big deep, scary barks. The car alarms were still going, and Vivian thought she heard another one flare up.

"Eleven's too late," Clotho said. "We'll have to explain."

"All right." Lachesis took a deep breath, and the others followed suit. They leaned toward Vivian in one swift movement.

Another bang sounded below, and all three women jumped.

"There are mortals, and then there are the magical," Atropos said, looking toward the door.

"You are one of the magical," Clotho said.

"Yeah, right," Vivian said.

"No, really," Lachesis said. Then she frowned. "That is the correct modern response, isn't it?"

"What?" Vivian asked.

"Never mind," Atropos said. "We'll update our slang later."

"If there is a later," Clotho said, and she too looked toward the door.

Vivian heard more banging, and then the sound of firecrackers.

"Oh, no," Lachesis said.

"He's found us," Atropos said.

"Quick," Clotho said. "We must wrap this place in tinfoil."

"What?" Vivian said.

"Tinfoil," Lachesis said. "Have you got tinfoil?"

Somehow that question seemed logical—at least coming from these women.

"I have some," Vivian said, "but not enough to wrap the apartment in, and besides, that would take all day."

The banging stopped, but the sound of firecrackers continued. It faded and blended into the sound of sparklers. Then smoke came in under Vivian's door.

"Oh, no," Atropos said.

The smoke filtered across the floor in tendrils, white and thick. The movement was orderly, and the smoke was odorless.

Vivian got up and ran for the phone. She had to call the fire department.

The three women climbed on their chairs.

"Your conventional friends can't help, Vivian," Clotho said.

"We need you to do something," Lachesis said.

Vivian picked up the phone. "I can't stop fire."

"There is no fire." Atropos peered at the floor. The tendrils of smoke were feeling their way over the couch, around the end tables. Once, it seemed like the tendrils stopped and sniffed the air.

"You must imagine this building encased in glass," Clotho said, her voice breathless.

Vivian started to dial 911.

"You must, Vivian," Lachesis said. "That's the only way to help us."

"Imagine it and project it outward, as if you were pushing the image out of you," Atropos said.

"Look," Vivian said, still clutching the phone. She hadn't quite finished dialing. "If you guys believe in magic, you do it."

"This isn't magic, per se," Clotho said. "It's a psychic's trick. But you have to do it."

Her voice went up as the tendrils got closer. Vivian's floor was lost in a sea of white. Throughout the sea, white telescopelike things poked out of the smoke and sniffed. Fingers felt the surfaces. This didn't look like any smoke Vivian had ever seen before.

"Please, Vivian," Lachesis said as she moved her feet away from a poking smoke finger. "Just try it."

"If it doesn't work, then dial your friends," Atropos said.

The other three glared at her as if she had just given bad advice.

The smoke curled around Vivian's legs. It was cool, not hot, and she thought she felt tiny pinpricks against her skin.

"Imagine a glass case?" she asked.

"Around the entire building," Clotho said.

"Then push it away from you," Atropos added.

Vivian closed her eyes. It took her a moment to envision the building—she'd never really looked at all of it, just the interior—and then she imagined slamming a glass box over it. She pushed the image away from her mind, and actually felt something leave her with the force of a sneeze.

She staggered, caught herself on the telephone table, then opened her eyes.

The smoke was gone.

"You did it!" Clotho shouted.

"I wasn't sure it would be possible," Lachesis said, sinking down into her chair.

"We're saved," Atropos said, reaching for a truffle.

"For the moment," Clotho said.

"I don't understand." Vivian set the phone down. She was shaking, and she felt a little weak. "What's going on here?"

"That's what we want to explain, dear," Lachesis said. "Now that you've bought us a little time."

Four

"What do you mean, they cut them off?" Eris leaned in the galley of the corporate jet, fingering the tiny half-made pastries the chef had been working on when she kicked him out. Her cell phone was pressed against her ear, but still she worried about the talent in the cabin overhearing her conversation.

"They did!" Stri's voice whined at her, so loud that it hurt. She slid deeper into the galley and pulled the privacy curtain closed. "I was using smoke feelers. They were in the building when this thing landed on them, cutting them off."

"Smoke feelers?" Eris took the tiny bottles of alcohol, arranged in alphabetical order, and began to move them around. "You were using smoke feelers?"

"Well, I had to make sure the Fates were in the building—"

"I told you to mark them and then leave them alone." In the very back, where it was hard to reach, she knocked down a few of the bottles.

The jet's engines droned and then cut back. It was climbing, trying to reach the right altitude for the flight to New York.

"Ah, Mom," Stri said. "We're talking the Fates here. They'd notice a mark."

"More than they'd notice smoke feelers?" Her voice rose. "What else did you do?"

"Nothing." His tone was sulky. It didn't matter what language he was speaking in—his native Greek, Latin, Russian, or English—he always sounded sulky when he was lying.

"What else did you do?"

The curtains twitched. Noah Sturgis shoved his square face, made unnaturally shiny by too much plastic surgery, into the gap. "You okay, Erika?"

He didn't really care about her. They both knew that. He wanted to know if there was some story brewing, something that would boost his career.

God knew it needed boosting. His biggest claim to fame was that he had once been groomed as Dan Rather's successor. But that had been years ago, and each major network had cut him loose. Eris had picked him up for a song, and pretended she didn't regret it.

"Go away, Noah," she said.

"If it's important—"

"If it's important, I'll tell Kronski." Kronski was KAHS's news director, and theoretically the person in charge of Sturgis. But no one was really in charge of Sturgis.

"Mom?" Stri almost shouted the word.

"Mom?" Sturgis mouthed. It was well known that Erika O'Connell was single, childless, and proud to be both.

"Go away," she said again, "or I'll cancel your fancy new contract."

"Mom?"

"Shut up for a moment," she said to her son.

"You'll have to tell me about this," Sturgis said and pulled the curtain closed.

"Now what?" Eris said to Stri.

"If I can't smoke them out, I'd like to go in after them. I hear they're powerless, and it would feel so good—"

"No," she said. "They're mine."

"I'm not bringing them to you."

She almost said that Stri wasn't supposed to bring them to her, and then she realized that he was right. Because he had screwed up, the Fates knew someone was out to get them. They'd be cautious at the very least, defensive at the very most.

And who knew which Powers That Be remained on their side?

"Of course you're not," she snapped, as if the change of plans had been her idea. "They dropped something on your smoke feelers, right?"

"Yeah."

"Is it a protect spell?"

"No," he said. "Something else. Sharper. Over the whole building."

How odd. She couldn't think of a spell that would do that. "You will stay there, monitor that building, and *not do another thing until I get there.* Is that clear?"

"Just pop in, Mom, and—"

"First of all, I can't *pop* in. I am at work. And secondly, your stupid errors might be drawing the wrong kind of attention. So I will be there as soon as I can get the pilot to fly north. And when I arrive, you will not call me Mom."

Stri laughed. "Okay. But I'm only doing what I do."

"That's what I'm afraid of," she said and hung up. She stuffed the cell phone in the pocket of her red suitcoat, and leaned against the galley wall.

She hated it when he was right. He wasn't named Strife for nothing. She had done that deliberately, hoping he would cause trouble, and he always had. She should have expected nothing less.

Next time, she'd send in a trusted minion. If there was a next time.

Stri was right about a few other things. Eris should pop in. But she was traveling with an entire bevy of reporters and news cameras. Disappearing from a jet in mid-flight was not a good idea in these circumstances.

But she would have to come up with some reason for diverting the plane. If there wasn't a news story in Portland, Oregon, she was going to have to make one up herself.

She hated doing that. Those stories usually ended up going on forever until she was so sick of them, she wanted to make them disappear—which, of course, she couldn't do.

Maybe it wouldn't matter this time. She was so close to the Fates that everything could change. And once she had gotten rid of them, the most important step in her plan would be complete.

That was what she had to focus on, not her piddly little international corporation. Sometimes she got so focused on the details, she forgot about the important things.

Like controlling the world—not just through the media, but in all things.

Including magic.

Dex sat up in his darkened bedroom, dislodging three sleeping cats and his familiar, an Irish wolfhound named Sadie. She stretched out in his warm spot. His Siamese cat, Nurse Ratched, was sitting on his nightstand, purring. She never purred.

"You woke me, didn't you?" he asked her.

As if in answer to his question, she jumped on his lap and demanded to be petted. He did so absently, remembering the dream he'd forced himself to wake up from.

He'd been dreaming of kittens, millions of abandoned kittens that someone kept leaving in his store. Every time he turned around, there were more kittens, and he finally realized that not only were they being abandoned, they were reproducing right in front of him.

Asexual reproduction, like worms did. The kittens weren't exactly dividing themselves in half, but they were doubling, like some computer program gone amok.

He realized that the doubling was going to go on until there were more kittens than space on the Earth—and just as the panic set in, the Fates appeared.

They were pounding on his front door and begging for his help. Yet it wasn't his help they wanted. He got the sense that somewhere, in this horrible place, there was something good. There was some-*one* good.

And even though he wanted to refuse the Fates, the kittens pulled the door open, sucking him into the trap. . . .

That was when he'd forced himself awake to find Nurse Ratched staring at him in the semidarkness. He glanced at the alarm clock—an old analog model he hadn't changed since the 1950s. Seven-thirty. Too late to go back to sleep, too early to open the store.

He stretched and slid back under the covers. Ratchy kept purring and butting his chin. She was hungry. So was he.

Time for his day to begin. Even though he didn't want it to. Even though he had a feeling that that dream was some kind of warning.

* * *

Somewhere in the middle of the Fates' explanation of the magical world, Vivian broke out another box of chocolates. Dark chocolate imported from Switzerland this time, the good stuff, the stuff she'd been saving for a particularly hard day.

This, she knew, was going to be that day.

All four of them still sat at her dining room table, picking over the chocolate and drinking too much tea.

The car alarms had stopped outside—at least for the moment—but Vivian didn't feel any safer. She kept checking the base of her door for more smoke, even though the Fates told her that she had taken care of it.

They told her many things. They told her that in addition to the world Vivian had seen her entire life, there was another world, one she'd probably heard of through myth, fable, and legend. Some of the people she saw on the street—indeed, some of the people she'd seen at Quixotic, the fancy restaurant next door—were mages who had lived hundreds, maybe thousands of years.

Most of these people were mentored. Men came into their magic at around age twenty-one, but women didn't come into theirs until menopause—giving them time to have children and live a little before the burdens of magic fell on them.

(*Burdens* was Atropos's word. Clotho and Lachesis disagreed with it.)

The magical were governed by laws, just like the non-magical were. Only the magical had one set of laws worldwide, laws that had been in existence for millennia. The Powers That Be (and as they said that phrase, the three women bowed their heads and spread out their arms in some sort of obeisance) created the framework for the laws and the Fates enforced them.

These three women claimed to be the Fates.

"The Greeks said that we spun the web of life," Clotho said.

"Atropos handles the shears, which can end the life in a moment," said Lachesis as Atropos looked at her empty hands.

"Lachesis assigns people their fates," Atropos said, still looking down.

"And I spin the web," said Clotho. Then her expression saddened. "Or I'm supposed to, anyway."

Vivian rubbed a hand over her face. The only reason none of this made her think they were crazy—or *she* was crazy, for that matter—was Aunt Eugenia.

This life is more complex than you'd think, Aunt Eugenia had said on more than one occasion. And one of her favorite phrases was, *You'd be surprised just how much magic there is in the world.*

"Okay," Vivian said as the Fates paused for breath. "If you have that much power, what do you need me for?"

"They've imposed term limits," Lachesis said.

"Who has?" Vivian asked.

"The Powers That Be," Atropos said.

"Although we think someone might be behind this," Clotho said.

"Just one of the Powers, lobbying the others," Lachesis said.

Vivian shook her head. She wasn't following this. "What do term limits have to do with this?"

"Our term is up," Atropos said.

"We must reapply for the job we've done for thousands of years," Clotho said.

All three women sounded indignant. All three

of them grabbed more chocolate. Vivian had never seen anyone eat so much chocolate in her life.

"And there are new requirements for the job," Lachesis said, "which I believe—"

"*We* believe," Atropos said.

"Were designed to keep us out forever," Clotho finished.

"Our last millennium wasn't our best," Lachesis whispered, and the other two glared at her.

"It was not our fault," Atropos said.

"I don't care about your history. I'm not even sure I believe everything you're telling me." Vivian looked out the window. The view had gone from clear to opaque since she thought of the building as encased in glass. She couldn't even see the street below, and the noise had ended almost immediately. "I certainly don't know how you think I can help you."

"Well," Clotho said, "you were the closest thing we could find to a mage at the moment."

"Besides, we really didn't know about Eugenia," Lachesis said. "Do you think that was another mistake on our part?"

Then the building shook. Vivian pitched forward, nearly hitting her head on the table. She caught herself with her right hand. "What was that?"

"A test," Clotho said, her face so pale that Vivian could almost see through it.

"You have great power," Lachesis said. "That's why you're psychic. Unfortunately . . ."

"You won't come into the magical part for another three decades or so," Atropos said.

"And we simply can't wait that long," Clotho said.

They looked at each other. Vivian frowned. The beginnings of a headache was building behind her eyes. "The restaurant won't open for another two hours, but I could try to call your friends."

"Aethelstan," Lachesis said.

"Darius," Atropos said.

Clotho shook her head. "They're good men, but they may not have forgiven us. We were harsh with them."

"Necessarily harsh," Lachesis said.

The building shook again. A pain shot down Vivian's nose. "I don't feel so well," she said, and sat back down, letting the tray bang against the table.

"Oh, dear," Atropos said.

"I knew we should have used the tinfoil," Clotho said.

"We're going to need assistance a lot sooner," Lachesis said.

"Vivian," Atropos said, and Vivian started. That was the first time they had used her name since they had come into the apartment.

"What?" Vivian continued to rub her nose. It ached.

"Do you know a way out of here that doesn't require stepping onto the street from the front entrance?" Clotho asked.

"The parking garage," Vivian said.

"Well, then, that's it," Lachesis said.

"What's it?" Vivian asked at the same time Atropos did.

Then all three women looked alarmed.

"We didn't have the same thought," Atropos said.

"Do you think everything is breaking down?" Clotho asked.

"I thought that we'd simply be without magic when we volunteered to go without magic. I didn't think that we'd lose ourselves," Lachesis said.

"Maybe it was a glitch," Atropos said. "Now I know what you thought."

"Well, I don't," Vivian said with irritation. Her headache was getting worse.

"Henri Barou," Clotho said.

"Yes," Lachesis said. "You must get Henri Barou."

Atropos shook her head. "He won't help us. Not after what we told him."

"We'll untell him," Clotho said.

"I don't know any Henri Barou," Vivian said.

"He lives here in Porttown," Lachesis said.

"Portland," Vivian corrected her absently as she got up. She picked up her new phone book and started to thumb through it.

"Now is not the time to read, girl," Atropos said.

"Haven't you ever heard of a phone book?" Vivian asked, finally finding the *b*s.

"Oh, dear," Clotho said. "There are so many details to learn."

"And I thought we were prepared," Lachesis said.

"We should have paid more attention to the films we watched," Atropos said.

"Or not gotten so involved in the stories—"

"Excuse me," Vivian snapped. "How do you spell his last name?"

Her headache was getting worse. She didn't know what she had done to deserve these women, this morning, this life here in Porttown, as they were calling it. Maybe she had stepped into her Aunt Eugenia's life without realizing it.

The women spelled the name, and Vivian looked for it. She looked in Portland, in Lake Oswego, in Beaverton, Tigard, and Tualatin. She looked at every *b* and every possible spelling of Barou.

She found nothing.

"I guess you're out of luck there," she said. "If he's here, he's not listed."

"Oh, he probably didn't use that name," Lachesis said.

Vivian rubbed the bridge of her nose with her thumb and forefinger, stifling the angry comment that she had been about to make.

"What name would he have used?" she asked.

"How should we know?" Atropos said.

"These mages make up new names willy-nilly," Clotho said.

"Sometimes they're variations on the real name," Lachesis said, "but every now and then they pick something completely different."

"We would have plucked the name from the air," Atropos said, "but, alas, we have lost that talent."

"Then we can't find him," Vivian said, "because I can't pull names from the air."

"Yet," Clotho said.

Vivian ignored that.

"There are no other mages here," Lachesis said.

"At least, ones that know how to use their powers," Atropos said.

"Or have come into them," Clotho said.

Vivian wiped a tear of pain from her left eye. She stumbled toward the bathroom and pushed the door open. It banged against the built-in linen closet, which made her headache worse.

She stepped inside, nearly slipping on the rug in front of the shower, and opened the medicine cabinet. Even though she knew she had Excedrin Migraine, it took her a moment to find it. It was behind some cough medicine she should have thrown out in Los Angeles.

Vivian opened the Excedrin bottle, poured out two pills, and swallowed them dry. Maybe she would have to call the police. She was getting ill, and there was no way she could continue to guard these women, even if she were well.

She wasn't even sure what she was guarding them against.

She peered into the mirror. There were deep shadows under her eyes, and her skin, which was usually the color of milky coffee, seemed to have more milk than coffee.

"Vivian!" one of the women called from the front room.

If only she had some friends here. If only Travers hadn't left. Or Kyle. Kyle would have some ideas.

"Vivian!"

"Just a minute," she said, and splashed cold water on her skin. It didn't help. Nothing seemed to.

The building shook, and she felt as if she were the one under assault.

"Vivian!"

They weren't going to leave her alone. She would have to get help; that was all there was to it. Maybe when Quixotic opened—

"Vivian." This time her name wasn't shouted. All three women were peering into the bathroom.

"It's rather small, isn't it?" Clotho said.

"I thought they were always larger than this," Lachesis said.

Atropos nodded. "In *Pretty Woman*, the tub was the size of—"

"It's customary to give someone privacy in the bathroom," Vivian said, without the force she would have used half an hour earlier.

"You're not well." Clotho came to her side and touched her forehead with a cool hand.

"He's trying a defeat spell," Lachesis said.

"Only he doesn't know where to aim it yet," Atropos said.

"We have even less time than we thought." Clotho put her arm around Vivian's back and led her into the living room. Clotho's support felt good. She was a surprisingly solid woman, considering how delicate she looked.

"Who is this he?" Vivian asked.

"We're not sure it is a he," Lachesis said.

"We're only basing it on Clotho's sighting," Atropos said.

"We were all looking at him," Clotho said. "He had a shaved head, and tattoos—"

"Just like everyone else in that park," Lachesis said.

"I didn't see anyone at all," Atropos said, and the Fates looked at each other in panic.

Clotho eased Vivian onto the couch. All the conversation did was make her headache worse.

"We remembered how to find Henri," Lachesis said.

"He has a shop," Atropos said.

"Oh, good," Vivian mumbled. "There aren't many of those in Portland."

"We believe it specializes in creatures," Clotho said.

"Like eye of newt and wing of bat?" Vivian closed her eyes. That only made her focus on the headache, so she opened them again. She didn't like the opaque light. She also didn't like the three worried faces surrounding hers.

"Like cats and dogs," Lachesis said.

"And fish," Atropos said. "He seemed to prefer fish, last time he spoke to us."

"Oh, yes!" Clotho said. "I remember. That's where we put Munin."

"Munin?" Vivian was following even less than she had earlier. "What's a munin?"

"A familiar," Lachesis said. "It was for Darius."

"Where was that?" Atropos picked up the phone book. "Is there a way to make this thing answer questions?"

"Not verbally," Vivian said. The Excedrin Migraine was beginning to work. Now it felt as if her eyes had shrunken and her thought processes were slowed, but the pain was receding.

"It seems to me that the store was in Beaverville," Clotho said.

"Beaver*ton*," Vivian mumbled.

"In a strip joint," Lachesis said.

"A strip mall?" Vivian asked.

"Near Kinky's," Atropos said.

"I hope that's Kinko's," Vivian said.

"And George Washington Square," Clotho said.

"Washington Square Mall," Vivian murmured, then sat up. "I know where that is. I've even seen the store."

"You know?" Lachesis said.

"Yes, but a pet store won't be open at this time of day."

"It just might," Atropos said. "Henri always worked early, even in the days when he was—"

"Shush," Clotho said.

Atropos closed her mouth and looked humble.

Vivian stood. "Let's go. I think I feel well enough to drive."

All she knew was that she wasn't going to let any of these women—whoever they really were— behind the wheel of her precious VW Bug.

"We can't leave, dear," Lachesis said.

"What?" Vivian asked.

"You'll have to go alone," Atropos said.

"And leave you in my apartment?" Vivian didn't have a lot to steal, but she still had a few precious things. She had no idea what these women would do if she left them alone with her stuff.

"The effort of keeping this place hidden is already paining you," Clotho said.

"You won't have enough strength to hide the transportation, and then another building or two," Lachesis said.

"Why don't we just call this guy?" Vivian said. "Give me the phone book."

"Wait," Atropos said. "Doesn't this phone device send information through the air?"

If these women were actresses, they were dang good. Aunt Eugenia at least knew how phones worked. And all sorts of other technology. Why would the Fates not know? Had they been kept in a bubble?

"I mean," Clotho said, even though Atropos had spoken originally, "can't other people overhear what's being said?"

"Sometimes," Vivian said, "when you're on a portable or a cell, and someone's determined to listen in."

"Or if you're bugged," Lachesis said.

"I'm not bugged," Vivian said, "but I do have a portable phone."

"No," Atropos said.

"Yes, I do," Vivian said.

"What I mean"—Clotho was speaking for someone else again, a habit that was driving Vivian nuts—"is that you can't use the phone."

"Why not?"

"Because someone will listen in," Lachesis said.

"Who?" Vivian asked.

"It's so complicated," Atropos said.

"Well, not really," Clotho said.

"You see," Lachesis said, "it could be anyone. There are so many who are angry with us, and—"

"Oh, never mind," Vivian said. She needed an escape from these women anyway. If they robbed her blind, then she could say they broke in while she was gone, and she wasn't certain if she left her apartment unlocked or not, Officer.

She shook her head. "I'm going to this store. What do you want me to do if they've heard of this Henri guy?"

"Henri Barou," Atropos said.

"Tell him what's happening," Clotho said.

"He'll believe me?" Vivian asked, wondering if this Henri person might have her committed instead.

"He'll know how to help us," Lachesis said.

"What if he's never heard of you?" Vivian asked.

"He's heard of us," Atropos said.

"He doesn't like us much, but he has heard of us," Clotho said, overexplaining again.

"He doesn't like you either," Vivian said. "Then how do you know you can trust him?"

"Because," Lachesis said, "if you can't trust Henri Barou—"

"—you can't trust anyone," Atropos and Clotho finished, then laughed.

"I don't see why that's funny," Vivian said. "I thought you were in trouble."

Lachesis put her hand on Vivian's. "We are in trouble, my dear."

"And," Atropos said, also putting her hand on Vivian's, "we're trusting you—"

"—to get us out of it," said Clotho, placing her hand on top of the pile.

Vivian looked down at their hand pile, hers buried beneath theirs. That was how she felt, her mind buried beneath the weight of the thing she had sent out, the thing that felt like a sneeze.

She had no idea what she was doing, but even without her sixth sense, she knew that she'd better do it quickly.

Time was running out.

Five

Dexter Grant brought his laptop to the store, along with the nursing mother and her kittens. The mother cat wasn't too thrilled with him. So far, he'd taken her and her brood to the vet, to his home, and now back to the store.

She'd actually tried to bite him when he picked up their basket this morning. He was keeping a close eye on her, knowing the ways of mothering cats. She'd had enough interference with her litter in the past twenty-four hours—and she probably remembered searching for them in the woods, that awful sense of panic when she couldn't find them. If he so much as looked at the kittens wrong, he knew she'd hide them somewhere inside the store.

The last thing he wanted to do was spend the day searching for a cat hiding place.

Dex rubbed his eyes. He hadn't gotten much sleep. Between caring for the kittens and having nightmares about kittens, he felt as if he were taking care of a whole brood instead of only a handful.

Because he'd arrived early, he had opened the

store, turning on the outdoor lights, and feeding the fish—a task that had almost gotten the mother cat's full attention. The only thing that kept her near her basket was the can of tuna-flavored cat food he'd given her. He could almost see her thought processes. She couldn't tell if he was a good or a bad guy, but she was willing to reserve judgment so long as he fed her well.

He was seated behind the counter, the basket at his feet. The computerized cash register hummed behind him, and his laptop was open on the other counter. The radio was playing a syndicated blues program that came out of Texas and whose DJ clearly knew what he was talking about.

Dex rarely missed the show, and it was keeping him company now. It certainly suited his mood. Even though the only lost loves he'd ever had had been beloved pets who'd died, he understood the blues. Maybe it was the loneliness that was a part of the music. In all his years, he'd never had anyone who had been able to help him, who had known him well enough to take some of the burdens of his life off him.

Like this burden. He was searching his database for customers who had bought cat food in the past five years, people who had multiple animals. He was running out of potential cat parents. He'd already asked all his friends to take previous kittens left at the store. He didn't believe in taking perfectly healthy cats to the shelter—dumping his problems on someone else—and he didn't have enough money to put a special ad in the paper.

The vet suggested that he look through his old client records to see who might be amenable to adopting a kitten, but the farther he got into this project, the more Dex realized he couldn't do it.

Maybe he should just do a bulk mailing—50 percent off cat food and cat supplies for the next three months if someone took a kitten off his hands. Of course, that didn't solve his real dilemma.

He didn't trust people he didn't know to take care of their animals. He gave his customers the third degree—and the fourth, and the fifth—and sometimes he used his magic illegally to spy on them. He'd even been known to take an animal back if he thought someone was abusing it.

Dex looked down at the basket. The kittens were nursing, except for one adventurous black-and-white who was crawling across the tile floor and mewing. Dex picked him up by the scruff of his fuzzy little neck.

"I know you want to explore," Dex said, "but this store isn't the best place for that."

The kitten mewled and pinwheeled its little back legs with their sharp kitten claws. Its eyes were still milky but filled with life.

Dex found himself grinning at the tiny thing. His real problem was that he wanted to make sure everyone in the world—from kitten to adult human—was safe and loved. If he could, he would adopt every stray cat that crossed his path. But he already had a houseful of pets. He didn't dare bring home any more or Nurse Ratched would find a way to eviscerate him in his sleep.

He put the kitten back in the basket and was helping it toward its mother's stomach just as the bell jingled above his door.

He sighed. It was his own fault. Even though it wasn't much past 8 A.M., a customer had found him. Probably some cranky customer with a stray Doberman she wanted him to buy.

"Excuse me?" A woman spoke from the door. She had a husky voice, warm and attractive. It sent a thrill down his spine.

He sat up slowly and peered over the counter.

The woman was small and bookish. She had curly brown hair that tumbled around her face, obscuring her features. Her oversized glasses magnified her brown eyes. And she had her arms wrapped around her waist like the teenage girls in his one-room school used to do ninety years ago, when they were asking the boys to the Sadie Hawkins Day dance.

Still he felt something—a curiosity, an interest— he had never felt before.

"What can I do for you?" Dex made the question friendlier than he normally would have because she looked so uncomfortable.

She came deeper into the store, and the light from the aquariums caught her face. Her skin was the color of the perfect tan, even though he had a hunch this woman never went outdoors. And she had bow-shaped lips, a pert nose, and cheekbones that were so high that they gave definition to her entire face.

In fact, if she brushed the hair away from her forehead, got glasses that suited her, and stood up straight, she would be a beautiful woman.

Or, more accurately, it would be apparent to the entire world that she was a beautiful woman. But somehow he was glad that the entire world had to work to see her that way. That way, he wouldn't have to share her.

Then he flushed. He never had thoughts like that. Never.

One of the kittens mewled. The woman came closer. She smelled of rosewater, a scent he hadn't smelled in fifty years. A scent he loved.

"Kittens?" she asked, peering over the counter.

Dex looked down. The black-and-white had escaped again. Apparently the little brat hadn't been hungry and had decided to continue on his search of the great tiled frontier.

"Some lady left them yesterday," Dex said. "I usually don't handle cats."

"I thought you were a pet store," the woman said.

He shook his head, wishing she hadn't said that. He found her so attractive, and she had uttered the most irritating phrase in his life. He wasn't the pet store. He was the pet store—

"I'm sorry," she said. "I meant, I thought this was a pet store. Jeez, I'm not at my best today."

Dex looked up at her, feeling stunned. It was almost as if she had heard what he was thinking. But she couldn't, could she? She would be a mage someday—the power fairly sparked off her—but she was too young to have come into it already.

"It's all right," he said. "I sell pet supplies. And fish. Lots of fish."

She nodded. "I would think getting rid of kittens would be hard, anyway. I mean, you never know who's buying them."

"Exactly," he said. "Why don't more people understand that?"

She gave a one-shoulder shrug. "I have trouble parting with collectibles. I can't imagine what it would be like dealing with living creatures."

Someone who understood. No one had ever given him perfect understanding before. They always thought of their own pets but never of all the others. Obviously this woman did.

Dex smiled at her and extended his hand. "I'm Dexter Grant."

She bit her lower lip. He got the sense, fleeting but powerful, that she had been looking for someone else.

Then she smiled. It lit up her entire face and brought out that hidden beauty. He felt slightly dizzy. Then he realized he had forgotten to breathe.

She took his hand, and her fingers were soft and dry. "Vivian Kineally."

Dex resisted the urge to take that slight hand and bring it to his lips.

Vivian Kineally stared at him as if she were daring him to do so. Then she slipped her fingers from his and pressed her hand against her right temple. "Things are never easy when you want them to be."

"Easy? So I take it you didn't come to adopt a kitten."

Her smile faded. Her fingers continued rubbing, as if she were trying to massage away a headache. "I wish. Actually, I came looking for someone."

"Oh?" He tensed in spite of himself. His sense had been right. She had been looking for someone else and she was disappointed to find him.

He didn't want her to be disappointed.

He also didn't want her to be with anyone else.

She nodded. "I'm not even sure this is the right place. I mean, it meets the description my friends—well, they're not really my friends, they're more like . . . intruders, but they're the ones who sent me, and—"

"Who're you looking for?"

"Jeez," she said again, and he found that he liked the old-fashioned slang term when he heard it from her. "I'm even talking like them."

"Who?"

She waved her left hand dismissively. "It's a long story."

Her skin had paled noticeably. She seemed to be going gray, as if the pain she felt was getting worse. He wanted to touch her temples and magic the pain away, but he didn't. He knew better. Sudden magic startled people.

"You can tell me," he said.

She shook her head, then put her left hand on

the counter, as if catching her balance. "No. I'd like to appear at least slightly sane."

The kitten mewled again, and then Dex felt needle-sharp claws digging into his calf. The damn thing had jumped onto his leg.

"One second," he said, and reached down. He scooped up the kitten, holding it gently, and raised it to his face. "I'm going to start calling you Marco Polo if you're not careful, little one."

The kitten mewled again, and his mother looked up from her basket. Dex put the kitten back into it, but Marco Polo marched toward the edge before Dex had a chance to sit up.

"Cute," Vivian said.

"They all are at that age. But I have a hunch that little guy is going to be a handful."

She had both hands on the counter now. He was wondering if she was dizzy.

"Do you need to sit down?" he asked.

"No," she said. "I just need to find someone. Do you know an Henri Barou?"

He felt as if he had been punched in the stomach. His real name was Henri Barou, but no one knew that. He'd left that name behind eighty years ago because he'd hated it so much. Since then, he'd stolen his names from movie characters he admired. This one came from C. K. Dexter-Haven, Cary Grant's character in *The Philadelphia Story*, a man who was decidedly wittier and smarter than Dex could ever hope to be.

"No," he said, but the answer was a beat too late.

Despite her obvious pain, she gave him a penetrating look. "Why are you lying to me?"

He wasn't sure how to answer. He hadn't covered well. Should he tell her that Henri Barou sold the store to him, or that—

"You're Henri Barou," she said. "Why did you tell me you're Dexter Grant?"

"I *am* Dexter Grant," he snapped.

"And Henri Barou." She rubbed the bridge of her nose. "They mentioned you might use a different name."

Dex frowned. Who knew his real name? Not many people. No one alive; at least no one he could think of. If people knew a mage's real name, they could have power over him.

He needed to know who gave this woman his name, and who pointed her in the right direction. Apparently he had enemies out there he wasn't even aware of.

"Who mentioned that my name might be different?"

She blinked, and he got the sense of real pain wafting off her. Normally he would have insisted that she sit down, but he was unnerved by the changes.

"Well, this is where it gets strange," she said. "This morning, three women appeared at my apartment, claiming they were in trouble. They say their names are Clotho, Lachesis, and Atropos, and they call themselves the Fates. It gets weirder than that. Are you sure you want to hear about it?"

He wasn't sure. But he remembered that dream, and the feeling of foreboding it had given him. Were the Fates warning him? That would make more sense than anything this Vivian was telling him.

He couldn't believe the Fates had come to her place. They never left their judicial court and quarters. Often they changed the look of the quarters. In fact, whenever he'd been there, it had never looked the same.

"What's really going on?" Dex asked.

Vivian shrugged. "I don't entirely understand it.

They say they're in trouble and they need your help.''

A surge of anger ran through him. They did this to test him. If they pleaded trouble, then they could see if he would rush to their rescue. Of course, they were involving a mortal. Well, technically, she wasn't a mortal, but she hadn't come into her magic yet. Which made it all the more likely that this was a Fate trick. They didn't like people who interfered with mortal lives.

"I'm sorry," he said. "I've never heard of these women and I don't know why they think I can help them."

"Why do you lie?" Vivian asked.

His gaze met hers. The pain in her eyes seemed unbearable. Before he even thought it through, he hurried around the counter and put his arms around her. She was soft, and tinier than he had expected. She leaned against him, almost as if she was having trouble standing up. He helped her to his chair, which was the only one in the front of the store.

"Should I call a doctor?" he asked.

She was vibrating with pain. The muscles in her shoulders were taut.

"No," she said. "No, really. I'm all right. This'll pass."

Then he realized what was going on. He should have realized it when he saw all that power sparking off her. "You're psychic."

She closed her eyes. "I'm sorry."

He hadn't expected that response. "Sorry? Why?"

"I didn't mean to cause trouble or to call you a liar. It's just that these women seem so desperate, and they told me to come here. You know who they are, right?"

No sense lying any longer. She would see through it all. "Yes."

"So they are magical?"

"Yes."

"And so are you." It wasn't a question. She was getting a sense of him. "You also believe that they're lying so that they can hurt you."

"Yes," he said, feeling inadequate.

"Why would they want to hurt you?"

He shrugged.

"Because they're bored?" She opened her eyes. "Are people in your world that cruel? No. They're crueler."

He was answering her questions without even speaking. He hadn't ever been around anyone with this much psychic ability. Or perhaps he was broadcasting his thoughts. He was upset, and that could cause broadcasting. And he found her so incredibly attractive that he could be forcing a connection where there wasn't one.

He hoped she hadn't caught that last thought. "Can I get you something for your headache?"

"No," she said. "I already took something. It'll get better. They always do. Why would they hurt you?"

It took him a moment to deal with the transition. *They* no longer meant headache. *They* meant the Fates.

"I'll deal with them," he said. "I'll be right back."

He went to the front door of the shop and locked it, turning the OPEN sign to CLOSED. Then he scooped up Marco Polo, who had followed him, placed the kitten on Vivian's lap, and walked to the backroom.

He needed a little privacy for this spell, and he didn't want to think about what he was going to do until he got back there, since he seemed to be shouting every thought.

The backroom was crowded with unloaded boxes of Science Diet and Iams cat food, books on all the various fish, and some aquariums ordered by a new restaurant but not yet picked up. He hadn't put an office back here, preferring to work out front, but there was an area for animals that he didn't want to sell, an area that dated from the time when he really took pets.

Directly in front of him was the outside door. He double-checked the deadbolt and pushed on the steel just to make certain it was closed tightly. Then he closed the door to the tiny bathroom as well.

Precautions, precautions. He hadn't used magic this powerful in the store in years.

Then he clenched his fists, trying to hold in all the anger he was feeling. He would save that until he saw those harpies face-to-face.

"To the Fates," he said, and disappeared in a puff of smoke.

Six

The headache was getting worse. It felt like someone was pounding on the inside of Vivian's mind. Or maybe on the outside of her mind, and it was echoing inside. Or maybe the entire percussion staff of every marching band in the country had decided to rehearse in her head.

Vivian plucked little Marco Polo off her lap and set him on the floor. The movement made her dizzy. She put a hand to her head and waited for the room to stop spinning.

Just her luck to meet the handsomest man she had ever seen when she had the worst headache of her life. She wasn't even certain she had been speaking English—and then when he seemed not to know about the Fates, she was afraid he was going to consider her crazy.

He just sat behind the counter, watching her with those amazing blue eyes. He had rich black hair and a square jaw. He even had a dimple in his chin. When she had seen that, she wished Kyle were with her so that she could point out how charming a dimple was.

But of course Kyle, being eleven years old and male, probably wouldn't have thought the dimple as charming as Vivian did.

The headache seemed to grow, as if it were alive. She had to do something about it—find out what had happened to Henri—or Dexter, which he seemed to prefer—and see if he had some aspirin or something, anything to make this pounding go away.

Vivian stood, careful not to step on the adventuresome kitten. She was glad that Dexter had locked the front door. The little one, Marco Polo, seemed to have inspired all the others into exploring. Mom didn't care; she slept after a particularly draining feeding session.

The store had strange lighting. The fish tanks provided most of it. Somewhere nearby a man with a Southern accent talked about bluesman Robert Johnson.

The radio. It was only the radio.

The scratchy sound of an old recording filled the store, clashing with the hum of the cash register. One of the kittens meowed, and it sounded like someone screamed—at least to Vivian's sensitive ears.

She needed to lie down. She'd got a sense that there was someplace for her to do it in the back. She'd had migraines before, often after a lot of concentration, particularly psychic concentration. The migraines usually passed after a short nap.

She used the counter, and then some displays, to help herself toward the back. The fish, moving in their tanks, seemed to follow her, as if they were concerned. She was imagining everything.

A short nap, and she could drive out of here, out of poor Henri/Dexter's life. The man had just been trying to live like a normal person, even though he clearly was not. Just the mention of those women had put him into a panic.

They had some kind of history—the women had even referred to it—and it wasn't something he wanted to revisit.

Vivian would return to them and make them go to that restaurant, Quixotic, instead. Or she'd go there herself, bring someone up to her apartment and get help.

After her nap.

She made it to the door leading into the back. The pounding on her skull grew harder, almost as if someone were trying to get into her mind. She pulled the door open and found herself faced with boxes, empty aquariums, and a lot of pet food.

In fact, the entire back had the meaty odor of dry dog food, and it made her instantly queasy.

She didn't see Henri/Dexter anywhere. The back door was locked, and the bathroom door was closed.

She called his name, but he didn't answer. Which was odd, because she hadn't seen him leave.

There was no place to lie down back here. She put a hand on the pile of boxes and leaned on them, feeling like an old woman.

Then she used the last of her strength to cast about with her mind for him. But she couldn't sense Henri/Dexter. She was alone here except for the kittens and the mother cat.

A shiver ran up her spine. Alone, and the headache was growing worse, worse than it had ever been in her life.

She wasn't going to be able to drive. She wasn't even sure she could walk any farther.

She was going to need some help, and she was going to need it fast.

* * *

Dexter appeared in a giant library. It smelled musty and the lights were dim. The floor was made of marble and there were long tables between the stacks. Ladders on wheels ran up the walls as far as the eye could see.

He looked up. The books seemed to run on forever. He wondered if every book ever written was in here and then supposed it was.

Behind him, gum snapped.

"Ew, gross," a young girl said.

"Don't do that. You almost got it in my hair," said another.

"Did not." The last voice was petulant.

He turned around. Three teenage girls sat on top of one of the tables, legs crossed. Stacks of books surrounded them, and they all had books open on their laps.

The girls wore crop tops, low-slung jeans, and too much makeup. Their feet were bare, but their toes were painted with glitter polish and decorated with fake tattooed butterflies.

"Excuse me," Dex said, keeping his voice down even though they hadn't. "I'm looking for the Fates."

The girl closest to him—a long-haired blonde with sky blue eyes—smiled at him. "That's us!"

"No," he said. "The real Fates."

The girl in the middle flipped her beaded cornrows out of her face with one beringed hand. "We are the real Fates," she said with a trace of annoyance.

He was the one who was getting annoyed. All he had wanted to do today was find a home for five kittens. He hadn't planned on spending his morning searching for three women he didn't even like.

"I meant," he said, enunciating carefully, "I'm looking for Clotho, Lachesis, and Atropos."

"Oh, them," said the last girl, who had trimmed her red hair so short it looked like a crew cut. "They're not the Fates anymore."

"What?" Dexter took a step forward.

"Yeah," said the first girl. "We are."

He felt his stomach twist. "What do you mean, they're not the Fates anymore?"

"Hey, bud, don't you pay attention in class?" the second girl asked. "They're done. We're the Fates now."

"Or we will be," said the third girl, tugging on the rings jutting out of her right eyebrow.

"What do you mean, you will be?" Dex was feeling the beginning of panic. As much as he disliked them, he couldn't imagine the magical world without the Fates.

The first girl pulled bubble gum out of her mouth, twisted it around her index finger, and then chewed the gum back in. She didn't look more than twelve. "Well," she said around the gum, "all we gotta do is a good job."

"Yeah," the second girl said, nudging the first girl in the ribs. "Right now, we're the Interim Fates."

"Whose bright idea was this?" Dex snapped, and all three girls looked stunned.

He could tell from the look on their faces that he'd just made a classic error.

"Don't tell me," he said. "The Powers That Be chose you."

"We needed fresh blood," said the first girl, speaking out of turn. Didn't she know that the Fates were supposed to speak in order? And the girls hadn't genuflected when he mentioned the Powers That Be.

The twisting feeling in his stomach had gotten worse.

"At least that's what we were told," she continued. "You know, they'd been doing it, like, for*ever*, and they were beginning to screw up, you know, so it was time to bring in new ideas, new thoughts, new *people.*"

"You?" he asked.

"Us," the second girl said with a grin. "Isn't that just the spiffiest news you ever heard?"

"Spiffy," he repeated. "I don't suppose you're Clotho, Lachesis, and Atropos, having a little joke on me."

"No way," said the second girl.

"Who gives their kids those weird names, anyway?" the first girl said.

"They were perfectly normal names in their day," Dex said, amazed he was defending the Fates. "What're your names?"

"Tiffany," said the second girl.

"Brittany," said the first, "and she's Crystal."

Crystal didn't seem to be paying attention. She had returned to the book she was studying, frowning at the page.

"You sound more like pop stars than Fates," Dex said.

Tiffany and Brittany grinned. "That's what we want to be. We want to bring the Fatedom into the Now. You know. It was so Last Week."

"Last Century," Brittany said.

"Last Thousand Years," Tiffany said, and giggled.

Dex didn't feel like giggling at all.

"But this is a lot harder than we expected," Brittany said. "You know, like, we're supposed to know who you are just when you arrive—"

"You're magic, right? Because otherwise you couldn't get here, right? They don't let, like, non-magic people in the door," Tiffany said. "Right?"

She was asking him? "No one trained you for this job?" he asked, then wished he hadn't. He wasn't sure he wanted to know the answer.

"Well, like, we, um . . ." Tiffany let her voice trail off. She looked at Brittany, who grinned at him.

"We lied on our application," she said. "Not lied, exactly, but we said stuff we shouldn't have."

"Yeah," Tiffany said. "You'd think they would've known."

"But I heard that the old Fates chose their replacements. That wouldn't be right, would it?" Brittany asked.

It would if they wanted to keep their jobs. "They weren't fired, were they?" he asked.

"Like, who knows?" Brittany said. "They're gone, we're here, and we're going to get the permanent job."

"Just as soon as we figure out what we're doing," Tiffany said.

"Or maybe not." Crystal slammed her book closed. "This is way harder than anyone said it would be. You know we're supposed to keep track of what all the mages are doing all the time? Most of them are *old* and, like, who cares?"

"Besides, we can't make that work any more than we can make the name thing work," said Brittany. "What's your name, anyway?"

"Never mind," Dex said, and spelled himself back to the store. As he did, he heard Tiffany say, "The old ones all have weird names."

"No kidding," Brittany answered, and then their voices mercifully faded out.

He appeared in the back of the store, right in

front of Vivian. Her face was gray and the circles under her eyes had grown deeper.

"You're back," she said. "Thank God."

And then she fainted.

Seven

Vivian was cradled against a man's hard chest, his muscular arms supporting her back. She kept her head against him, and her eyes closed. If she didn't move, it didn't hurt, but she had the sense that it would if she did anything out of the ordinary. Anything at all.

The smell of pet food was strong here, but if she kept her face turned toward him, she caught his nice clean scent instead. Masculine, with just a hint of something—sandalwood?—buried faintly in his aftershave. Attractive, whatever it was.

She'd always wanted to be held like this. Fantasy cuddling. She would have to choose though: Superman? Batman? She'd even settle for Wolverine if he looked like Hugh Jackman had in the movie. But not Spider-man. She'd never been real fond of Spider-man.

"Vivian?" He had a deep superhero voice too. Bass, with just enough tenor. What'd they call that? Baritone. Rich and warm tones, masculine without the scary Darth Vader vibe. "Vivian, are you awake?"

"No," she said, without moving.

"You have to tell me what's going on. I can't spell your pain away, which means it's coming from an external cause."

Spell. Pain. She didn't want to think about that. Or about the fact that the man holding her was— Superman. She smiled a little. Maybe Batman. Golden Age, anyway. Not Silver Age, not Bronze Age. Collectible. D.C., not Marvel.

"Vivian, please. Don't fade out. I need you to stay with me."

A cool hand on her face. Large hand, long fingers. Gentle. She could stay like this forever.

"Tell me what's going on. Did the Fates do this to you?"

Fates. The pain whooshed back into her head twenty times stronger than before. She must have moved somehow.

She opened her eyes. Dexter—he preferred Dexter—was looking down at her. Maybe she had made him up. Maybe he was a vision from Kyle's comic book. Square jaw. Dimple in his chin. Electric blue eyes and hair so black that there was blue in it too. It curled over his forehead just so.

How could a man be that good-looking? It wasn't right.

Maybe it was right. He had strong arms too. He wasn't struggling with her weight. She felt like she was floating.

"Vivian," he said. "Stay with me. Did the Fates do this to you?"

"Do what?" she asked.

"Hurt you somehow?"

She shook her head, then wished she hadn't. She must have moaned, because his arms tightened around her. "No."

He didn't believe her. How come she knew what he was thinking? She sometimes knew what people were thinking, but only flashes, strong flashes, and then rarely.

"I think it's the glass," she said.

"Glass?"

"Around the building . . ."

He frowned, squaring his face even more. His eyebrows were two straight lines across his perfectly horizontal brow ridge. He didn't understand.

She would have to explain. She wasn't sure she had the words to explain. Her mind was too busy for words. Except the few she was sparing now, and they were forced, difficult, something she had to struggle with.

Then his eyebrows rose. "Are they in a building? The Fates?"

"My building," she said.

"And you always keep it guarded?" he asked. "Using a psychic's glass jar image?"

"Never done that before," she said. "It's harder than it sounds."

"Oh, crap," he said, clutching her closer. "Those stupid women are trying to get out."

"No," Vivian said. "I think someone's trying to get in. . . ."

And then she closed her eyes again, letting the words fade, and darkness take her once more.

The private landing strip at Portland International Airport was as far away from the terminal as it could get. Eris stepped onto the tarmac, the stench of jet fuel in her nose, and wished she hadn't adopted this identity.

Erika O'Connell was internationally famous. She couldn't spell herself around the planet willy-nilly. She had to use her magic with circumspection—

and she usually did, often channeling her power through mages with less power than she had, or even the occasional unsuspecting mortal.

But she couldn't do that now. She had to walk, catch a cab, and somehow find a reason to go downtown—create some kind of crisis, do something that would be worth her A team's time.

Noah Sturgis was right behind her, his deep announcer's voice carrying over the whine of the jet engines. "I have dinner at the Rainbow Room tonight, and I'm not planning to cancel the reservations. It took me a week to get them. Me! Imagine."

Imagine that he wasn't as popular as he thought he was or as big a star as he thought he was. Eris moved farther away from him so that she couldn't hear any more of the conversation.

A young maintenance worker hurried toward the jet, his orange jumpsuit so large that it bagged around his body. Eris caught his arm.

"Where do we get a taxi?" She had to shout to be heard over the noise.

He was thin and blond, with that open friendliness so common to the West Coast. "Where're you going?"

"Downtown."

"That's what I was afraid of. You'd better just stick around the airport for an hour or so. There's some kind of thing going on."

Eris glanced over her shoulder. Sturgis was still talking to Kronski at the base of the jet's stairs. Suzanne Gilbert, the real reporter of the group, bent forward under the weight of the overnight bag she had slung over her back.

The camera operators—all three of them women—lugged their gear down the stairs, their arms looking as muscular as a man's in the morning sunlight.

"What kind of thing?" Eris asked, turning her attention back to the maintenance man.

"Dunno. Radio says car alarms have been going off, and there've been like instant fires that just spring up and go away. They think maybe there's been a gas leak or something. So they're quarantining the downtown."

"Really?" Eris knew it wasn't quite a gift. Strife was screwing up again. But it would help her get her team down there.

"Yeah, and at least one building's shut off. No one can get in or out. It's weird. We've been watching it on TV when we're not dealing with all this." He gestured toward the tarmac.

Another jet passed by overhead—a commercial jet that had just taken off. Its silver side winked against the clear blue sky.

"Perfect," she said softly.

"What?" he shouted, leaning closer to her.

She smiled. Her smile could be charming when she wanted it to be. "Thank you."

He nodded—no one said "You're welcome" here—and hurried off. Only then did she realize he hadn't answered her original question: She had no idea where to get a taxi—particularly one driven by someone willing to go downtown.

"What's the scoop?" Sturgis asked as he reached her side.

That had been a nice trademark line twenty years ago, but it wasn't now. Eris ignored him.

"Where're we going?" Kronski asked.

"We're going to rent a car," Eris said, "or a van, something large enough to carry all of us. And you're going to figure out how to get us downtown. Apparently, the entire main area is cordoned off."

"You weren't kidding when you said something big was going on," Kronski said as he hurried away from them.

Sturgis watched him go. The jet engines behind them wound down and the whine faded. Eris's ears ached.

"You're the only person I know with sources this good." He looked at her sideways, which in his pulled-tightened-and-tucked face made him look slightly evil. "How do you do it?"

"Trade secret." She smiled. "And don't bother to ask anymore, because it's a secret I'm not planning to share."

Vivian was going to die, right here in his arms, standing among the bags of cat food and the empty boxes in the back of his store. Dex smoothed her curls away from her face. Her skin was clammy and cold. If someone from outside broke through that glass she had built around her building, they would destroy her mind. And it looked like they were close.

He couldn't believe someone was harming her. He cradled her against him. He had just found her and he might lose her.

What was wrong with the Fates? Why were they making a novice who hadn't even come into her magic defend a building?

He didn't have time to figure it out. He just had to solve it. He clutched Vivian even closer and did a location spell. He centered the spell on Clotho, Lachesis, and Atropos. If that didn't work, then he'd try to find the building Vivian was talking about.

For a moment, he continued to stare at the unfinished walls in the back of the store. Then the world whirled, and he was crouching on the hardwood floor of a newly remodeled apartment.

The Fates sat at a glass-topped table, picking through a nearly empty box of chocolates. The light from the floor-to-ceiling windows behind them was opaque, and outdoor noises—someone's car alarm kept going off—were muted.

"Henri!" Clotho stood and held out her arms as if he were her long-lost son.

"Not a moment too soon," Lachesis said as she stood also.

"Someone keeps trying to break in," Atropos said.

Dex rose, Vivian draped in his arms.

"Oh, no," Clotho said.

"What did you do?" Lachesis asked.

"I didn't do anything," he said. "Someone's trying to break through the glass she put around this building."

"And she's not strong enough," Atropos said, as if she were having a revelation. "Of course."

Lachesis came over to him and touched Vivian's forehead, as if she were trying to spell the pain away. But Vivian didn't open her eyes. He could still feel the pain radiate through her back and into his skin.

It was as if they were hooked up somehow, as if there was a direct pipeline from her personality to his.

He had no idea what was causing it, but it had become important to him.

She had become important to him.

"You ladies need to get the hell out of here," he said. "Vivian is in no condition to be part of your game."

"Oh, Henri," Atropos said, "it's no game."

"We have no powers," Clotho said.

"What?" This day was getting worse by the minute. "You have more powers than the rest of us combined. What's going on?"

"Had," Lachesis said.

"We gave them up," Atropos said.

Vivian didn't stir. She seemed to be getting weaker. He couldn't worry about the Fates at the moment. He had to worry about Vivian or she might die. If the Fates were testing him, he would fail. He wasn't going to let Vivian die because the Fates had some misguided sense of justice.

Dex carried Vivian to the blue and gold couch pushed against the wall. With one hand, he grabbed all the matching pillows and placed them against the couch's arm. Then he eased Vivian onto the cushions, careful to protect her head so that her pain wouldn't get any worse.

The gray color of her skin hadn't changed. The circles under her eyes looked deeper. The vibrancy she'd had when she had shown up at the store not an hour before was fading fast. And, considering how much pain she had been in then, that vibrancy couldn't have been close to the kind she had when she felt good.

The Fates watched him closely, as if he were some kind of test subject. He turned his back on them, smoothed the curls from Vivian's forehead, and kissed her ever so lightly. Her skin vibrated with agony, and he couldn't absorb it, the way he sometimes absorbed other people's pain.

This pain was something else, not internal but external. The mark of an attack that Dex couldn't see or hear.

He had to fight magic with magic. And then he would be able to help her recover.

He clenched a fist and uttered a protect spell. Weaving it carefully, he spread his protection around the building, making certain the spell included Vivian's glass jar vision as well. He wanted to make certain nothing could break her image from the outside. He cared more about that than he did about protecting the building itself.

Or the Fates.

He made the spell as strong as he could. In all his years of fighting crime and evil, he had learned how to make spells even more powerful than his so-called mentor had taught him.

Dex didn't know if the Fates had seen this extra power of his, or what they would do once they knew it existed.

But they had seen it now.

He was sacrificing everything for Vivian—a woman he had just met.

A woman, it seemed, he had been waiting for all his life.

Beside him, Vivian sighed. Her color was improving. Some of the pain had to be easing.

Before he congratulated himself on finishing the spell properly, though, he checked it—mentally testing its walls and shields so that nothing could get through.

He had woven the spell as tightly as he had ever woven a protect, and it seemed to be effective. He hoped it would hold until he had time to deal with whomever or whatever was out on the street, trying to break in.

Then he sat down on the edge of the couch and stroked Vivian's forehead. He had expected her to come to after he had taken the pressure off her vision. But, of course, she didn't know he had done that.

The shadows under her eyes were still deep, and there were lines around her delicate mouth. She seemed so tiny to have so much psychic power. She clearly had been able to read him. He'd come across a lot of psychics in his day, but none of them had the ability to read him—particularly when they were at a disadvantage, like she had been.

"Vivian?" he said, running a hand along her cheek. Her skin was soft. She stirred under his touch but didn't awaken.

Had the pain been so bad that it had destroyed part of her?

He eased his hand to her neck and found the problem. Her muscles were rigid, as they had probably been the entire time she fought the pain.

The external cause of the pain was gone, but the internal one apparently remained. And that was something he could solve.

The Fates were being unusually quiet during this crisis. He expected them to give him advice, to step in, to shove him aside, to do the work for him, or even to criticize what he was doing. Instead, they hovered, blocking his view of the rest of the apartment and making him nervous.

He shifted on the couch, determined not to let them interfere with his concentration.

Dex bent over Vivian. He slid his hand across her face again. The pain resonated through his fingers. The psychic link was there—faint, because she was unconscious, but there.

He pressed his thumb against the bridge of her nose and put his forefinger on her temple. Vivian leaned into his hand. He closed his eyes, reached through his hand to her mind, and found the pain.

This time he was able to touch it, and because he could, he recited a very simple spell that would transfer the pain from her to him.

It took a moment for the spell to work. Then his fingers seemed to sink into her skin, and pain shot up his arm. It struck his brain.

The intensity was blinding. Dex nearly toppled off the couch. He had no idea how one person had survived that much anguish. He bound the pain, wrapped it in a ball, and forced it outside the building, into the Willamette River, where it wouldn't harm anyone.

Even feeling the pain for that short a time had

been staggering. He wanted to put a cold compress over his face and lie down.

But he couldn't. He had to make sure Vivian was all right.

He opened his eyes. Vivian's skin wasn't quite so gray. There was a flush of red in her cheeks. It gave her a startlingly warm appearance, as if she were about to open her eyes and smile. Some people's faces in repose looked solemn. Vivian's had an impishness to it, as if she had fallen asleep in a particularly good mood.

The Fates had moved even closer, and they weren't looking at him. They appeared to be watching Vivian with concern.

It took him a moment to catch his breath enough to speak. "Vivian?"

Her eyelids fluttered. She raised a hand toward her forehead, then let the hand drop.

"Vivian?" he said again.

Her eyes opened. They seemed clear for the first time since he'd met her, and he was struck by the intelligence in them. He revised his opinion upward: She wasn't beautiful—she was strikingly beautiful. And it was the intelligence that made her so.

"Dexter," she said, frowning just a little. "Right?"

"Right," he said.

She smiled. "It suits you better than Henri."

He thought so too. "How're you feeling?"

"Fine." She put a hand to her head. "Amazingly."

"They had no right to ask you to create that vision," he said, unable to keep the anger out of his voice.

But Vivian didn't seem to hear him. Instead she was looking around her—at the couch, the artwork above it, the end tables, and then, finally, at him. "I'm home."

He nodded. The Fates were still pressed against him, saying nothing.

"How did I get here?" She eased herself up on her elbows, a movement that would have made her face pale even more in agony a few short minutes ago.

"I brought you," Dex said, uncertain how much to tell her.

"How did you know where I lived?"

"I didn't," he said.

"Then, how—?"

"Magic," Clotho said.

Dex braced himself. They were going to launch into him now, the inappropriateness of helping humans no matter what the circumstances. He even knew the speech: *If we gave you permission to help them, then we'd have to allow others to harm them. We'd have no control at all. Don't you think things through, Henri?*

Vivian looked at him, as if trying to sense whether or not he was telling the truth. She seemed awful accepting of his short—but apt—explanation.

None of the Fates said anything else. They didn't make the speech.

"So my car is still at your store?" she asked.

The question surprised him. He expected more discussion of the magic. Maybe she was already being mentored. She was old enough.

But if she were, she would have known the dangers of the glass jar vision and wouldn't have tried it.

Unless the Fates forced her to. He clenched his other fist. He would get to the Fates in a moment. No matter who they were, they had no right to interfere in lives like this.

"Yes, your car's there," Dex said, "along with a group of unsupervised kittens. I suppose I should be getting back."

"No, Henri," Lachesis said. "We need your help."

Dex didn't even face her. He continued to watch Vivian, who, despite her recovery, still looked a bit wan.

"I don't have time for games," Dex said to the Fates. "I've followed your rules. I don't think it's fair that you used Vivian to test me."

"We haven't done anything of the sort," Atropos said.

"Although you are correct," Clotho said. "We recognize the irony of asking for your help when we have denied it to so many others."

"Even if we were right," Lachesis said.

Vivian was frowning, as if she didn't entirely understand what was happening. She was the innocent victim in this. Dex wanted to take her in his arms, hold her, and comfort her, letting her know that nothing—absolutely nothing—would harm her again.

Dex stood slowly, menacingly. He'd done that once before with the Fates, only to feel small. This time, he towered over them.

He had never been taller than they were before. It was disconcerting, just like this entire conversation had been.

"I met your replacements," he said.

Atropos rolled her eyes. They were almond-shaped, accented by kohl. Very Greek. All three women looked very Greek. He hadn't realized that before either.

Was their claim to have lost their magic correct, then? Was he actually seeing them in their real forms?

"What did you think of them?" Atropos asked.

For a moment he thought she was referring to their forms—a question he didn't ever want to answer, in case they did get their positions back—

and then he realized she was asking about the Interim Fates.

"They didn't seem to have a solid grasp of the rules," he said.

"Such a surprise," Clotho said, even though she didn't sound surprised.

"Imagine what a mess they'll make," Lachesis said, putting a hand to her cheek in mock dismay.

"Save it," Dex said. "They told me that you picked them."

"Out of a candidate pool of three," Atropos snapped.

"Although we didn't tell them that," Clotho said.

"They're Zeus's daughters," Lachesis said. "They have an in with the Powers That Be."

"Zeus?" Dex raised his eyebrows. Somehow this amazed him, and it shouldn't have. "Zeus must have a million children by now."

"Seven-hundred-and-seventy-five thousand," Atropos said. "Not that anyone's counting."

"Do you see why we made it so that men can't father children after they've come into their powers?" Clotho said.

"Most men wouldn't abuse the privilege," Lachesis said.

"But every once in a while, you get someone like Zeus," Atropos said.

"No matter how much you tell him," Clotho said, "he simply doesn't grasp the idea of birth control."

"Well, he does," Lachesis said, "but he doesn't appreciate it."

"Last time we told him, he said something about socks." Atropos shook her head.

"Let me guess," Dex said. "You haven't even tried to talk to him for the last hundred years."

"And we should have," Clotho said. "Those children really are children. Because he had his powers when he fathered them, they were born with powers."

"We've had to monitor them from the beginning. Imagine a baby with the ability to change the world with the wiggle of a toe?" Lachesis said.

Vivian was still leaning on her elbows, frowning as the conversation continued around her.

Dex had lost control of it, and quicker than he had expected. The Fates, even though they might not have their magical powers, still had the power to confuse.

"They seem to think that just because they've had constant schooling since birth, they know enough to govern the world," Atropos said.

Dex was cold. "Don't tell me. They really are teenagers?"

"They might as well be," Clotho said, "for all the learning they've done."

"They're actually not much younger than you, Henri," Lachesis said. "Not much older than sixty, if my memory serves."

"I hate relying on memory," Atropos whispered to Lachesis. Lachesis nodded.

"Sixty?" Vivian sat up even farther. She looked at Dex as if he'd sprouted two heads. "You're sixty?"

She made it sound so old. He didn't want to seem old to her. He wanted to seem perfect. He said, "Actually—"

"Yes," Clotho said. "They're just babies."

"I don't think anyone can make informed decisions until they're well past their first century," Lachesis said. "These girls are going to be a disaster."

"You hope," Dex said, happy the focus had been taken off his age. He was 105, barely within the realm that the Fates considered old enough to make an informed decision. Although Vivian would probably find 105 even more shocking than sixty.

The Fates were staring at him as if he had said something profane. He had to think back. He wasn't quite sure what had come out of his mouth.

"No," Atropos said. "We do not hope. We have spent millennia preventing disasters. We do not want one."

Clotho nodded. "However, we could not explain to the Powers That Be"—at this the Fates extended their hands and bowed their heads with respect, just like they were supposed to—"how important we are."

"They seem to think anyone can do the job," Lachesis said.

"So long as these anybodies follow the new rules for application," Atropos said.

"Did we tell you that we must reapply?" Clotho asked.

He was feeling dizzy with information. The Fates weren't playing a trick on him—or if they were, it was a successful albeit elaborate one. They really were in some sort of trouble.

"Is that why you have no magic?" Dex asked.

Clotho's mouth thinned. Lachesis crossed her arms. They both looked at Atropos, who shrugged.

"We don't have magic," Lachesis said, "because Atropos believed we should try to fulfill all the silly new requirements."

"Now you blame it on me," Atropos said. "You agreed to it."

"That was before we were attacked," Clotho said.

"Attacked?" Dex asked.

"It's a long story," Lachesis said. "Let us tell it to you in order."

So they did.

Eight

Northwesterners were tough. No matter how many media badges Eris flashed at them, no matter how many autographs Noah Sturgis signed, the police would not let Eris's rented van past the cordon. Other media trucks sat outside, their little satellite dishes revolving, and cameramen hurried into nearby buildings, hoping to get on the roof. Helicopters flew overhead, their whap-whap-whapping a constant distraction.

Eris put Sturgis in charge of arguing with the authorities and then inched her way around the side of the van. The rest of her team stood behind Sturgis, listening to his argument—all except mousy little Suzanne, who was interviewing the handful of nonmedia personnel in the crowd.

Doing their jobs, as if the jobs were important. Eris would leave them to it. She had a real life to consider.

For the first time in months, she did actual magic. She slipped into the van and snapped her fingers, spelling herself to Stri's side.

Her son stood on a sidewalk in the middle of the cordoned-off area. His shaved head glistened in the sunlight. He had a skateboard under one booted foot, and the other foot rested on the ground. He wore tight jeans, a jacket covered with zippers and snaps, and no shirt. His tattoos appeared to be gone. In their place were more piercings than Eris wanted to think about.

Around him, car alarms blared, their screeching bleats half of a step off from each other. The cacophony was irritating.

People peered out of nearby buildings—all of which appeared to be apartments—but when they saw her looking at them, they eased back in, as if afraid to be seen.

That was when she realized Strife was alone on the street. She snapped her fingers, changing her outfit and hair color immediately, so that no one would recognize her as Erika O'Connell.

"Took you long enough," Strife said. He wasn't looking at her. He was staring at the building across the street.

She followed his gaze. The building—an eight-story brick building that appeared to have apartments on each floor—was winking in and out, as if it were part of a malfunctioning computer program.

The only thing that would cause a reaction like that was if a mage's spell and a psychic's vision collided. Someone had already put a glass jar shield on the building, so someone else—someone powerful—had to have countered with a protect.

Eris cursed. "When did this start?"

"About five minutes ago," he said.

"Who got in?"

"Dunno," he said.

"How'd he get in?"

"Dunno that either."

"Did you do a relocate? Centered on the Fates?"

"The Fates," Stri said calmly, "are those babies you talked Zeus into spoiling."

Eris smiled at the beauty of her own plan. Then her smile faded. "Did you try a relocate using their real names?"

"Whose?"

"The Fates?"

"The Interim Fates?"

She cuffed him on the side of the head. "The Fate Fates."

Strife cringed away from her. "What'd you do that for?"

"Did you?"

He kicked the edge of the skateboard, popping it upward and catching it with one hand.

"Strife?" Her eyes narrowed. She could feel some real temper coming on. "You didn't, did you?"

He shrugged. "Didn't think of it."

"You didn't think of it? You tried fire, you tried smoke feelers, you tried—what? minor explosions to set off those car alarms?—and you didn't think of the easiest spell of all? The relocate spell?" She grabbed one of the hoop earrings he had put into his right eyebrow and tugged just enough to hurt. "Are you really that stupid?"

"Leggo," he said, reaching for her hand.

"Strife? Are you that stupid?"

"No. Mom. Please, leggo."

"Then why didn't you do the spell?"

"Because," he said, "I couldn't remember their names."

Eris let go in surprise. "You couldn't remember the Fates' names?"

Strife was clutching the right side of his face and backing away from her. "No."

"It didn't occur to you to call and ask me?"

"I thought you'd be mad," he said.

"It didn't occur to you to go to the library and look up the myth?"

"Forgot about the library," he said. "Haven't used one in fifty years."

"Or the Internet? You couldn't walk down the block and hop into one of Portland's six billion Internet cafes?"

"I screwed up, Mom. I did. I'm sorry."

"Sorry." She cursed again. It would have been so easy. If some other mage had been able to get into the building with a relocate spell, then Strife would have been able to too. She would have been able to, if she'd been willing to use her magic on that plane. "You're sorry."

"Don't hurt me, Mom," he said. "Please."

She backhanded him anyway, just for old times' sake, and walked across the street.

"Ma'am." An amplified voice reached her from nowhere and everywhere at the same time. *"Back away from the building. You could get hurt."*

So the police were monitoring this. Great. That was all she needed: her transformation from Erika O'Connell to this punk chick who hit Stri all done in front of reliable eyewitnesses.

But she couldn't think of that. She kept walking.

"Ma'am. Back away—"

With a flick of the wrist, she shut off the noise. She reached the building, created a little magical fog, and looked for the edge of the protect spell.

If she guessed right, whoever had done it had done it quickly, and would have left a hole or two.

But as much as she looked, she found nothing. This was the tightest spell she had ever seen. And it looked a little familiar. She would save part of it, and look for the signature later.

What she needed was a bit of that glass shield. Just a piece.

"Stri?" Eris said, beckoning him forward.

He came, carrying the skateboard under his left arm and covering the side of his face with his right. He looked like a modern Quasimodo, only with a jean jacket instead of a hump.

He stayed just outside of arm's reach as he asked, "What?"

"Did you do any damage to that glass jar shield?"

He frowned. Or partially frowned. Or hid half of his frown. She couldn't tell with his hand there. She was tempted to grab it and move it down, but she didn't. She wanted him to answer her.

"No," he said after a moment. "But when it started out too big it crashed onto the sidewalk. There should be pieces somewhere."

Eris smiled at her son. "You can be such a good boy when you want to be," she said.

He gave her an uncertain smile. Her own smile faded.

"Well," she said. "What are we waiting for? Help me find those pieces—*now.*"

The Fates settled around the glass-topped table as if they were going to recite Homer's *Odyssey* in the original Greek. Vivian, who was looking better, decided to make herself some tea, and offered Dex some. He wasn't much of a tea drinker, but he knew he'd better fortify himself. He had a hunch the story the Fates were going to tell might take the rest of the day.

As the Fates spoke, he watched Vivian work around her apartment—her delicate hands gathering the remains of the chocolate box, the sway of her hips as she walked into the kitchen. He had to force himself to concentrate on the Fates' words, because he really wanted to think about Vivian.

Apparently, the Fates said when they finally had

Dex's attention, the Powers That Be were dissatisfied with the Fates' performance since—well, they weren't sure. They argued about the date until Vivian came into the dining room, bearing tea on a tray and more cookies than Dex had seen since he'd helped some Girl Scouts save a dog in the 1970s.

Anyway, doing the math, and subtracting a little for the vagaries with which the Fates seemed to regard mortal time, Dex figured the Fates's trouble started either in 1700 or 1960. He wasn't going to narrow it down any farther. The Fates were notified recently (which Dex guessed to be about two years ago mortal time) that they would be forced to step out of their positions due to newly imposed term limits.

("They laid you off, then," Vivian said as she sat down at the table, and everyone glared at her except Dex, who had to bend his head to hide a smile.)

The Fates were told that there were new requirements for their job and that they didn't meet any of those requirements. The Powers That Be (the Fates paused for genuflection) would contact the legal-minded mages, encourage some to apply, and then open the process to application. The application process wouldn't start for some time.

"How much time?" Dex asked.

"Just shush and listen," Clotho said.

"It's important, isn't it?" he asked. "What if they've already started the application process."

"They haven't," Lachesis said.

"I doubt anyone has even noticed we're gone yet," Atropos said.

"I noticed," Dex said glumly.

Beneath the table, Vivian put her hand on his. The brush of her soft skin sent a tingle through him. He turned his hand upward so that he could hold hands properly. Their fingers meshed, and he rubbed his thumb along her forefinger. Touching her felt good, and eased the sense of frustration he was getting from this conversation with the Fates.

"Maybe you'll get it if we explain the application process," Clotho said, and before he got to weigh in on that idea, they did:

According to the Fates, the Powers That Be (genuflect) promised to examine each applicant, pick a few good candidates (maybe fifteen, five for each position) and interview, interview, interview.

So the Fates decided that they would reapply, but first, they would gain experience in the areas they lacked. Those new areas sounded simple enough: They needed to understand other cultures; they needed to learn diplomacy; and they needed to experience powerlessness.

"The problem," Lachesis said, "is that the makeup of the governing council of the Powers That Be—" Here the women genuflected again. Vivian looked at Dex as if she wondered if she should too, but he shook his head. "—has changed in the last two thousand years. They argue a great deal about cultural heritage. We have Egyptians, the Norse, of course, Japanese, Native Americans—"

"Frankly, I put much of this change on that Coyote person. He seems to enjoy stirring things up, which is not what we're about. How he got on the governing council I'll never know." Atropos squeezed her teacup so hard that her knuckles turned white.

"I told you," Clotho said. "He can be reasonable when it's in his own best interest."

"I have a hunch this isn't the kind of cultural understanding they all want," Dex said. He kept moving his thumb on Vivian's hand, enjoying the feel of her.

"It doesn't matter," Lachesis said, "at least not yet."

"Well, it does," Atropos said, "if we're going to understand all of this. After all, the Powers That Be"—another genuflection—"believe that we're too Greek, even though the country didn't exist yet when we were born."

"They meant our heritage is too Mediterranean," Clotho said.

"And too old," Lachesis said. "I got a real sense of ageism from them."

Dex shook his head slightly. Discrimination within his ruling government. What a shock.

"I don't understand." With her free hand, Vivian picked up the teapot, shook it, and seemed satisfied with its slosh. "How did that lead you all to me?"

"We decided to go after all of this backward," Atropos said.

"We figure we can learn cultural diversity and diplomacy," Clotho said. "After all, how hard can it be? A few books here and there, maybe a few movies, and we're covered."

This time, Dex did roll his eyes. Vivian squeezed his fingers, as if she agreed with his disbelief.

"But powerlessness," Lachesis said. "That's the real trick. We've never been powerless, and we're not sure we understand it."

"Although I think we're getting evidence," Atropos said.

"What?" Vivian asked.

"A clue," Dex whispered to her. "They're getting a clue."

Clotho didn't seem to hear. "We arrived in Porttown this morning—"

"Port*land,*" Dex and Vivian corrected in unison.

"—and it's been nonstop crisis ever since. First we get zapped with some sort of fire ray."

"Then we run, screaming, and nearly get hit by an unsympathetic car," Lachesis said.

"Unsympathetic?" Dex asked.

"We were in crisis," Atropos snapped. "The driver should have known and been more careful."

"Then this creature appears in front of us, grabbing for us," Clotho said.

"Only he got hit by a more sympathetic car," Lachesis said.

"It took us a while to figure out that we needed help," Atropos said.

"So you came here?" Dex asked.

"Actually, we'd arrived outside Quixotic, but the doors were locked," Clotho said.

"We're going to have words with Aethelstan about that," Lachesis said.

"The restaurant hadn't opened yet," Vivian whispered.

"I got that," Dex said.

"That creature attacked us again," Atropos said, "and I stabbed him with my shears."

"Breaking them," Clotho said. "I'm not sure what the Powers will think of that."

The women pondered that for a moment, apparently forgetting to make obeisance to the Powers That Be with that mention. Or maybe it wasn't necessary when the name was shortened.

Lachesis sighed and the others followed, as if her response awoke them all from their reverie. "Then Clotho remembered Eugenia, only we couldn't remember where she lived."

"But we knew where Vivian was because we had just gotten her change of address," Atropos said.

"Right before we left," Clotho said. "I believe it was on the very last day."

"And lo and behold, the address was right here in Porttown," Lachesis said.

"Port*land,*" Dex corrected, but he was alone this time. Vivian looked startled. She let go of his hand.

He felt the loss. It was almost as if she had, in her surprise, closed herself off from him.

"Change of address?" she asked. "What change of address? I haven't sent out any forms yet, and I wouldn't have sent any to you anyway, because I didn't know any of you before this morning."

She sounded almost angry. Not that he blamed her. He remembered when he found out he was going to have magical powers. He had gotten angry too, wondering why no one had told him sooner, why they hadn't made the transition easier, why nothing in his life could be simple.

And of course it had gotten even more complex.

"Oh, you don't send them, my dear," Atropos said. "We just sort of know."

"Or we used to," Clotho said. They all sighed again.

"And when we came up here and tried to explain what was going on," Lachesis said, "we realized that Vivian knew nothing—"

"—and the attacks continued," Atropos said. "Which is why we sought you."

Dex rubbed his forehead with his hand. He was the one getting a headache now. Or maybe he just wished he was so that he could conveniently pass out on the couch—next to Vivian. Alone.

"What kind of creature was attacking you?" Dex asked.

"Well, it wasn't a creature, exactly," Clotho said.

"It was a person," Lachesis said.

"Although he was dressed like a creature," Atropos said.

"Not to mention he hadn't bathed in—oh—weeks, maybe," Clotho said.

Vivian wrinkled her nose. It was a cute reaction. Dex looked at her fondly. She raised her eyebrows at him, as if she expected him to ask another question.

It took him a moment to remember what the group had been discussing. "Was this so-called creature a man or a mage?"

"A mage," Lachesis said.

"Definitely," Atropos said.

"And a familiar one," Clotho said.

"Sort of," Lachesis said. "He was dressed differently."

"Lots of metal," Atropos said.

"And he'd lost all his hair," Clotho said.

"If you recognized him, tell me who he is and I'll stop him." Dex tensed as he spoke. There were many mages, especially dark mages, who were more powerful than he was, but he had fought powerful dark mages before. And won.

Vivian looked at him sideways, as if she had heard that thought and it surprised her. He extended his hand under the table. She took it.

"We said he looked familiar," Lachesis said.

"But that doesn't mean we recognize him," Atropos said.

"That power seems to have disappeared with our magic," Clotho said.

"And we need it," Lachesis said.

"Who knew we weren't very observant?" Atropos asked.

Dex knew, but he said nothing. Vivian watched them avidly, her hand warm in his. He loved this instant connection between them. She had a familiarity. It wasn't as if he'd known her all his life. It was as if he'd expected her all his life.

"And you don't even have a guess as to who this could be?" Dex asked.

"It could be anyone," Clotho said. "We seem to anger people."

"Maybe that's why you need to learn diplomacy," Vivian said, with an admirable lack of tact.

The women ignored her.

"How long are you going to be without your magic?" Dex asked.

"Until we decide to return to Olympus," Lachesis said.

"Why don't you decide to return now?" Dex asked.

"Because we've just gotten started," Atropos said.

"This is simply a—how do you say it?—a hitch," Clotho said.

"A glitch," Vivian corrected.

"That too," Lachesis said.

The phone rang, startling all of them. Dex nearly knocked over his teacup. Vivian stared at the phone as if she had forgotten it existed.

It rang again.

Vivian's hand slipped out of Dex's. She got up like a woman sleepwalking and crossed the floor. Dex held his breath. He didn't know if the mage or mages who were searching for the Fates would think to call this apartment. Or even if they knew who to call.

Vivian picked up the phone as if she expected it to be too hot to touch. Apparently she was leery too.

"Hello?" she said, sounding so timid that Dex found himself wondering if she was the same woman who had called him a liar.

The Fates stared at her. They appeared to be holding their breath as well. They did seem diminished somehow, or maybe he was just reading that into them. He only thought they were less without their magic.

But then, he'd only had his for eighty-some years, and he would feel lost without his magic too. Theirs was more powerful, and they hadn't been without it for millennia. In fact, they hadn't even left their compound during all that time until this morning.

Considering they'd been under attack from the start, they'd done remarkably well. He hadn't really figured that out until now.

"Yes," Vivian said. "That is my address."

She had carried the phone toward the large television set that she had beneath a wall covered in comic book art. With all the turmoil, Dex hadn't noticed the TV or the art before.

He stopped watching Vivian and got up from the table. He walked toward the art, a shiver running through him.

He found himself staring at the yellow cover of Superman #1, with its chesty superhero in his blue tights and red cape flying over a building.

The complete story of the Daring Exploits of the one and only SUPERMAN lined the bottom. He didn't have to see the date to know when that was published. 1938: the beginning of the end.

"That's just not possible." Vivian turned on the television with her remote. The Fates got up and crowded around her. They looked fascinated with the TV, even though Dex knew they'd seen one before. They'd watched a lot of television since Stalin had given them one to stay on their good side.

Not that Stalin's ploy had worked, of course. He was rotting away in some kind of Fate-induced hell.

The screen image winked on and Vivian thumbed up the channels until she found CNN. News crews were huddled on a city street as a building winked on and off like a giant firefly.

Dex recognized the street. It was in Portland.

"It's got to be some kind of special effect," she said into the phone.

And then Dex knew what was happening. "That's no effect, Viv," he said. "We're doing that."

"Well, I'm not," she said, then she frowned as whoever had called spoke. "Look, I'm sorry, Travers, but I have to go. Yes, I'll call you when I know what's happening. On your cell. I remember that you're driving."

She hung up and set the receiver on a nearby table. "I can't be doing that," she said to Dex.

"You're not doing it alone," he said. "We're doing it together."

"So stop," she said.

"If I stop, then whoever is trying to get the Fates will be able to get into this building."

"Huh?" She blinked at him.

"The winking effect only happens when a mage's spell collides with a psychic's creation, usually designed for the same purpose. I put a protect around the building, but you already covered this place in glass. Now it's time to take the glass away."

She frowned, clearly not understanding. "How do I do that?"

"Imagine it gone," Atropos said.

"Hurry," Clotho said.

Dex wondered how they felt, being the cause of such a huge revelation of magic in the middle of a weekday morning.

Vivian closed her eyes. Then she staggered backward, clutching the end table for balance. When she opened her eyes, she looked surprised.

On the television screen, the building reappeared, solid and dark. No winking. He could hear a gasp from the crowd—both on the screen and ever so faintly outside.

"At least that's over," Vivian said.

"Actually, it isn't." Dex took the remote out of her hand. The entire world had seen that building flash like a malfunctioning Christmas tree. "Now whoever's been searching for the Fates knows exactly where they are."

"They knew that before," Vivian said, "if the pounding in my head was any indication."

"Maybe," he said. "But they also know what kind of spell I cast around the building."

"It's hard to counteract a protect," Lachesis said.

"But it can be done," Dex said, "given enough time."

"You've got magic, though," Vivian said, putting her hand on his arm. "You can stop anything."

He shook his head. "I wish I were that powerful."

"We were," Atropos said.

"Just yesterday," Clotho said.

"But we're not anymore," Lachesis said.

"What an ignominious end," Atropos said, sinking into a chair, hands over her face.

"We really should think things through," Clotho said, sinking down beside her.

Dex stared at them, not liking this admission from a group once assigned to administer justice.

"Don't panic yet," he said, trying to sound reassuring. "I have a plan."

They all looked at him, their expressions filled with hope. He let out a small sigh. He had no idea what had just possessed him.

He had no plan.

Now, he supposed, he would just have to make one up.

Nine

Dex's panicked gaze met Vivian's and she knew, as clearly as if he had spoken, that he had no plan at all. She glanced at the clock she'd hung above her comic book art: the Incredible Hulk's arms pointed to ten and twelve.

Only an hour until Quixotic opened for lunch. Maybe someone would be in the restaurant.

She actually sent the thought to Dex, hoping he could receive it. This trick rarely worked with other people. Only her baby sister Megan seemed able to understand Vivian's thoughts when she sent them like that.

But Dex smiled. She could feel the warmth in his gaze. His lips didn't move, but she heard him say *thank you* as clearly as if he had spoken the words aloud.

"We need to get you out of here," he said to the Fates, "now that everyone knows where you are. They're going to try to trace any magical trail I make, and since we don't know who's after you or how powerful they are, I think it might be good if we have some help."

"Who, though?" Lachesis said.

"Quixotic is just next door," Dex said. "Seems to me there should be at least one mage inside."

"They're closed," Atropos said.

"We already told you that," Clotho said.

"Just a few minutes ago, as a matter of fact," Lachesis said.

"They have hours like other restaurants." Vivian smiled at the Fates. "They should open at eleven."

The Fates looked up at her clock, just like she had done. The minute hand hadn't moved much.

Her gaze slipped from the Hulk to her framed comics: her prized Batman original, signed by Bob Kane; the line art for an early issue of Swamp Thing; and her most prized possession, a carefully framed copy of Superman #1. Once upon a time, that comic book had been worth more than everything else she owned put together.

The value of the comic book hadn't declined, but she had come into money since Aunt Eugenia had given her the book. (Aunt Eugenia again. Vivian felt her heart twist.)

Then she frowned. That cover had given Dex quite a jolt when he had first seen it. He had studied it as if it were the enemy.

She loved the cover. Superman over Metropolis, his marvelous body curled as he stopped in the air mid-flight to study the city below. His lantern jaw and solid profile gave him an all-American handsomeness that she so admired. The blue-black hair curled over his forehead. The only thing she couldn't see was that beloved dimple in his chin.

The dimple. In his chin.

Vivian looked at Dex.

Dex had Superman's face. Or rather, Superman had Dex's face. Dex flushed.

"I can explain," he said.

"You're—?"

"No," he said. "They were just a couple of teen-agers who didn't know what they saw was magic. They were—"

"Henri!" Atropos said.

"You're not to talk of that," Clotho said.

"You are forgetting our warning," Lachesis said.

And even though the Fates had no power, Dex seemed unnerved enough to stop talking.

"I think he can tell me," Vivian said, a little unnerved herself. Dex looked like Superman. Whenever Vivian envisioned the perfect man, she envisioned Superman. Or, if the situation called for an intellectual, Clark Kent. Kent always looked good in a suit.

Just like Dex would.

"I think we should take Henri's suggestion and leave this place," Atropos said.

"And that artwork," Clotho said, as if there were something wrong with it.

The back of Vivian's neck itched. She ran a hand over it, wondering if this was an aftereffect of the strange headache that glass jar had given her. She scratched at the base of her skull, and the itch went away.

"You all right?" Dex asked.

She wasn't sure if he was asking about her reaction to the art and the news, or if he was concerned about her health. She didn't have time to dwell on either. The Fates had to be the priority. "I think we should go."

"You don't have to tell me twice," Dex said, and waved his arm in a circle. Instantly, Vivian's apartment vanished. For a moment, she appeared to be in a void with the Fates and Dex, and then she was inside Quixotic.

She'd been to Quixotic before with Kyle and

Travers, the day after she moved to Portland. She wanted to treat them after all the help they had given her.

The meal had been special. Wonderful service that caught every detail, but no one hovered. Excellent food, rivaling anything she'd ever had in L.A., and a congenial atmosphere, which her hostess had called upscale Northwest, laughingly adding that it was upscale because the tablecloths were linen.

The restaurant had been packed that day. It was empty now, and colder than it had been. The air was still fragrant, though. Some of the scents lingered from the night before—or had probably always been there—a hint of garlic, a bit of vanilla, some exotic spices she couldn't identify. But over all of it was the rich, warm smell of baking bread, a smell that made her feel at home.

The group had arrived in the front of the restaurant, near a long bar that brushed up against floor-to-ceiling windows. Everyone was standing in the same positions they had been in: Vivian near Dex, and Atropos near the empty hostess station. Clotho and Lachesis had the worst of it. They had both been sitting on the couch, and when they arrived, they toppled to the hard tiled floor.

They didn't look upset, though. Instead, they both cast glances at the darkened windows, which had an excellent view of the street.

"I'm not sure this was a good idea," Clotho said.

"Let's get away from here," Lachesis said.

They stood, brushing themselves off, and headed into the restaurant. The tables, made of wood, had runners going across them, with rose centerpieces. The dishes, already in place, were stoneware, and the silverware beside them had a distinctly knotted pattern.

Apparently lunch here was a lot more casual than dinner.

Vivian glanced at the street before following the group. She could still see police vans, news trucks, and a crowd of people, most of whom had surrounded her building and were touching its brick sides. She wondered if CNN was still broadcasting the strange news, wondered if she should call Travers back, and then decided to do it later.

Atropos had stopped in the middle of the restaurant. She was touching one of the floral centerpieces, her hand lingering on the rose's petals. Clotho and Lachesis moved forward, apparently not realizing that they were alone.

Dex stood near the hostess station, watching Vivian.

"This is a bit much for you, isn't it?" he said.

She gave him a small smile. Superman. Wow. But his kindness seemed more personal than the Man of Steel's had ever been. Vivian often got the sense that Superman never really got involved emotionally with anything—not even Lois Lane.

It was clear that Dexter Grant didn't have that problem. Vivian already felt involved with him, and she had only known him a few hours. He was clearly wrapped up in her as well.

"I feel like I'm in a different world," she said.

"You are." He extended his hand. "Come on. Let's see if we can resolve this so you can go home safely."

She froze. She hadn't thought about that. Her apartment wasn't safe because whoever was looking for these women had known they were there.

"Do you think I'm in danger?" she asked.

He studied her for a moment. She got a sense he was going to lie to her—tell her everything was all right, when it really wasn't. And then, clearly, he changed his mind.

"I'll know more when I know who we're dealing with," he said. He kept his hand out, and she took it. His fingers were warm and dry. They wrapped around hers, and she felt a jolt.

Dex glanced at her. He seemed to feel it too. It was odd that she couldn't tell if he actually felt it or not. For a moment, he seemed closed to her.

Did he have the ability to shut her out? She'd never met anyone who could do that before. Either they didn't let her in at all, like the Fates, or they were completely open to her if she wanted them to be.

Of course, she wasn't usually this hooked up, either, where she could hear actual thoughts.

Dex led her toward the back. Clotho and Lachesis went through a double door, and she could hear voices rise. Atropos picked up the rose and brought it to her nose, inhaling deeply. Then she held the rose away, staring at it with a frown.

"It's a hothouse rose," Dex said as he and Vivian reached Atropos's side. "It has no scent."

"Then what's the point of having a rose?" Atropos put it back into the vase.

Vivian had never seen her away from the other two. Atropos seemed smaller than she had before, as if she weren't really a full person, even though Vivian couldn't really say what was different.

"Come on," Dex said.

They headed toward the back. At that moment, the double doors opened again. Clotho beckoned Atropos forward. Atropos sighed and hurried ahead.

"I've never seen them apart," Dex said. "I didn't think they could be separated."

His words echoed Vivian's thoughts from a moment before, except that he sounded worried. "Is that a problem?" she asked.

"I don't know," he said, but he sounded confused. His hand gripped hers tightly, his pressure gentle.

"I still don't understand all this talk about interims and governing bodies and powers," Vivian said. "If there were powers in charge, why would they let someone attack these women?"

"I'm not sure the Powers That Be know what the Fates are doing." Dex had slowed down. He wasn't walking as fast as he had a moment before. It was almost as if he didn't want to go into the back, didn't want to get involved with the other mages.

"When do you think we can leave?" Vivian asked.

He smiled down at her. "You really do read minds."

"No," she said. "Usually I just get a sense impression. You and I seem particularly in tune."

Then she blushed. She hadn't meant that the way it sounded. Or maybe she had. She wasn't really certain. She just knew that this man attracted her and made her feel safe all at the same time.

Then the double doors banged open. A tall, black-haired man wearing blue jeans, a crisp white shirt, and silver-toed boots walked into the room. He had odd silver eyes, and a narrow, classically handsome face, so perfect that Vivian would have thought he was airbrushed if she'd seen his photograph in a magazine.

"So you're the infamous Henri Barou," the man said in a deep voice that had a hint of a British accent.

Dex sighed. "Let's go with Dexter Grant, shall we?"

The man's eyebrows went up in amusement. "All right. If we're going to do that, I'm Alex Blackstone."

"Aethelstan." Clotho came to the double doors. Her tone made the name sound like a reprimand.

"He insists that we don't use real names. I think he's right," Blackstone said. "We have no idea who's listening."

"I say we make sure no one is." A broad-shouldered man with the whip-thin athleticism of a long distance runner stopped beside Clotho. He had blond curls and eyes so blue they reminded Vivian of sapphires.

The blond man was beautiful. Vivian almost felt as if she'd seen him before—and then she realized she had. At the Getty Museum, she'd seen a touring exhibit of Greek sculpture. He looked like one of the young athletes caught mid-run.

"To keep things level," the blond man said, "my real name is Darius, but you will call me Andrew Vari."

Vivian wasn't sure how much more of this she could take. Both men had strong personalities, and she got a sense of them, clearer than anyone except Dex. With Dex she felt a connection. With them, she had a sense she could be overpowered at any moment.

"I think we should meet here in the dining room," Blackstone said, "since we seem to have quite a crowd."

His silver gaze passed over her, and if she hadn't had a sense of him, she would have thought he hadn't seen her. But she knew he had, and she also knew that he saw her magical power just like Dex had.

"Besides," Blackstone said, going to a large table, "if we talk out here, we don't have to worry about my kitchen staff overhearing anything unusual."

He reached into the pocket of his shirt and removed a box of matches. Then he lit a fat candle in the middle of that table's large centerpiece.

"Alex." Another blond woman pushed her way

past the group at the door. "You're not thinking of opening today, are you?"

The woman was tiny and had the cute, open face of a high school cheerleader. In fact, if she hadn't spoken first, Vivian would have thought she was a high school student. But the woman's voice had a strength that only came with age and experience.

When Blackstone raised his head and looked at the woman, his expression softened, easing the angles and planes of his face. He suddenly looked approachable.

"I think it would be more suspicious if we remained closed, don't you, Nora?"

Nora, the blonde, shook her head. "Not with all those cops and news organizations out there."

"Publicity," said Andrew Vari. "It's always good to be open when members of the press are around."

"Except when you have three Fates in your dining room," Dex said dryly.

Vari shrugged one shoulder. "We could spell them so no one saw them but us."

Dex let go of Vivian's hand. She felt the absence as if he had left her. "Before we go any farther, I need to know if this place is protected."

Blackstone's eyes hooded, and Vivian couldn't see their expression any longer. "Why?"

"These women have been under assault all morning," Dex said. "I need to know they're safe."

"They're safe for the moment," Blackstone said. "We'll have a problem when we open for business."

"So you do have a protection spell on this place?"

Vari crossed his arms. "How we protect this place is none of your business."

The back of Vivian's neck ached. She wondered

if she had twisted it funny when she passed out. She rubbed it absently.

"Right now, it is my business," Dex said. "I didn't bring everyone here to make matters worse. I suspect the Fates are up against some pretty big powers, and I am a rather young mage compared to you two. I thought I could use some help."

"This is the part where you say, 'But I was wrong' and then stomp off, right?" Vari's face, however beautiful, was not kind. Vivian had been right to compare him to a sculpture. He had all the warmth of stone. "You'd like to leave them here with us. You've had enough trouble with your heroic tendencies. Better to let bad boys who've already served their sentences mess with the Fates, just in case this is some kind of trick."

Dex's expression didn't change, but Vivian could feel his shock. No one had ever spoken to him about his magic like that except the Fates themselves.

"The ladies came to you for help," Vari said.

"Actually," Dex snapped, "they came to you first, but you two were unavailable."

"Actually," Vivian said, putting her hand on Dex's arm in an attempt to calm him down, "they came to me first. They didn't know how to find Dex and they couldn't find you two either. I did what I could. I'm not able to do any more. I don't know if Dex can either. So maybe we should just leave this up to the rest of you."

No one had sat down around the large table. Everyone was standing near it, like houseguests who weren't sure if the party had started yet.

Blackstone stared at the Fates as if he could see through them.

"I'm not real keen on helping them," he said as if they weren't there. "There's a thousand years of my life spent carting a coffin around that I'd like to get back."

Vari's arms tightened, showing the muscles in his biceps. He didn't look at the Fates at all, but directed his remarks to Dex. "They're not my favorite people either. They made me look like a garden gnome for nearly three thousand years."

Clotho, Lachesis, and Atropos stood near the swinging doors, arms around each other. As they listened, the hope on their faces slowly faded.

"Your punishments were justified," Clotho said.

"Particularly yours, Darius," Lachesis said. "You nearly destroyed true love for everyone."

"I never had that power," Andrew Vari said.

"And as for you, Aethelstan," Atropos said, "you misunderstood our prophecy. That is not our fault."

Blackstone took a step toward the women, his face filled with menace. Vivian felt the repressed anger in him, now boiling very close to the surface.

She took a step back even though she was nowhere near them. Dex put his hand against her spine, holding her in place. He didn't want her to call attention to herself.

Nora grabbed Blackstone's arm. "It turned out all right, Alex. It turned out the way it was supposed to. You know that."

Blackstone glared at the three women for a moment, then bent down and kissed Nora on the top of her head. "Right as always, my beautiful wife."

Vari rolled his eyes and Nora glared at him. Even though Vivian got no sense of magical power from her, she suddenly had the feeling that Nora was the strongest person of the three.

"Everything turned out all right for you too, Sancho," Nora said, obviously using yet another nickname for Andrew Vari. "Better than all right. And you're usually the first to admit it."

Vari grimaced, then shook his head. At that moment, yet another woman came through the double doors from the kitchen. She glanced at the Fates as if she didn't recognize them, then walked around them, looking with surprise at the large group.

She had a sweatband around her forehead, and her red hair was tied back into a ponytail. She was wearing Lycra running shorts, a Lycra top, and expensive running shoes.

She looked very familiar.

"Is my husband causing trouble?" she asked, using a towel to wipe the sweat off her face.

"I don't cause trouble, Ari," Vari said. "I prevent it."

She grinned. "In what world?"

He grinned too, but Vivian didn't like the expression. It hid scheming, which she could sense from him. She tilted her head sideways, still trying to ease the ache in her neck.

"Ari," Andrew Vari said, "I don't think you've ever met the Fates."

He swept his arm toward the three women near the one he was calling Ari. She whirled toward them, her green eyes flashing, her mood completely different.

"You! You're the ones who hurt my husband. Didn't you know what a good, kind man he is? Don't you know what you put him through, how unfair it all was? Do you know what you did to him, making him suffer like that? It's not right and not fair, and I've been meaning to tell you all this for a long time now, but he wouldn't let me. Now I can, and believe me, if I had magic, you women would pay for what you did. You'd—"

"Ariel." Blackstone's voice was sharp. "Don't ever threaten the Fates."

"It's all right," Dex said, his tone laconic. "They don't have any power anymore. Or have they forgotten to tell you that part?"

Nora, Blackstone, Vari, and Ariel turned toward him, their shock so overpowering that Vivian would have taken another step backward if Dex hadn't still been holding her in place.

Vivian had no idea why Dex had told the group that the Fates had no power. She could sense it was important—at least as far as he was concerned. He was thinking that no one would help the Fates if they still had their magic.

Given the anger radiating from the men across from Vivian, she realized that Dex might be right.

"We were going to get to that," Clotho said.

"It's not something you announce the moment you come into a room," Lachesis said.

"Besides," Atropos said, "it's not permanent."

"You hope," Dex said.

Vivian felt a prickling run up her spine. She glanced at the front door. They were being watched; she was certain of it.

But she couldn't see anyone standing at the door. She could barely see through the darkened windows. Only shadowy forms existed out there, and none of them seemed to be close to the restaurant.

Yet she knew that someone was watching. Someone from outside. Someone who shouldn't have been watching at all.

"Excuse me," she said.

Dex glanced at her, but no one else seemed to notice. The rest of the group was looking at the Fates.

"No power?" Vari said, a gleam in his beautiful blue eyes as he looked at the Fates. "You mean I can turn *them* into garden gnomes?"

Vivian felt Dex stiffen beside her. He was worried about the Fates. He'd been worried about how they would treat him, and now his innate kindness made him concerned for them.

Vivian wanted to slip her arm around his back and reassure him that everything would be all right. But something in his body language told her that he didn't want to be touched like that. He wanted to focus on the conversation around them.

"You know," Blackstone said as Vari came to his side, "they've always opted for beauty whenever they've changed forms. Maybe we should let them know what it's like to be at a disadvantage."

"Like you've known," Vari said.

Blackstone shrugged. "They had me deal with other issues. Prolonged fights, failed spells."

The prickly feeling grew, and exacerbated the pain in Vivian's neck. Her sense of another presence, a powerful presence, grew.

"Excuse me," she said again, but no one looked at her, not even Dex.

He was watching the Fates, who were cringing against the kitchen door.

"You know, I've never been one for vengeance," Vari said, "except, well, when I was young, but—"

"I have, even now." Blackstone wasn't smiling. In fact, his expression terrified Vivian. They weren't going to help the Fates. They were going to harm them.

"Gentlemen," Nora said, "you deserved the punishments you got and you know it. Let's move on."

"I don't know, Nora," Ariel said. "I'm not real fond of these ladies either."

"They did their jobs. They rehabilitated Sancho and they—"

"Stop sounding like a lawyer," Blackstone said.

"I am a lawyer," Nora snapped. "And what

you're proposing will get you in trouble with the Fates.''

"Who are standing right here," said Blackstone, narrowing his gaze.

"But their replacements aren't," Nora said. "And believe me, your Powers That Be—"

As she said this, the Fates did half of their genuflection. They spread their arms, but they didn't lower their heads. They kept their gazes on the men they'd come to for help.

"—won't allow your magical system to go without its judiciary-slash-law enforcement wing."

"Actually . . ." Dex started, but Vivian poked him in the side. She was developing a fondness for the Fates, and she didn't want this crew to know that they'd been replaced by some helpless teenage girls.

Dex gave her a look, then said nothing more.

"Punishment in this case," Nora was saying, "might be a lot more severe because you should know better."

"And it would be your second offense," said Ariel, tapping a finger against her teeth as she thought about this.

"No, Blackstone's second. I'm well past three-strikes-and-you're-out country." Vari sighed and pulled out a chair with one foot. Then he sat down rather heavily, keeping his arms crossed and glaring at the Fates. "I'm not really willing to help you."

"I don't think it matters," Vivian said. The tingling on the back of her neck had grown worse. "Because—"

"Neither am I," Blackstone said to the Fates. "I won't get in your way, but I'm not real fond of you ladies.''

"You asked us for help," Clotho said.

"At the end, with Ealhswith. And we helped," Lachesis said.

"We didn't have to," Atropos said. "We bent some rules for you."

The tingling was almost unbearable. "Please," Vivian said. "Will someone listen—?"

A thick skein of rope dropped from the ceiling and lassoed all three Fates. Ariel reached for them, then backed off as if she had been burned. Dexter dove forward, reaching for the rope as he did, but he seemed to be moving in slow motion.

The lasso tightened around the Fates and yanked them upward, just as Dex reached them. He grabbed for them, but his fingers missed their kicking feet.

The Fates were pulled into the air. They screamed, snapping their fingers, probably trying to do a spell.

Blackstone watched, his mouth open. Vari tilted his head back in surprise.

"Stop sitting there!" Nora shouted as she ran forward. "Do something!"

The Fates disappeared through the ceiling. Dexter slid across the floor, and slammed into the wall, the thud echoing throughout the building. He lay there, hunched, eyes closed.

Vivian hurried to his side. She had no sense of him, and no sense of the Fates either.

They were gone, as if they had never been. The rest of the group was staring at the ceiling, but Vivian looked at Dex.

She couldn't tell if he was breathing.

She wasn't even sure if he was still alive.

Ten

Eris sat on the warm concrete steps and leaned against the metal railing. Anyone watching her would have thought she was observing her anchor describe the changing scene for the camera trained on him.

In truth, she could have cared less how Noah Sturgis described the changes occurring in Portland. She was concentrating instead on manipulating her puppet.

The woman she had chosen had been an elderly schoolteacher (now retired) who had emerged from her apartment to watch the chaos in the streets. She had attracted Eris's attention because the woman, with her formidable chin, silver-gray hair, and regal manner, looked like a stereotypical witch.

So Eris had made her one just for the day. *Witch for a Day*—probably not a concept show that would work on her cable network, but one that she aired privately every now and then.

Eris smiled. The magic she used to control her

puppet, once mastered, was simple and required little energy. What required energy was keeping a mental eye on her puppet's progress while Eris pretended she was doing nothing at all.

She had sent Strife into the building across the street to see if he could find the Fates. Eris had already known they were gone, but she wanted to keep Strife busy and out of her way. The last thing she needed was her son to distract her at the wrong moment.

The crowd still milled in the street, occasionally glancing at the building that had been winking all morning. The winking had stopped, of course, once whoever had done the protect had figured out what was going on, but that didn't stop the crowd from hoping that the magic would continue.

No one noticed when Eris made her elderly puppet disappear, and no one noticed when the old woman popped up again on the roof of Quixotic's building, carrying a length of rope that Eris spelled to this location from a nearby hardware store.

Eris dumped most of her magical abilities into the puppet, and then controlled the woman from a distance. With the flick of a thought, she got the woman to spell the rope, and then complete a series of complex maneuvers that eventually allowed her to lasso the Fates.

Once those creatures reached the roof, Eris would have the puppet spell them to Eris's own secret hideaway—her lair, as her son always called it.

The Fates were sliding up through the building, floor by floor, terrifying tenants and screaming for help. Eris particularly liked hearing the Fates scream, and she wished she could prolong the sensation.

The terror in their voices gave her great pleasure. Eris rested her elbows on the step behind her and enjoyed these last few moments. She was nearly there. And once she had the Fates far from here, her revenge would really begin.

Dex huddled against the wall. His head ached, and he had floor burns on his elbows and knees, but he had succeeded. In his hands, he clutched the end of the magic rope.

Whoever was wielding it didn't seem to know quite what she was doing. She had lassoed the center of the rope, not one end, and left an end dangling. He had seen it as he jumped, and when he hadn't been able to grab the Fates, he caught the rope instead, holding the end in place with his body weight and praying that would be enough.

Around him, he could hear discussion and feel Vivian's concern. He wanted to reassure her, but he needed to concentrate on holding the rope.

The moment it went taut, he yanked with all his strength. The rope vibrated and then went completely slack. Dex grinned. He could hear the screams of three women grow closer and closer until—

The Fates fell through the ceiling. Vivian stumbled backward to get out of their way. They zoomed past her, the breeze from their fall blowing her hair away and nearly knocking her glasses off her face.

Then the Fates landed on the floor with a decided splat. The rope was wrapped around them, but not as tightly. They lay on it, their arms and legs entwined, moaning.

Vivian looked for Dex, but didn't see him. For a moment, she was afraid he'd been buried beneath the three women. Squashed by Fate, as it were.

That last thought didn't feel like hers. It had too much puckish humor. She scanned the room and finally saw Dex, wrapped in a rope, even farther from the wall than he had been.

I'm okay, he sent to her, and she felt a relief deeper than any she had ever known.

Nora and Ariel were at the Fates' sides. The two mortal women bent over the three immortal ones, smoothing hair, untangling limbs, making sure nothing was broken.

Blackstone was looking up at the ceiling as if it had been ruined. Vari stood slowly. He was also looking up.

Vivian hurried to Dex's side. He was wrapped in the rope and grinning as if he had just been on the ride of his life. Vivian reached down to help him unravel, but he shook his head. He wanted to do this himself.

The Fates didn't seem hurt either. They were already talking—only they weren't taking turns. Their voices overlapped: Clotho worrying about being bruised; Lachesis wondering if she had a cut on her face; Atropos convinced she'd have a lump on the back of her head the size of Athens.

Over the din, Vari said, "What happened? How'd they come back?"

Blackstone crossed his arms and loomed over the Fates. Vivian could feel his menace from across the room. "You really haven't lost your magic, have you?"

"If we had any magic, we wouldn't have fallen like that," Clotho said.

"It's not dignified," Lachesis said.

"And we always try to be dignified," Atropos said.

Dex had finally unwrapped himself. No one but

Vivian was looking at him. She helped him wind the rope around his hand and elbow, like cowboys did. She was shaking. She had been so worried about him. She had a sense—just for a moment—that she had found the man of her dreams only to lose him again.

"I really don't care about your dignity," Vari said. "I want to know how you got back into this restaurant if you don't have any magic. I wasn't done with my spell."

Dex stood. "I think this had something to do with it."

He nodded toward his right arm, wrapped in rope. The rope trailed to the Fates, who were still lassoed in it. The other end of the rope had pooled on the floor like a giant snake.

"How'd you get that?" Blackstone asked, sounding suspicious.

"I caught it," Dex said, "and tugged. No magic involved. Just good old-fashioned effort."

"Tugged?" Vari asked.

"Tugged," Dex said. "You know the old saying. 'What goes up ... ' "

"Yes." Clotho pulled herself off the pile of Fates. "But I never expected clichés to be so painful."

She was rubbing her backside. Nora untied the lasso, freeing the Fates from each other.

"Did you see who did this?" Nora asked.

Lachesis shook her head. "I was trying to free us, but I was doing it wrong. I was trying to use magic I no longer have."

"It really was a dumb idea to come here without powers." Atropos had a hand on the back of her head. The rope was still wrapped around her waist.

"Grabbed it, huh?" Vari asked, as if he couldn't quite understand that. He crouched near the Fates and touched the rope, as if he were testing it for magic. "A quick jump and a grab."

"A quick jump, a grab, and a tug," Dex said.

"You must be very strong," Ariel said, looking at him with admiration.

Vivian didn't like the admiration. She wanted Ariel to move away from Dex. Vivian also didn't like the way Dex smiled at Ariel. It was a roguish grin, filled with a bit of joy and pride.

"Not that strong," he said. "The rope was going up by magic. Anything can interfere with that sort of spell. Which reminds me. We'd better put a good protect spell on this place or we'll be in for more of this."

Blackstone glared at him, as if Dex were calling Blackstone's magic into question. But Vari clapped his hands, and Vivian saw just a bit of light leave his fingers. The light seeped into the walls, ceiling, and floor, sparkling before it faded into nothing.

"There," Vari said. "Nothing bad can get in here."

"That's subjective, isn't it?" Dex asked.

Vari shrugged one shoulder as if he didn't care. Vivian continued gathering rope. There was a lot more of it than she had originally thought. She had no idea how Dex had managed this. A regular man couldn't have.

No wonder he got mistaken for someone with super powers. Traditional comic book super powers. Even when he wasn't using magic, he was impressive.

"How're we going to open for lunch?" Nora asked.

"We'll worry about that when the time comes." Blackstone smiled at her. Then he bent over and, to Vivian's surprise, helped Lachesis up.

"Let's go sit down," he said. "I have some vegetable soup I've been experimenting with and some French bread. That should make us all feel better."

"Experimenting?" Clotho asked as Nora helped her up.

"Don't worry," Nora said. "He tries to re-create meals he's eaten over the past thousand years. So when he's experimenting, we get a hundred really good versions of the same meal."

"Re-create?" Lachesis asked. "Why doesn't he just conjure the recipe?"

"And take all the fun out of it?" Blackstone pulled back the chairs at the table he had originally been leading everyone to. The Fates limped over there and Vari returned to his seat, patting the chair beside him for Ariel.

Vivian and Dex finished coiling the rope. When they were done, Dex slid it up his arm to his shoulder, the way a cowboy would. He started for the table too, not looking injured at all.

He seemed so confident. Vivian watched the way he walked, the tension in his body. His muscles rippled as he moved.

She made herself look away from him. She hadn't followed him because something had changed. It took her a moment to realize the change had been in Blackstone.

His attitude toward the Fates seemed to have shifted. It was almost as if he wore a layer of charm over his real personality. She could see it, like a mask, making his handsome features even more attractive, his eyes brighter, his smile wider.

Everyone else seemed fooled by it, but she still sensed confusion beneath the charm. Blackstone wasn't certain whether he was going to help these women or not.

"I'll help you serve the food," Vivian said, not trusting him.

Blackstone glanced at her in surprise, as if he had forgotten she was there. "No need."

He clapped his hands together, and before the

sound faded the table had changed. White stoneware soup tureens and matching bread plates
appeared before each chair. Three loaves of
French bread sat on cutting boards in the middle
of the table, along with a huge pot of steaming
soup.

It smelled wonderful, rich and garlicky. Vivian's
stomach growled, but she still hadn't moved. She
didn't trust any of this. Blackstone bothered her.

Dex put the rope over the back of his chair and
sat down as if nothing were wrong. But he was
watching with the same wariness Vivian felt. Only
his wariness wasn't as obvious. He masked it with
feigned indifference.

"Food is a good idea," Vari said, leaning forward
and grabbing the ladle. "I'll serve."

Dex wasn't going to speak up. He probably
thought it wasn't wise. But Vivian had nothing to
lose.

"Wait a minute," she said, and this time she
spoke with enough force that everyone turned
toward her. "This isn't about food or conviviality.
These three women could have died."

"You don't know that," Blackstone said. "For
all we know—"

"I do know that." The anger Vivian had been
feeling since she arrived in the restaurant finally
boiled over. "And if you people hadn't been so
damned self-involved, this could all have been prevented. I knew it was going to happen. I could
sense it. And you all ignored me to go on with your
silly little argument."

Vari let the ladle fall back into the soup. Blackstone's eyes narrowed. The Fates watched Vivian,
small smiles on their faces. Nora and Ariel seemed
surprised.

Dex was reclining in his chair, his arm over the
back. It looked like he was resting. But Vivian felt

him again, as if he were inside her mind. He was amused and proud of her, all at the same time.

His approval gave her strength.

"You couldn't have known anything in advance," Blackstone said. "You haven't come into your magic yet. You were just nervous."

"Nervous?" Vivian walked toward him, this tall, pompous man who had lived for centuries. "I wasn't nervous. I felt something. I knew that we were being watched, and I felt the danger. I tried to tell you people, but you kept interrupting me with your petty argument."

"Petty?" Blackstone seemed taller than he had a moment before.

"Petty." Vivian shoved her hands in the back pockets of her jeans and stopped right in front of him. She was a lot shorter than he was, but not as short as his cheerleader/lawyer wife.

Blackstone looked surprised. Apparently people rarely called him on his behavior.

"These women came to you for help," Vivian said. "They worried about it too, knowing you had a history. And all you and your friend there, Sancho or Darius or Vari or whatever his name is, did is try to figure out ways to make them pay for some punishment they meted out to you hundreds of years ago. Punishment that was, from what I understand, deserved."

"You don't understand," Blackstone snapped.

"I think I do," Vivian said.

"Vivian," Clotho said, with a warning in her voice, but Vivian chose to ignore her. Chose to ignore everyone else except this cold man in front of her.

She didn't even look at Dex.

"What I understand is this," Vivian said, raising her chin slightly so that she could look Blackstone in the eye. "You use charm like it's a magic spell.

You pour it on so thick that people think you're better-looking than you really are, and nicer than you really are. And what has your attention at the moment is the fact that these three women scare you and—"

"They do not," Blackstone said.

"They do. You're worried that they're going to punish you again for some imagined slight. Which—" Vivian started to add that Dex had been afraid of the same thing and then changed her mind. That was his secret to tell if he wanted to— "they are in no position to do."

"I am not afraid of them," Blackstone said, but his voice shook, belying his words.

The Fates looked amused. Dex leaned slightly to the left, the rope coiled behind him like a tamed snake. His right fist was clenched. He didn't seem to notice. His entire body vibrated with anger at Blackstone, for the way the man was treating Vivian.

Dex would jump to her defense in a moment, and she didn't want that. She wanted to do this on her own.

"I've never seen Blackstone afraid of anyone," Vari said, "and I've known him the longest."

"You don't need to defend him," Vivian said. "You're just as bad, maybe worse, because you're acting out of an anger that you know is misdirected."

Vari's pale cheeks flushed. The red accented the blue of his eyes.

Dex shifted in his chair. Vivian made sure she avoided eye contact with him. He would take that as an invitation to help her.

Instead, she glared at Andrew Vari. "You know you were wrong all those years ago, and still you blame them for all you suffered in between."

"I do not!" Vari said.

"Well, you certainly did when they arrived," Vivian said. "You're still broadcasting your desire for revenge. You never thought you'd get this chance. Of course, you're a little appalled because you didn't realize you were this angry."

"You can't know that," Vari said. "It's not possible. You don't have magic yet."

"She doesn't need magic." Dex's tone was laconic. "She's psychic."

"No one's that psychic," Vari said.

"You mean she's right?" Ariel's voice rose. She frowned at Vari.

"You were angry at them too," Vivian said to Ariel. Vivian wanted to include all of them in this. She was furious that they had dismissed her because they thought she had no super power.

Well, she had a strong super power, and it had saved the Fates when they arrived in Portland. These mages and their wives wouldn't ignore her again.

"You think the Fates hurt your husband unnecessarily," Vivian said, "and you're not happy about that either. But you'll help them if someone else does."

"Boy." Ariel winced. "That makes me sound like a humanitarian."

"It wasn't meant to," Vivian said. "There is only one humanitarian in the room and it's—"

"Quite obviously Vivian." Dex interrupted her before she could say his name. "She took on the Fates even when she thought they were crazy women. I think we should give her the benefit of the doubt and listen to what she has to say. You'll be surprised at the depth of her knowledge."

Vivian turned to him, startled by the way he'd taken control of the conversation away from her. Her anger turned on him for just a moment, until she sensed the emotion beneath his words.

He didn't want these people to get to know him.

He didn't trust easily, and nothing anyone in this room had done made him trust them.

Vivian frowned. He believed he didn't trust easily, yet he had trusted her from the moment they met. His expression thawed just slightly and his eyes held a warmth just for her. *We're different.* His thought reached her as if it were her own.

And it almost felt like one of her own thoughts. She'd had some similar ones earlier. This feeling she had for Dex—this instant sense of him—was unlike anything she had ever experienced.

"I already am surprised at her knowledge," Blackstone said. "I should apologize."

His words took Vivian's attention away from Dex. The anger returned. "No," she said to Blackstone. "You shouldn't apologize. You wouldn't mean it."

Vivian walked past him toward the table. Blackstone watched her with something like awe. Dex's mouth twitched as he tried to suppress a smile.

She was shaking. She hadn't lost her temper like this in nearly a year—and that incident had occurred at the hotline after months of build-up.

She had never gotten this angry this fast about anything.

"We'll be all right, dear," Lachesis said. "If they don't want to help us, they can spell us to someone who will."

"There aren't many who will," Atropos said. "We've never made friends outside of our circle."

"Surely you haven't threatened to punish everyone," Nora said.

The three women faced her as if they were surprised by her comment.

"You work in law, young lady," Clotho said to Nora. "You know that judges are often feared and mistrusted, especially by people who do nothing wrong."

"That's true," Nora said. "I hadn't thought of it that way."

"It's the same for us," Lachesis said. "Either we're hated for the punishments we've doled out or we're feared for the ones we might."

Dexter winced. He had been worried about something that hadn't happened too.

But, unlike the other mages in the room, he seemed to be able to get beyond his feelings. He had been helping the Fates.

"Well," Vivian said to the Fates, "I'm not afraid of you, nor am I angry at you. And after all I've seen today, I certainly believe you are who you say you are. I'm willing to help, whether anyone else here is or not."

She sat beside Dex, who was now leaning forward, his head down. Her sense of him vanished again, and she felt oddly alone. Did their connection wink in and out like the building had? Was he doing it?

Or was she?

"And if none of the rest of you are willing," she said into the silence, "help us figure out who might be."

The silence grew around her. She was beginning to wonder if she alone would be responsible for three formerly magic, extremely naïve, and somehow experienced women. The idea scared her. She was out of her depth, and the people who understood that depth weren't willing to help.

What was that about fools rushing in? Was Clotho right? Were clichés a lot more painful than Vivian could imagine?

She waited. But no one said a word.

Not even Dex.

Eleven

Finally, instead of speaking, Blackstone came over to the table. He grabbed the soup ladle and picked up Vivian's bowl. Then he poured some steaming broth into it and set the food in front of her.

He meant it as a peace offering. She didn't even need her psychic powers to know that. And it was a good offering. The steam wafted toward her, smelling of beef broth, bay leaves, and thyme, as well as spices she couldn't identify.

Her stomach growled. She was a lot hungrier than she'd realized.

Blackstone grabbed Dex's bowl and filled it. Dex watched the movements with scarcely any expression at all, but he was suspicious. Even more than he had been a moment ago.

Blackstone was all about subtlety. Dex was not. Dex preferred open, honest reactions, even though he was hiding his own emotions now. He only did that sort of thing in a group like this one, where his honesty might not be appreciated.

Vivian was astonished that she knew so much about him by just a fleeting touch of their minds. They were winking in and out, but she appreciated even the occasional hint of his emotions.

She hoped he appreciated hers as well, because she knew he was feeling them.

Blackstone was working his way around the table. When the soup was served, he sat down.

"I thought Nora was the only woman who saw me clearly," Blackstone said. "I'm sorry, Vivian. I misjudged you, and I handled this situation incorrectly. I forgot the most important thing about our Fates."

"What's that?" Vivian asked, mostly because she was supposed to.

"That all of their work is about love."

That sounded like New Age bunkum to her. She started to object when Dex put a hand on her knee. His touch sent a tingle through her.

"He's right," Dex said. "They give us all prophecies when we're born and we're to try to fulfill them."

"Lachesis assigns the prophecies," Atropos said, then shrugged. "You know. Dispenser of Lots."

"Although sometimes they're pretty misleading," Vari said as he reached for the French bread. "Like the one about Cupid. Calling that fat idiot the God of Love is like calling Ghengis Khan a Uniter of Countries."

"Actually, Cupid is one of the reasons we're here," Clotho said.

"Shhh," Lachesis said, looking alarmed.

Atropos bit her lower lip. "I don't think you can blame our situation in this restaurant on Cupid."

Vivian frowned. Atropos was lying. Purposefully lying.

Did this Cupid person have something to do with

the attacks on the Fates? Or was Atropos lying about something else?

"I thought you took care of Cupid," Vari said.

"He's serving time again," Clotho said. "But he's been involved in some pretty nefarious—"

"But ultimately unimportant deeds." Lachesis kicked Clotho under the table. The movement was not subtle; everyone saw it.

"So you think Cupid's the one who attacked you?" Blackstone asked, spooning some soup from his own bowl.

"Impossible," Atropos said. "He's imprisoned."

"But you mentioned him," Vivian said. She felt a bit odd accusing a cherub whom she thought of as the God of Love of attacking the Fates.

Clotho shrugged. "We have many enemies."

She seemed so calm about it.

"We have to figure out who is after you if we're going to help you," Dex said. He hadn't removed his hand from Vivian's knee. She had no desire to slide his hand away either.

"I didn't hear anyone volunteer to help the Fates," she said.

"I just did." Dex gave her a warm smile. It made her feel as if he had volunteered only because she was involved.

"We're all going to help," Blackstone said, as if he were the one in charge of the others.

"Nice of you to ask our permission before you volunteered us," Ariel said. "I'm training. I don't have time for this. I have a race in a week."

Vivian froze. That's where she recognized Ariel from. Ariel Summers, the marathoner. She had an endorsement contract with Nike, and her picture was on the side of one of the old brick buildings in downtown Portland.

Ariel was really famous. Which made sense, with all the magic available to her.

"Didn't realize who she was, huh?" Vari asked. His voice was kind, though. He seemed to have softened since Vivian yelled at him.

"I knew she looked familiar," Vivian said.

"It's all right," Vari said. "And now it's my turn to read minds. No one knows about us and the magic. I help her train, but I don't use my powers. That would be cheating. Ariel has no magic."

"None?" Vivian said.

"She has a sort of sixth sense about it," Nora said. "She can see magical edges of things."

"You tend to glow green when you're thinking," Ariel said to Vivian. "Or maybe it's when you're receiving other people's thoughts. I haven't observed long enough."

Vivian's cheeks grew warm. "I didn't mean to imply that you were doing something wrong."

"It's all right," Ariel said. "I would wonder the same thing in your shoes."

"And in case you were wondering," Nora said, "you didn't breathe a word."

"It was just your expression that gave you away," Vari said with a grin. "Don't ever play poker."

"Oh, I don't know." Dex liked to use that I'm-just-an-ignorant-cowboy tone. It made him seem less perceptive than he really was. "I have a hunch she'd be really good at it."

He squeezed her knee. Vivian looked at him and got lost in his blue eyes. They were so stunning, and the lashes were so very long. An intelligence shone through his eyes that gave him a confidence most people didn't have—couldn't have, really. Most people weren't that smart.

"If she played poker," Blackstone was saying, "she would have an unfair advantage."

Vivian turned, breaking her gaze from Dex's. Blackstone had been talking about her.

Nora hit his arm. "If you're going to stay this

grumpy, you can go back to the kitchen. The rest of us have work to do here."

"I'm sorry," Blackstone said, and this time his apology was completely sincere. He turned to the Fates. "Why don't you tell us exactly what's going on?"

As the Fates launched into the story for the third time—at least from Vivian's perspective—she tuned them out and focused on the soup.

It was delicious. The flavor was robust, the vegetables crisp, and the broth just thick enough to give the meal the right texture.

"You know," Dex said softly, his voice sending a pleasurable shiver down her spine, "Blackstone is something of a legend."

Lachesis's voice rose indignantly as she described the Interim Fates.

"I've heard of him," Vivian said.

"No, no," Dex said. "He's not that Blackstone. From what I've heard, that Blackstone stole his name—"

"He's not a chef, then, after all?" Vivian asked. "I mean, this stuff is good."

Atropos had taken up the story now. She held knives in both hands and brandished them like shears as she described her last few days at the job.

Dex frowned. "Of course he's a chef. He's just not the—you've never heard of William Blackstone, have you?"

"Vaguely," Vivian said.

Clotho was standing now, waving her arms in big circles, talking about their arrival in Portland.

Vivian listened for half a moment and realized the Fates were telling the same story in the same way using the same language. She wondered how they did that, then decided she didn't want to know.

Dex scooted his chair closer to hers. "You're amazing, you know," he whispered.

Vivian flushed, flattered by his compliment. Then she smiled at herself. Part of her felt like she had known him forever, and another part felt like a giggly schoolgirl on a first date. She kind of liked the combination. It didn't take the uncertainty from the flirting—the what-kind-of-future-would-we-have feeling— but it added a level of trust that Vivian had never had with anyone outside her family before.

Dex leaned closer. Their heads were almost touching. "You are. They say Blackstone can charm a snake. In fact, they say he has."

"Oh." Vivian wasn't impressed with Blackstone. Some of this stuff sounded like myths the man had made up for himself. Suddenly a pain flared through her neck. She put her hand on it, rubbed it absently, and the pain died away.

"People don't stand up to him," Dex said.

"Well, they should." Vivian finished her soup. It was the best vegetable soup she'd ever had. "He can't always be right."

"That's what I'm saying." Dex's shoulder brushed hers. She was so aware of his touch, of the scent of him, of his warmth through his shirt. When he was this close, he made her breathless. "What you did took guts."

"No." She turned her head toward his so that their eyes met. His were open and honest and full of admiration. Hers were probably the same way. She hoped they were. "What *you* did took guts."

He blinked, then broke the eye contact. "I didn't do anything."

"Oh, let me see." She set her spoon down. "You saved my life this morning. Then you saved the Fates from being roped into oblivion, probably saving their lives. Yeah. You're right. That wasn't anything."

He shrugged, the color in his cheeks high. "It's not the same."

"You're right, it's not," she said. "It's much more important."

"No," he said. "Ultimately what you've done is. It shows so much courage—"

"Excuse me," Andrew Vari said. "This mutual admiration society is nice and all, but we're through with the history lesson. You can start paying attention in class again."

Both Vivian and Dex jumped at the same time. The entire table was looking at them. They hadn't realized that the Fates had stopped speaking.

"Who's your yenta these days?" Vari asked the Fates.

"I don't think they need one," Nora said, putting her hand on Blackstone's.

"Sometimes these things work without divine intervention," Clotho said.

"What?" Vivian and Dex asked in unison.

"Long story," Vari said. "Mostly involving me, a garden gnome, a man in a diaper, and lots of arrows. Not something worth repeating over the lunch table."

"Do you get the feeling we walked in on act three?" Dex said to Vivian.

"It's not act three." Nora buttered a slice of French bread. "This is a whole new play and it's about the Fates. Ladies, I didn't hear anything in your story that tells me who is after you."

She directed this last to the Fates, all of whom were on their second bowl of soup.

Vivian took a deep breath. The fluttery, flirty feeling was wonderful, but she had to concentrate now on the task at hand: saving the Fates.

Still, Dex remained close to her, brushing against her side. She leaned into him and listened.

"I think our behavior shows it could be anyone," Blackstone said.

"Or a lot of anyones," Vari said.

"It's just one person," Vivian said. The pain rose again in the back of her neck. She rubbed it absently.

"How do you know?" Ariel asked.

Vivian shrugged. "I just know. I never get the sense of diverse actors in this campaign. Just one person, focusing on the Fates."

"I saw several different people," Clotho said.

"There was a man watching us when we arrived," Lachesis said.

"And I thought I saw a woman at the end of that rope," Atropos said.

"Ah, the rope." Dex turned around in his chair and grabbed it. Vivian felt the loss of his heat as if a cold breeze had struck her.

Dex didn't seem to notice. He was focused on the rope. It was made of thick, heavy jute, but he moved it as if it weighed nothing. He didn't just have magic; he had strength and speed as well. He put the rope on his lap. "Let's see what it tells us."

Everyone leaned forward, except Vivian, who leaned back. She wasn't sure what was going to happen, and she was half afraid the rope was going to burst into flame.

Dex ran his fingers along the woven strands. "There's no glamour left in it."

"I might be able to find it," Blackstone said, holding out his hand.

But Dex ignored him. "But there is something . . ."

He passed a finger across the center strand, then touched it with a finger of his left hand, muttering something in a language that sounded suspiciously like Quebecois.

An image rose off the rope and moved toward the center of the table. A woman sat on a cloud, the rope wrapped around her waist.

The woman looked like an English teacher Vivian had had in middle school—with the thin lips, arched eyebrows, and snotty attitude Vivian often associated with uptight British matrons. The woman—now even older than she had been when Vivian knew her (if, indeed, Vivian had known her)—took the end of the rope, held it up, and waved it, as the flesh on the back of her arms wobbled back and forth.

Then she swung the end of the rope over her head. It formed a lasso that snaked through her fingers and zoomed downward, unwrapping itself from her waist as it did.

She held her fingers out, controlling the un-lassoed end, as screams echoed from below.

Vivian recognized those screams—she'd heard them when they originally happened, when Clotho, Lachesis, and Atropos were dragged from the restaurant.

Dex pushed his fingers together, and the image vanished into the rope. The screams continued to resound, until they faded into nothing.

"Well," Vari said. "We should trust our young friend here. One person."

Condescending idiot. Vivian thought she had cured them of their bad attitude toward her, but apparently not.

"That's not the person I've been sensing," Vivian said. Her tone was sharper than she had intended it to be. Dex, whose head was still down, smiled. She hoped she was the only one who had seen his reaction.

"I thought you said there was only one person." Blackstone was frowning.

"There is, but apparently there are others working for him," Vivian said.

"You're sure it's a him?" Dex asked.

"No," Vivian said. "I'm just sure there's one mind in charge of all this."

"Did you recognize that woman?" Nora asked the Fates.

"No," Clotho said, her brows furrowed.

"But she doesn't have any magic," Lachesis said.

"You can tell?" Nora asked.

Atropos shook her head. "If someone that old had magic, we would recognize her."

"You're sure?" Vari asked.

All three Fates glared at him.

He shrugged. "I guess you are sure, then."

"You can't do that rope thing without magic," Blackstone said.

"There are ways," Clotho said.

"Now is not the time to be mysterious," Nora said to the Fates.

They studied her for a moment, then nodded in unison. "Someone could use a puppet," Lachesis said.

"A puppet?" Dex asked. His hand returned to Vivian's knee as he spoke. She relaxed slightly at his touch.

"It's dark magic," Atropos said. "Strictly forbidden."

"And not used for hundreds of years," Clotho said.

"That we know of, anyway," Lachesis said.

"In other words, no one has been caught doing it," Atropos said.

"I've never heard of it." Blackstone took a piece of bread and broke it apart with his long fingers. He was still nervous; Vivian could sense it.

"The mage funnels his magic through a nonmagical person," Clotho said.

Lachesis took some more bread for herself. "It can be done through one person or a string of people, so that the mage won't get caught."

"So whoever's doing this is making mortals perform magic?" Vari asked. "They'll notice, right? I mean, the press is out there."

"They won't remember," Atropos said.

"And," Clotho said, "if the magic is done right, then the mage won't get caught."

"It's a very sophisticated trick," Lachesis said.

"Only someone very old and very powerful can do it," Atropos said.

Vivian moved her shoulders. The tension from her neck was running down her back. "Define *old* for those of us who just this morning thought the human life span was a mere hundred years."

Vari looked interested in this part too.

"Over a thousand at least," Clotho said.

"Probably closer to three thousand," Lachesis said.

"I'm that old," Vari said.

Vivian looked at him, and felt something deeper than surprise. She was so shocked that she wanted to joke—something along the lines of he looked no older than a hundred—but she kept quiet.

He was saying, ". . . know that Ealhswith wanted to take over her body, but that wasn't temporary. This is temporary?"

"And a brilliant way to keep us from knowing what the mage is doing," Atropos said. "If, of course, we could still know."

The Fates looked at each other sadly.

"Can we trace the spell backwards?" Blackstone asked.

Clotho shook her head. "If the mage is sophisticated enough to do the spell, then he's sophisticated enough to wipe all trace of himself away when the spell is through."

"That's true," Dex said. "The spell I used should have shown us who cast the spell. If the Fates are right, and this woman was just a puppet, then we should have seen the spellcaster, not this mortal."

His hand rubbed Vivian's knee. She caught his fingers, holding them still.

At that moment, the kitchen door swung open. A middle-aged man in chef's white stepped tentatively into the restaurant. "Mr. Blackstone, sir? I'm sorry to disturb you, but we're supposed to open in fifteen minutes and we still haven't finished prepping the lunch special."

Blackstone swore quietly. "Thanks, Marcel. I'll be right in."

The chef went back into the kitchen, the door swinging closed behind him.

"Want me to put up the CLOSED sign?" Ariel asked.

Blackstone shook his head. "I don't think the answers are going to be easy on this one, but the problem is that we can't keep this place defended much longer. We're going to have to find a way to protect you ladies."

The Fates nodded.

"It might be easier if you split up," Vari said. "We have three powerful mages here. If one of us watches one of you, we might actually have a chance at this."

"Along with some thinking, remembering, and research," Nora said. "We have to find out who is behind these attacks."

Vivian felt her stomach twist. She was nearly done here. But she wasn't certain if she could return to her apartment or not. Would the attacker—whoever it might be—leave her alone?

And beyond that, she still wasn't sure she trusted Blackstone and Vari with the Fates. Dex could handle himself just fine, of course. She had complete faith in him.

"Dex," she said turning toward him, and then she stopped speaking. He wasn't looking at her. He was looking at the Fates, an expression of concern on his face.

"What is it?" she asked.

"I don't know," he said.

She followed his gaze and found herself completely stunned. The Fates had their arms around each other, silent tears streaking down their faces.

"What's wrong?" she asked.

That got everyone else's attention. "Did something happen?" Ariel asked.

"There isn't another attack, is there?" Nora asked.

The Fates shook their heads.

"Then what's going on?" Blackstone asked.

Atropos closed her eyes and leaned even closer to the other two women. "We can't split up. We tried. If we're separated for more than a day, we'll die."

"That's got to be a myth," Vari said.

"Like everything else around here," Nora snapped. "Give them the benefit of the doubt."

"I'm not sure we can, honey," Blackstone said. "Protecting all three of them for more than a few hours takes more magic firepower than any of us have."

"Dar and Ariel have a pretty big house," Nora said. "You guys can put a spell on it."

"We could," Vari said, "but it's in the middle of a neighborhood, and some of these evil mages don't care about destroying entire acres of property. I like my neighbors. I don't want to lose them."

"Do you live in the country?" Nora asked Dex. He shook his head, but didn't volunteer any more. Vivian got the sense that he was embarrassed, but she couldn't tell why.

"You have an apartment," Nora said to Vivian, clearly not expecting a response, "And we have a loft. All of which are in the middle of the city."

"Your cabin might work," Ariel said to Vari.

He shook his head. "That place is impossible to spell properly."

Blackstone sighed. "I could try contacting the Powers That Be."

As the Fates tried to do obeisance, they nearly slapped both Blackstone and Vari.

"But," Blackstone continued, leaning back to get out of the way of the Fates' hands, "I don't think they've talked to a real mage in centuries."

"You won't be able to see them," Clotho said. "You must go through the Interim Fates."

"I've met them," Dex said. "I'm not sure they know who the Powers That Be even are."

This time, Vari and Blackstone ducked as the Fates did their obeisance.

"Then we're out of options," Nora said.

The prickling sensation Vivian had had earlier, just before the Fates were taken, returned. So did the feeling of being watched.

"We're not only out of options," Vivian said, "but I think something's going to happen."

"It can't," Blackstone said. "We've protected the place."

"I'm only telling you what I sense," Vivian said.

"That's odd," Vari said. "This shouldn't be happening."

"It doesn't matter," Dex said. "It is. If the three of us shield the Fates, that might protect them for the next few minutes. Then we can figure out what to do."

The men raised their hands, and power sparked off their fingertips. A shield, multicolored in the same way that an oil slick was, formed over the Fates.

The shield stayed visible for a few seconds and then faded into nothing.

"Okay," Blackstone said. "Let's resolve this. We have five minutes."

Vivian looked at Dex. Even without reading his mind, she knew what he was thinking. They'd been discussing a solution for nearly an hour now and had gotten nowhere. There was no way they would figure out what to do in five minutes.

If things didn't change, and change quickly, the Fates were doomed.

Twelve

What it came down to was, simply, that Dex didn't trust Blackstone or his friend Andrew Vari. They seemed to be interested in helping the Fates now that Vivian had yelled at them. But how long would it take for the two men to remember their animosity and conveniently forget to check their protection spells? Or let it slip in a conversation with some other mage that they knew where the Fates were?

The Fates still had their arms around each other, faces wet with tears. The tears had unnerved Dex the most. He thought of the Fates as powerful and unfeeling creatures. He hadn't realized how attached they were to each other, and how human they were underneath.

Blackstone kept looking at Vivian as if he were seeking her approval. Nora was concentrating on the Fates. Andrew Vari had shoved his plate away and seemed to be contemplating the crumbs on the tablecloth. His wife, Ariel, rocked restlessly in her chair as if she couldn't keep still.

Vivian was nervous, her worry for the Fates palpable. He loved her kindness. In a sense, the Fates were strays, and Vivian had already adopted them, even though she hadn't realized it.

Pots banged in the kitchen and voices occasionally rose, reminding Dex that they were not alone, that a group of mortals worked just behind the door, and more waited outside, some of whom probably had plans to come here for lunch.

Vivian's apartment wasn't safe, and neither was this place. And Blackstone was right—they had only a few minutes to decide what to do.

Dex wished he had met Vivian before this morning. She had a good head on her shoulders, and she would have been an asset to him even if she hadn't been psychic. He admired her strength and her ability to confront the others.

His confrontational skills had never been good. He'd always solved problems once they arose, but never had he prevented them before they happened.

Yet another detail those two teenagers had missed when they had confused Dex with a superhero.

"There's got to be somewhere we can move them," Nora was saying. She was moving the silverware in front of her plate, sliding the fork back and forth as if she were trying to decide the proper position for it.

Dex twined his fingers with Vivian's. She gave him a sideways look, combined with a worried smile. She had no idea what to do next, and why would she? All of this was new to her.

"This isn't like hiding an object," Andrew Vari was saying. "The Fates will need food and shelter and—"

"No need to discuss us in the third person," Lachesis said. "We are here and can take care of ourselves."

That was the problem, wasn't it? The Fates believed they could take care of themselves, but they had no experience with the modern world and didn't know how to survive without magic.

Dex had an idea, but he wasn't willing to implement it until he knew a few things. He squeezed Vivian's hand, wishing he could consult with her. Wishing she knew everything about him, even the stuff he had purposely blocked from her once he learned she could read his mind.

"If we figure out who is doing this and manage to stop that person," Dex said, "will someone else appear and come after you in the same way?"

"I should hope not," Atropos said.

"That's a good point," Andrew Vari said. "Can you petition for your magic back?"

The three Fates sat up straighter, as if the question offended them. Vivian's hand trembled in Dex's. With her free hand, she rubbed the back of her neck.

"I suppose we could," Clotho said after a moment.

"But you don't want to," Nora said, revealing the unspoken answer. "Why not?"

"We have a purpose here," Lachesis said.

"To find out what it's like to be powerless?" Blackstone said. "Now you know."

"We're wasting time," Dex said. "All I want to know is whether or not we're helping you for the short term or the long term. It makes a difference in what we plan."

"Good point," Ariel said. She had stopped fidgeting and was leaning toward the table.

The Fates frowned, as if they were considering what Dex had said.

"Short term." Atropos's words sounded final, as if she had made a decision for all of them.

Dex sighed. He could feel the time running out. He glanced at Vivian and wondered what she would

To start your membership, simply complete and return the Free Book Certificate. You'll receive your Introductory Shipment of FREE Zebra Contemporary Romances. Then, each month as long as your account is in good standing, you will receive the 3 newest Zebra Contemporary Romances. Each shipment will be yours to examine for 10 days. If you decide to keep the books, you'll pay the preferred book club member price of $15.95 – a savings of up to 20% off the cover price! (plus $1.99 to offset the cost of shipping and handling.) If you want us to stop sending books, just say the word… it's that simple.

If the Free Book Certificate is missing, call 1-800-770-1963 to place your order. Be sure to visit our website at www.kensingtonbooks.com.

BOOK CERTIFICATE

Yes! Please send me FREE Zebra Contemporary romance novels. I only pay for shipping and handling. I understand I am under no obligation to purchase any books, as explained on this card.

Name _____

Address _____ Apt. _____

City _____ State _____ Zip _____

Telephone (___) _____

Signature _____

(If under 18, parent or guardian must sign)

Offer limited to one per household and not valid to current subscribers.
All orders subject to approval. Terms, offer, and price subject to change. Offer valid only in the U.S.

Thank You!

CN013A

ll..l..lll...lll.l.l.l..l.l.l..ll.l..l.l.l..lll.l..l

Zebra Contemporary Romance Book Club

Zebra Home Subscription Service, Inc.

P.O. Box 5214

Clifton , NJ 07015-5214

think of him as he revealed more of himself. He liked the easy camaraderie they had now; would it change when she realized just how much he had influenced the comic books she loved?

Then he shook his head. She already knew he was the prototype for Superman, that Siegel and Schuster had thought their weird neighbor who could run fast and pull off feats of amazing physical strength was an alien, abandoned here from another planet. They mistook his magic for great physical powers, and mistook his character for the open, all-American Superman.

Dex was more like Batman—secretive and protected, not willing to let other people in. Or maybe the better analogy came later, from the comic book artists who had never met him—the Stan Lees, Len Weins, and Frank Millers of the world, who seemed to know what it was like to be an outsider with an outsider's vision.

Vivian was watching Dex closely. He could feel her concern.

"You all right?" she whispered. No one else seemed to notice his pensiveness. The conversation still continued to run its circles around him.

He nodded, squeezed her hand, and let go. Then he looked directly at the Fates. "I have an idea, if you promise me I won't get into trouble."

Everyone turned toward him in surprise. Apparently, he had interrupted Nora, and his comment seemed to come out of the blue.

He ignored the others and just concentrated on the Fates—and Vivian, of course. He couldn't delete her from his consciousness even if he tried.

"We have no power over you," Clotho said.

"Right now," Dex said.

"We're not as rigid as you people seem to think," Lachesis said.

Dex swallowed hard. They were that rigid and

they didn't even realize it. It was very possible that once he saved them and they returned to their jobs, they would punish him for disobeying the law.

Vari shot the Fates an irritated glance. "What's your idea?" he asked Dex. "Because we're out of time."

Dex nodded. He looked at the Fates. They had wiped the tears off their faces, but they still appeared fragile. He couldn't get used to how small they were, and how very human they looked.

"Okay," he said. "I can take you to the cave."

"The fortress?" Atropos's voice rose.

He felt his cheeks grow warm. Vivian turned toward him, her expression surprised.

"I never called it a fortress," Dex said. "You did."

"Those books did," Clotho said.

"Those books were fiction," Dex said. "They had nothing to do with me."

"You started them," Lachesis said.

"I didn't even know the boys had written the first one until they'd sold it," Dex said. "And then they sold all their rights to it, so I thought it was over. Some big company was going to deal with it, and the company didn't know me."

"You're talking about Siegel and Schuster?" Vivian asked, awe in her voice.

"No," Dex said, "we're talking about whether or not I violated some sacred oath I didn't even know about."

"Everyone has heard of the comic book offender," Blackstone said.

"You're not helping," Nora whispered.

"The comic book offender?" Vivian asked.

"There's enough about our people in various comic books that we knew someone had blown the whole secrecy thing." Andrew Vari shrugged. "Of course, you could say that about myths, or Shakespeare, or any writer worth his salt—"

"We will not get into your indiscretions." Clotho glared at Vari.

"You're one of the reasons we had to crack down on later offenders," Lachesis said.

Dex leaned back in his chair, feeling discouraged.

"I don't understand the problem," Vivian said. "Dex is offering to help you. Stop fighting him."

"By sending us to the fortress," Atropos said.

"Which you promised you would get rid of." Clotho had turned her glare on Dex. He had been wrong a moment ago. She could be just as formidable, even in her smaller, more human state.

Dex clenched his fists. He would not let anger get the best of him. It took all his control to speak calmly. "See? This is what I was afraid of. You just don't understand."

"It was an order." Lachesis's tone had a bite to it that Dex had heard only once before. "No one disobeys our orders."

"Disobeyed." Vari glanced at Dex, obviously hoping Dex got the message. "Get your tenses right."

"You already compromised your position among mortals," Atropos said, as if Vari hadn't spoken. "You risk doing even more."

That was it. He'd had enough. If the Fates hadn't put Vivian in such danger, he'd walk out the front door and let whoever do their worst. But he was afraid it would ricochet on Vivian, who didn't deserve it.

And he had to protect her too. In fact, he wanted to protect her more than he wanted to protect anyone in his entire life.

"First," Dex said, "the comic book thing happened a long time ago. The boys, as we've been calling them, are dead now. No one remembers but us. Second, no one has found my cave in all the decades I've had it. Third, that property appreciates every year, and I'm not a rich man. I'm not willing to sell it. Fourth, if people believed comic books—which they emphatically do not—then my cave would be a damn fortress and it would be in the Arctic. And fifth, whether you like it or not, I think taking you there is our only option."

"To the Arctic?" Clotho asked.

"We're not fond of the cold," Lachesis said.

"I think he means the cave," Atropos said softly.

"What kind of fortress?" Blackstone asked. He had been watching the entire interchange with interest. Dex found it odd that even though Blackstone wanted to be in charge, he let this entire conversation continue without interference.

"It's not a fortress," Dex said. "It was an experiment. It's a home built inside a cave."

But he wasn't about to tell Blackstone where the cave was. Dex didn't trust the man enough to do that.

"They called it a fortress," Clotho said.

"Who?" Nora asked.

"The mortals. Those boys."

"The boys who are dead?" Ariel asked.

"Siegel and Schuster," Vivian said. "But they didn't come up with the Fortress of Solitude."

"That's right," Dex said. "That's what I'm trying to tell you."

"You told someone else?" Lachesis asked.

"I got the idea from the comic book!" Dex raised his voice.

"I thought you said no one got ideas from comic books," Atropos said.

"I said no one believed comic books were real," Dex said.

"But if no one believes they're real, why take ideas from them?" Clotho asked.

"You've been accusing me of putting ideas into them, not taking them out," Dex said. "I never told anyone about the caves, not until you decided to punish me for every leak that made its way into the D.C. and Marvel offices. And most of those didn't come from me."

"You just started the problem," Lachesis said.

"I did not," Dex said. "Half the stuff came from world mythology anyway."

"Yeah." Andrew Vari grinned. "And you guys can blame yourselves for that."

"This isn't helping," Vivian said.

"No, it isn't." Dex stood. He was shaking with anger. He pointed a finger at the Fates. "You see why someone has chosen to attack you? You're unreasonable. I'm trying to help you and you're angry—"

"Because you violated a sacred promise," Atropos said.

"It wasn't sacred," Dex said.

"You made an oath to us that you would never interfere with mortals again. You promised to get rid of all the accoutrements, and still, still, you have this place." Clotho stood too. "If I had power—"

"If you had power, you wouldn't even know I still had the cave," Dex said.

Vivian rubbed the back of her neck. Dex frowned. He didn't like that gesture. He had a hunch it was connected to this entire mess.

"We were out of time five minutes ago," Vivian whispered to him.

But the others heard and the conversation stopped. Finally, Blackstone took a deep breath.

"A cave?" he asked Dex.

Dex nodded. "It's really a vacation home now,

and no one knows I have it. The only way in is through magic. I've been fixing it up. It's nice."

"It sounds perfect," Blackstone said. "Let's get the Fates there."

"If we continually use magic to go in and out," Dex said, "there'll be a trail. Anyone with powers can find it. We bring the Fates in once and they stay until we find whoever has been attacking them."

"You don't need to discuss this as if we're not here," Lachesis said.

"Yes, we do," Vari said. "You're being petty. So he didn't follow your rules. Or maybe he did. Who cares? It's not relevant at the moment. And you know, you guys can make mistakes."

"That kind of logic has gotten you into trouble more than once," Atropos said.

The Fates might have gotten rid of their magic, but they hadn't gotten rid of their arrogance. Blackstone's arms were crossed. Ariel's mouth was in a thin line, and Vari looked as angry as Dex felt. Vivian was watching the Fates as if she hadn't seen them before.

Then she rubbed her neck again. The gesture seemed involuntary.

Dex sent a small reveal spell her way. A greenish glow tingled against the back of her neck and then vanished. Someone had touched her with magic, but he wasn't certain what kind.

Maybe his sense in the pet store had been right. Maybe Vivian was the evil mage's link to the Fates. But he wasn't sure how that could be. He certainly didn't sense any evil coming from her. She seemed to be the only person who cared.

Of course, she was the one who knew the Fates the least.

"Well," Dex said to the Fates, "you get a choice. You go to the cave and you don't complain about it. You stay until we say it's safe to leave and you never, ever punish me, nor do you tell anyone else to punish me, for keeping that cave. Or you walk out that door now and survive on your own."

Vari smirked, crossed his arms, and leaned back in his chair. Blackstone raised his eyebrows. Nora's gaze caught Vivian's and Vivian looked away. Dex felt her nervousness. She was worried that this would turn out badly for everyone.

Lachesis stood beside Clotho. Then Atropos stood. They stared at Dex, their gazes flat, their faces expressionless. They had looked at him like this the first time they had called him to them, before he had realized he had done anything wrong.

He had found their expressions terrifying then. They were still unnerving now, even though he knew he had more magic than the three of them combined.

"You dare challenge us?" Clotho said.

"You take advantage of our vulnerability?" Lachesis said, almost at the same time.

"You treat us like mere mortals?" Atropos said.

"Which you're supposed to be right now," Dex snapped. "Didn't you say you wanted to learn what it was like to be powerless? Well, welcome to that world, and make your damn choice."

His words echoed in the restaurant. Everyone looked at him in surprise, as if they hadn't expected it from him. He hadn't expected it from himself either, but someone had to take the lead. Someone who would ensure that Vivian wouldn't be hurt any worse than she already had been.

One by one, the Fates sat down. They didn't speak. Blackstone took Nora's hand. Ariel laid her head on Vari's shoulder.

Dex still stood, his arms crossed, his face set. He had taken quite a risk, and the Fates might make him pay for that risk at some point.

"All right," Clotho finally said. "Do what you must."

"But we'll stay there no longer than a month," Lachesis said. "Your time."

"And we'll need some sort of communication system that's impossible to track. We'll need to know what's going on," Atropos said.

Vari tossed Dex a cell phone. Dex caught it with his left hand.

"Take them now," Vari said, "before they change their minds. Then come back here. We'll have it all figured out by then."

That was all the permission Dex needed. He was going to take them to his private cave, and he was going to take them alone. If this went wrong, he didn't want Vivian anywhere near the Fates.

If this went wrong, he would take care of the problem himself.

Thirteen

Dex vanished, taking the Fates with him.

The room, which had seemed full of overwhelming personalities, suddenly seemed empty. And Vivian felt abandoned. She hadn't known Dex when she woke up that morning, so why should she feel empty just because he left?

Although, granted, he didn't just leave. He vanished, along with the three Fates, who had been the cause of her difficult day. And he'd abandoned her to Blackstone, Nora, Ariel, and Andrew Vari, people she still wasn't sure of.

She stood near her plate, staring at the three empty chairs across from her, feeling the emptiness of the chair beside her. She felt more unsettled than she had all day—which was saying something, considering what had been going on. Partly, it was because she had no idea where Dex was or when he'd be back (*if he'd be back,* her insecure subconscious was saying to her), and partly it was because she missed his presence—in her mind.

She hadn't really realized it had been there. Not

completely, anyway. She had recognized the psychic connection and had even noticed when Dex blocked his thoughts from her. But she hadn't realized that his being—his personality—had been inside her mind, like background music, something she wasn't aware of until it was gone.

Odd that realizing how close they'd been in the short time they were together didn't bother her. She used to hate being hooked up—as she called it—to anyone, not that it happened often. It happened with Aunt Eugenia, but as Vivian's mother used to say, Aunt Eugenia was a Presence. No one could ignore her. It also happened sometimes with Vivian's sister Megan, but they were as close as siblings could be.

It had never happened with someone outside her family.

"Are you all right, Vivian?" Nora asked. Nora stood alone on her side of the table. A few moments ago, she had seemed surrounded by Fates.

Vivian rubbed the back of her neck. That ache had become almost a headache. "I'm still not used to people popping in and out of my life."

Both Nora and Ariel smiled. "You'll get used to it," Ariel said.

Blackstone stood and put his napkin over his plate, as if the conversation offended him. "I've got to get into the kitchen."

"That can wait," Vari said. "We still have work to do."

Work? What kind of work would they have to do? It looked like Dex was doing all the work. And like Vivian was now out of the equation.

"Am I done?" she asked. "Can I go home?"

"Good question," Blackstone said. "Maybe I'll have an answer after I've ducked into the kitchen for a moment."

He hurried from the group, as if he couldn't

get away fast enough. Nora stood too, and started busing the table. Ariel took another slice of bread.

"They'll work this out," she said to Vivian.

She wasn't so sure. That feeling of being watched had returned. "I hope so."

Nora took a pile of soup dishes into the kitchen, then returned with a bus cart. Ariel helped her clear off the table. Andrew Vari grabbed the rope. Vivian almost stopped him, feeling protective of it, as if Dex owned it, instead of some mysterious evil mage.

But she didn't stop Vari. Instead, she watched him examine each strand, as if he were reading information in the jute.

"Guess we don't need the extra protection spells anymore," he said, raising his hand to call it off.

"Keep it for a moment." Blackstone spoke from the kitchen door. "We don't want to clue the enemy into the fact that the Fates are gone."

"The enemy?" Nora set a stack of bread plates in the bus cart. "Isn't that a bit dramatic?"

"I don't think so," Blackstone said. "I think whoever it is wants to kill the Fates."

"And that person is still out there," Vivian said. "I can feel him."

Vari dropped the rope. "Where do you feel him?"

Vivian shrugged. "It's just a sense."

"It's more than that." He sounded certain, even though they were discussing her body, her feelings.

"She is psychic, Sancho." Nora's voice held wry amusement. "Maybe it is just a sense."

"Is that true?" Vari asked. "Is it the same as your usual psychic experiences?"

No one had ever used the phrase *usual psychic experiences* with her before. Vivian would have smiled at it if the situation weren't so strange.

"It's not really the same," she said. "Just before

the rope came down, I felt this prickling in my spine. And then, there's this feeling of being watched—"

"Does your neck bother you?" Vari asked.

"I've had some major psychic experiences today," Vivian said. "I think it might be the beginnings of a migraine."

He frowned. "Maybe. But it might be something else. Mind if I check it out?"

"Check what out?" Vivian asked.

"Your neck."

She looked at Ariel. Ariel raised her eyebrows and shrugged, as if to say that her husband was always odd. "Just go with it," Ariel said. "He'll explain when he feels the need."

"All right." Vivian felt nervous about this. She wondered what Dex would say. Then remembered that Dex wasn't here, and she didn't know when he'd be back. If the pain in her neck was, literally, something evil, she wanted it taken care of sooner rather than later.

Vari walked over to her, started to put his fingers on her skin, then paused. "May I?"

"Sure," Vivian said, not certain what he was about to do.

He pressed his thumbs against her spine, then ran them upward to the base of her skull. The pressure made her shiver. If Dex had touched her like that, the shiver would have been with delight. But she found Vari's touch impersonal, almost cold.

Then the air sizzled, and Vari cursed. A smell, like burned electrical wires, floated around them.

Vivian turned. Vari had both thumbs in his mouth. Vivian touched the back of her neck. The pain was gone, but some of her neck hairs felt coarse and dirty.

"Are you okay?" she asked Vari.

He shook his head. "Efslakafaaut."

"What?"

He took the thumbs out of his mouth and shook them. They were both blackened on the tips.

Vivian stared at them. She got no sense of pain from him, but he wasn't that easy to read. Her heart was pounding now. Something had been wrong and she hadn't even known it.

"You want me to get some ointment for that, or can you take care of it?" Ariel asked Vari. She didn't seem concerned at all.

"I got it," he said, and the blackness disappeared. Still, he rubbed them together as if they hurt.

"What did you say a minute ago?" Vivian asked, sensing that it was important.

Vari grinned. "What I said was 'It's like I thought,' only it came out not like anything I thought at all."

"I should hope not," Ariel said dryly, "since what you said was unintelligible."

"What's like you thought?" Vivian asked. She didn't want to participate in banter. She wanted the scary part of this day to end. And, if she were honest with herself, she wanted the nice part—the part with Dex—to go on for a long, long time.

"Whoever this is has latched onto you. They're not focused on the building. They're focused on you." Vari stared at his thumbs, as if they could tell him who had done the magic. He seemed both bewildered and puzzled.

Vivian wasn't bewildered or puzzled. She was scared. She didn't remember seeing anyone in the past few days who'd seemed remotely evil. She knew that no one had touched the back of her neck.

"What do you mean, focused on me?" she asked.

"I mean that it was a good thing Dexter didn't take you with him," Vari said. "Or whoever it is who's doing this might have a shot at knowing where the Fates are.''

"I'm the reason they almost got killed?'' Vivian asked, sinking back into her chair.

"No,'' Vari said. "At least not at first.''

"Dar, stop that,'' Ariel said. "You're scaring her.''

"I'm being honest.'' Vari sat down. "I'm pretty sure you weren't targeted until you did that glass shield spell. Then it would be pretty easy for anyone to figure out who you are. But most mages would have attacked you. That was a real subtle spell I found, and one not often used.''

Vivian touched the skin on her neck. It felt unfamiliar, as if it had been sunburned or dried somehow. "Then how did you find it?''

"I've been around a long time, kiddo,'' Vari said. "I may be slow, but I get there eventually.''

"Meaning what?'' Vivian asked.

"Meaning I remembered someone else, a long time ago, doing the same thing to her neck that you were doing. That's why I thought I'd see what I could find.''

"Do you think the same person cast the same spell?'' Ariel asked.

"Not likely, Ari,'' Vari said, "since that mage is long dead.''

"You're sure?''

Vari nodded. He looked both serious and dangerous. "I'm sure.''

"How could they magic me without me knowing it?'' Vivian asked.

"It's a very subtle spell,'' Vari said, "but one that a person who can use puppets would be capable of.''

"What is?'' Blackstone came out of the kitchen. He was wiping his hands on a towel.

"Vivian's been targeted. That's why she knew

when the attack was going to come. I touched the back of her neck and shorted out something." Vari sniffed. "See? You can still smell the singed hair."

"Okay." Vivian took a deep breath, trying to stay calm. "Tell me how I could have gotten targeted."

"Someone used the signature of the imaginary glass you put over your apartment building to figure out who you are. Since you haven't come into your powers yet, and if the Interim Fates are as incompetent as Dexter says they are, then whoever did this has some powerful magic of his own." Blackstone moved the bus cart away from Nora and pushed it toward the kitchen. He was clearly thinking about what he had just said. "An incompetent mage couldn't have done this, nor could someone who has just come into his powers."

"Didn't I just say that?" Vari asked.

Blackstone shrugged. "I wasn't here."

"It's not even as simple as Alex makes it sound," Vari said. "I'm not sure I could do it."

He grabbed one of the tables and pulled it away from the other table. Ariel got a cloth and wiped both tables down.

Vivian understood that they wanted to open the restaurant, but their focus on business bothered her more than she was willing to admit. She still felt like there was a crisis going on, and these people were cleaning tables as if it were a regular day.

"Yes," Blackstone said to Vari with obvious affection, "but that's more a reflection of your level of practice than your abilities."

"That's my point." Vari grabbed a runner from a stack on a nearby shelf and put it on one of the clean tables. "I spent most of my life doing parlor tricks for reluctant lovers. It takes someone with a serious dedication to magic to target a woman who hasn't come into her powers yet."

This entire discussion was making Vivian nervous. "So what do I do now? How do I get untargeted?"

"We have to catch this person first," Blackstone said.

"But I have a life. I have some stuff I need to deal with, and my apartment, and my family—"

"Your family's not here, are they?" Blackstone asked.

"No," Vivian said. "They left yesterday."

"And the Fates arrived this morning?"

Vivian nodded, wondering how she was going to explain this to Travers on the phone. Kyle might get it, but Travers seemed very reluctant to believe in something that he couldn't see.

"Then I don't think you have anything to worry about. Do you agree, Sancho?"

Vari shook his head. He was watching Ariel set the tables. She was moving with the swiftness of someone who did that job often.

"I think Vivian's going to need a guardian just like the Fates do," Vari said.

At that, Nora gave him a suspicious look. "You're not reverting to form, are you, Sancho?"

"Of course not," he said, but his eyes twinkled.

"What form?" Vivian asked.

"Early garden gnome," Nora said, and got a growl from Vari. Then the twinkle left his eyes.

Vivian didn't understand the reference—or at least all of the reference. She remembered that someone had said the Fates had made Vari change his appearance for a few thousand years. Had they turned him into a garden gnome? A real gnome, or one of the ceramic kinds? And if he had been ceramic, he couldn't have been a garden gnome for several thousand years. She knew that they didn't have garden gnomes long ago, and she wasn't even sure when ceramic was invented.

"I'm serious, though," Vari was saying. "I think

Vivian is the one who needs protection, as much or more than the Fates.''

"You don't think I can protect myself?" Vivian asked, not sure she wanted to do it and yet also not sure she wanted to remain with these people.

Blackstone sighed. "I don't mean to offend you, but asking if you can protect yourself is like a toddler asking if she'll survive a boxing match with Evander Holyfield. This mage might go easy on you because you're without training, skills, or strength, but he might also decide to use you to teach the Fates a lesson."

Vivian sank into her chair. "I can't believe this happened to me because I opened my door this morning and let some strangers into my apartment."

Vari gave her a sad smile. "It's not that simple."

"Sure it is," Vivian said. "If I hadn't let them in, I wouldn't be here right now."

"I wouldn't be so sure of that," Vari said. "Remember who those women are. Fate. Destiny. An uncontrollable force with total control over your life. You're here now because they meant you to be here now."

"But they have no power," Vivian said.

"I'm still not sure of that." Vari's gaze met Blackstone's. "I'm not sure of that at all."

Fourteen

A *zzzzt!* went through Eris. Her entire body felt as if she had received a strong electric shock.

She had been sitting on the stairs, watching Quixotic while she was pretending to watch Sturgis wrap up his voice-over on the winking building. The voice-over would air during the afternoon newscasts, with promises of more to come later.

Sturgis was watching his replay on the video monitor, Kronski peering over his shoulder. Suzanne was off somewhere, trying to find out the scientific cause of the winking. The camera operators were anxious to go to the local affiliate—probably so they could escape Sturgis's presence.

The crowds had thinned now that the building was solid again, and many of the other news teams had left. The story was, for all intents and purposes, over.

Until the *zzzzt!*, Eris had been contemplating the next few days, planning to let the team return to New York while she remained here, ostensibly to meet with stockholders. She figured it would only take a few days to wrap up her business, so to speak, with the Fates.

The rope trick's failure hadn't angered her. With that many mages in the room, she had been surprised to get as far as she had. Although if Dexter Grant hadn't been there, she would have had the Fates.

Grant was the one to watch; Eris knew that now. And he seemed a lot more interested in pretty little Miss Kineally than in the Fates themselves.

Amazing what kind of information a connection gave her. It wasn't as if she watched everyone, and it wasn't quite a psychic link either. It was more like a radio in a neighbor's apartment, tuned to a staticky talk station. If she wasn't paying attention, she wouldn't have gotten any information at all.

Then the connection ruptured. She'd never felt anything like that *zzzzt!* before. It was painful and left her tingling all at the same time.

And more than a little angry. Grant hadn't severed the connection. Eris had been paying too much attention to Sturgis and hadn't been listening in as closely as she should have. Someone else had severed it, and it had hurt.

"Erika?" Sturgis was peering at her over the video replay. His own tiny image—looking much better than his large one—was nattering on about mass hallucinations and tricks of the light. "You all right?"

"Of course," she said, sounding as calm as she could under the circumstances.

"It's just . . ." He waved a hand over his head. "Your hair . . ."

She touched her hair. It was sticking out straight, and it felt coarse, just like the fur on those cartoon parodies of cats with their claws stuck in light sockets.

"The wind," she said, a bit of panic in her voice. "Hadn't you noticed how strong it is?"

Sturgis touched his own hair, as if he were afraid the light socket effect was contagious.

"Wrap it up," Eris said, nodding toward the video replay. "I want to get to the hotel and clean up before lunch."

"Okay," Sturgis said. "Why don't you go and we'll meet you somewhere?"

She raised her gaze toward the restaurant across the street. The neon lights turned on as she watched, and the vertical QUIXOTIC sign came to life in all its art deco glory.

"Meet me there," she said.

"Across the street?" Sturgis turned toward the restaurant. "Why?"

"Because it's famous, stupid." Kronski handed Sturgis the handheld mike. "You have to do your outro again. Truck noise."

Sturgis kept staring at the restaurant. "If it's so famous, how come I've never heard of it?"

Kronski's gaze met Eris's, and for a moment she knew they had shared a thought. She wasn't sure she appreciated it, or the fact that Kronski considered himself her equal. Then, as she watched, his eyes moved upward, his gaze traveling to her hair.

"What happened to you?" he asked.

"My crème rinse gave out," she snapped. "It's only an eight-hour treatment."

"Oh," he said, and turned away. She stood up and brushed herself off. People nearby were looking at her hair. It had to be pretty spectacular. She would wait until she rounded the corner before spelling her hair back to normal.

Then she would check into her hotel, change, and prepare herself for meeting the sources of those faraway radio voices. They wouldn't know who she was, of course. She would use her blocking magic and no one would be the wiser.

But she would see what she was up against.

She had a hunch that, without Dexter Grant, she wasn't up against much.

Dex appeared in the center of the cave, snapped his fingers to light candles, and clapped his hands. The Fates landed on the floor beside him, still standing side by side like they had been in Quixotic.

They looked just as angry as they had before.

He didn't say anything to them. Instead, he lit the fire in the hearth he had built by hand. The great room was his favorite. It had a natural arched ceiling, a flat floor (again the result of his own painstaking work), and thick fake fur rugs that covered everything. The couch was deep and comfortable, the easy chairs reclined, and the walls were covered with books.

A fully equipped modern kitchen stood off the entrance, and five bedrooms were down the hall. All of the bedrooms had tiny windows that overlooked the cliff face. The view from those windows was spectacular—waves breaking against the rocks below—and isolating at the same time. Nothing was visible except rocks and the sea itself, extending all the way to the horizon.

Dex went into the kitchen and flicked on the electricity. He'd wired that in during the last ten years, and it had been the worst job of his life. The electric company thought he was getting service to the acre of grass on the other side of the cliff face, not wiring inside natural caves.

So far, no inspectors had shown up, and he hoped none ever would. At one point, he'd had to use his magic to connect circuits through fifty feet of solid rock. There was no way he could explain to a mortal how that had been done.

When Dex got back into the great room, Atropos was reading the titles on the books in the bookcase. Lachesis was sprawled on the couch, her arm over her eyes, and Clotho was tending the fire.

"Okay," he said. "I'm the only person alive who knows that these caves are here. The guy who sold this property to me died in nineteen forty-seven, and I've kept the caves hidden since then. You can get out if you need to by following a passage off the kitchen, but it will take you days, and at times you'll have to crawl on your bellies. I don't recommend it."

"We're stuck here?" Clotho asked.

"You said you'd stay a month," Dex said.

"No windows," Lachesis said.

"No television," Atropos said, somehow making that sound worse.

"There are windows in the bedrooms—you can open them for fresh air. There is no beach below us, so no one will see you from the ground, although you have to watch out for the occasional ship. From the sea, those windows look like natural openings in the rocks, so you have nothing to worry about there either. There's also a small built-in balcony off the master bedroom, if you feel the need to go outside."

Dex felt awkward. He had never brought anyone here, no matter what the Fates believed. This was his private place, so private that he had built everything by himself, most of it by hand. He'd had to spell the furniture in here, but that had been easy.

"Who will bring us our meals?" Clotho asked, peering into the dining area. His table was made from the stump of an old growth tree, but the chairs were ladderbacks with upholstered seats.

Meals. He hadn't even thought about it. "No one. We can't continually pop in and out of here."

"Then we have a problem," Lachesis said. "There's no way to eat."

"Can't you cook?" Dex blurted before he thought the better of it.

"I believe Clotho tried," Atropos said, "decades before she came into her powers, which would put that . . . how many centuries ago, Clotho, dear?"

"Too many." Clotho sat on one of the dining room chairs. "We're going to need food."

"I'll make sure the kitchen's fully stocked before I leave. I'll put fresh foods in there, as well as frozen and microwavable. There are instruction manuals and cookbooks. You have a month. You'll have to learn how to cook—modern style."

"Cook?" Lachesis said, as if he had proposed she strip naked and jump into the ocean.

Dex nodded.

"Can't you send us a chef?" Atropos asked.

"Aethelstan will do," Clotho said.

"I don't have control over Blackstone," Dex said, thanking any god he could think of that he didn't. He didn't want to be part of that controversy.

"We have not learned anything nonmagical in centuries," Lachesis said. "We will starve."

Dex smiled. "I'm not too worried. Anyone can microwave a pizza."

"I'm not even sure what a microwave is," Atropos said.

Clotho twisted her torso so that she was draped over the back of her chair. "I had thought we would come to this place, have adventures, and then return to our job. I did not expect to come here, have a half day of panic, and be stuck in a cave for a month."

Dex clenched his fists, struggling not to lose his temper. He hated their lack of gratitude, their sense of entitlement, their—he forced the thoughts back, took a deep breath, and said, "It's not my problem, ladies. I had a solution to your predicament. As I said at Quixotic, accepting that solution is entirely your choice."

"Books and cooking are not enough," Lachesis said.

"We need to stay occupied," Atropos said.

"Then work on who could be doing this to you." Dex did a long-lasting power spell on the cell phone Vari had given him, and added a boost so that the signal reached the closest tower. "When you figure it out, call Quixotic."

"I hope you have instructions for that thing too," Clotho said.

"Nice try." Dex handed the phone to Lachesis. "But I'm the wrong person to give that line to. I know you keep track of modern culture. You may not know how to use a stove, but you know what one is for. And you've watched enough movies to know how a phone works."

Lachesis didn't say anything as she took the phone from him. She set it on the table beside him.

"Movies would help," Atropos said.

"Anything to keep us busy," Clotho said.

"There's a DVD player in the master bedroom, along with the only TV," he said. "When I spell in the groceries, I'll spell in enough movies to keep you busy for a month."

"That's at least three per day," Lachesis said.

"And be careful," Atropos said. "We've seen a lot."

"I'll try to get the director's cut where I can." Dexter went into the kitchen. It was big and warm, with a flat-cooktop stove and a water-in-the-door refrigerator. He loved this room and spent a lot of time here, usually baking for himself.

The cave was special. Part of him couldn't believe he would let anyone else inside. This was the place he went when the world got to be too much for him. This was his haven, his favorite hideout, his most secret lair. Now the Fates would move things, scatter things, break things. He'd have to resign himself to the fact that nothing in here would be the same.

At least they weren't in his store. That, at least, remained his and his alone.

Then he froze. He'd left the mother cat and the kittens in there, unguarded, for hours. They could fend for themselves, but he couldn't continue running off and leaving them. He would have to find them homes sooner rather than later.

"Cooking, movies, books, and thinking," Clotho muttered. "As if those things will take up our time."

"We can't even do idle magic," Lachesis said. "I'm not sure I know how to run a remote."

"There's a lot we can learn," Atropos said, clearly trying to remain upbeat. "I'm sure we'll do fine."

Dex snapped his fingers, and the box with the mother cat appeared. All the kittens except little Marco Polo were inside. Dex snapped his fingers again, and Marco Polo appeared halfway across the room.

"Troublemaker," Dex said, going to fetch him. He picked up the kitten, rubbed its fluffy fur against his nose, and handed it to Clotho.

She smiled. "What's this?"

"Something to keep you busy," Dex said, snapping his fingers a third time. "If I'm going to help you, I won't have time to take good care of them. I just spelled you a stocked kitchen and movies, along with cat food and litter. Don't let these guys out of your sight in the bedrooms—they might climb out the windows and fall to their deaths—

and don't let them wander around the house until you're sure they're box-trained."

"Box-trained?" Lachesis asked, clearly not understanding the reference.

Dex went to the bookshelf and pulled down a book on cat care. "I suggest you all start with this book. Do the best you can. I'll be back as soon as possible."

He got ready to spell himself out before they could complain about anything else. He was half-way through the arm arch when he heard Atropos say, "When you do come back, be a good man and bring us a chef."

"Preferably a famous one," Clotho said, her voice fading as she did.

Lachesis added something too, but Dex ignored it. He didn't want to know what she said. All he wanted now was to return to Vivian.

He hoped nothing had happened to her while he was gone.

Fifteen

Vivian stood behind the bar at Quixotic, her back to the three men in business suits who laughed as they discussed their latest business deal. No one else sat at the bar. All the other customers were inside the restaurant, seated or waiting for the maître d'.

The bartender was working around Vivian as he tried to keep up with the larger than usual number of mixed drinks being ordered at lunch. He blamed it on the disappearing building ("Did you see that?" he asked Vivian, and she could honestly answer, "Only on TV."), but he hoped the trend would continue. He liked being busy.

She wished things would slow down so she could talk to someone. Dex hadn't come back, and everyone else was busy with the lunch crowd. Vivian had asked permission to use a phone, and Blackstone had told her to use the one behind the bar, since the kitchen was already overcrowded.

So Vivian had made her way past all the full tables, surprised at how many faces she recognized.

Most belonged to the news reporters she'd been watching on the local channels this past week, but she also recognized Noah Sturgis, who had been around since she was a little girl. He looked somewhat plastic in person, as if he'd glued his face back, a feature she'd recognized from L.A. Plastic surgery looked good on camera, but it certainly looked awful in person.

Sturgis was sitting right in the center of the restaurant with a scruffy man in jeans and a young woman who looked out of her depth. Sturgis seemed to enjoy the positioning, signing autographs and talking to people who passed. Vivian made certain she avoided that table as she made her way to the front of the restaurant.

Which was where she stood now, trying to stay away from the floor-to-ceiling windows. She was still nervous about going outside. She had moved the phone as far away from the windows as she could, but she still felt oddly exposed.

The crowd din was less here, but the occasional laughter from the celebrating businessmen jarred her. She wrapped the phone's cord around her hand, wishing for a portable phone instead, and dialed Travers's cell phone.

He answered on the fifth ring—or rather, Kyle did, sounding breathless. "Got it," he said into the receiver, then apparently realizing what he had done, added, "hello?"

"Hey, Ky," Vivian said.

"Aunt Viv! How're you? We've been really worried. Hey, Dad, it's Aunt Viv!" Kyle said all of this so quickly that Vivian couldn't get a single word in.

"Gathered that." Travers's voice was faint but audible. Someone else was talking—yet another reporter, probably on the radio—and then that voice cut off. "Give it to me."

"Wait," Kyle said. "You okay, Aunt Viv?"

"That's what I was calling to tell you," she said. "I'm just fine."

"She's just fi—" There was a sudden crackling, a rap, and then the squishy sound of hands rubbing on plastic. A horn honked in the distance, Kyle cried, "Da-ad!" and then Travers said, "Vivian, what the hell's going on?"

"What do you mean?" Vivian asked, unwrapping the phone cord from her hand. She knew exactly what he meant, but she wasn't sure how to talk with him about her day.

"That whole building thing." Another car honked, the sound moving past, as if Travers was driving away from the problem. "I thought you were going to call me right back."

"I said I'd call you as soon as I could. This is the first chance I got."

"It was your building, right?"

"Hey, buddy! Watch it!" a man yelled, the voice startlingly close.

"Dad, let me talk to her."

"Are you driving?" Vivian asked. "I thought you weren't supposed to drive and talk on the phone at the same time."

"I'm not in L.A.," Travers said. "No way is some state cop going to know about my previous citations. I paid the—well the same to you, jerk face!"

"Nice talk with your son in the car." Vivian turned around and leaned against the back bar. The bartender grinned at her—apparently he'd heard that last comment—and pulled a highball glass off the nearby display.

"Lay off," Travers said, and Vivian couldn't tell if he was talking to her, Kyle, or some faceless driver.

"Do me a favor and pull over," Vivian said.

"I'm not—"

"Do it, or I'll hang up. And I'm not at home, so you won't be able to find me."

The phone crackled again, and she heard Travers's voice, fainter now, say, "Here, you talk to her."

"Aunt Viv, we nearly hit a semi." Kyle sounded breathless. "And some guy in a Mazerati swore at us."

"Is your dad pulling over?"

A crowd of people had gathered outside the restaurant. Vivian had the sense they were looking at her. Then she realized they were studying a posted menu.

"There's no place to pull," Kyle said. "He'll find somewhere, though. He's been really worried, Aunt Viv. He said he shouldn't've left you up there all by yourself. You gonna be okay?"

"I'll be fine," Vivian said. "I've met my neighbors and they're . . ."

She glanced at the swinging kitchen door. Ariel had just come through it, holding a tray of steaming plates like a pro.

"What, Aunt Viv? I missed that."

"They're okay," Vivian said, feeling like *okay* was a completely inadequate description of the crew at Quixotic. The bartender, who had just put three rum and Cokes on a cocktail waitress's tray, gave Vivian another grin, as if he too found the word *okay* an understatement.

"We see an exit," Kyle said. "It's a mile and a quarter. Dad says to wait."

"I will."

A woman walked through the main glass doors. She was tall and slender, dressed in a tasteful red business suit that seemed too upscale for Portland. She was in her mid-fifties and had done nothing to hide it, unlike most women of her age in L.A.

She carried a clutch purse in one hand and a

cell phone in the other. Her close-cropped hair was dark, and her features were familiar. But she wasn't an actress. Vivian had lived in the L.A. basin long enough to recognize one of those.

". . . Aunt Viv?"

"What?" Vivian asked. She had missed everything Kyle had just said to her.

"Have you looked at my comic book yet?"

"I've looked at it," Vivian said, still watching the woman. She radiated power, and not the confident power that some businesswomen had. Power—wattage—like Blackstone did. Or Andrew Vari. But unlike them, Vivian got no sense of magic from this woman.

Besides, the others would've noticed if someone magical had walked in, right?

"Aunt Viv!" Kyle shouted in her ear.

At that moment, the woman looked at her, and Vivian got the sense they had met before. In fact, the woman's features weren't familiar because Vivian had seen them on television or in a movie. They were familiar because Vivian had—

"Are you Erika O'Connell?" the maître d' asked the woman, breaking Vivian's train of thought.

The woman turned away from Vivian, and the feeling passed. Vivian wasn't sure what she had been thinking or where she had known the woman from. Or, exactly, why it had suddenly seemed so important.

"Aunt Viv?" Kyle was still shouting.

"I'm here, Kyle," Vivian said, missing the woman's response to the maître d'.

"What'd you think of my comic book?"

"You're burning up money here, kiddo." Travers's voice dominated the line as the phone crackled again.

Vivian was only half listening. She watched the maître d' take the woman to Noah Sturgis's table.

Of course. Erika O'Connell was supposed to be the twenty-first-century female version of Ted Turner. She owned several cable stations, and she was trying to create her own empire. But her focus was on news, on making it viable, profitable, and still honest.

Or so she had said in the interviews Vivian had seen.

"So what happened with your building and why aren't you there?" Travers asked.

"I'm having lunch," Vivian said. "And no one seems to know what happened. Personally, I didn't notice anything different. I think it was a trick of the light."

"Weird things always happened around Aunt Eugenia, Viv, and I'm wondering if she gave that legacy to you. You've never been the most stable—"

In the back of the restaurant, a woman screamed. Vivian set down the phone and hurried toward the sound.

Dex was sitting on an elderly woman's lap. The woman was sitting in the chair he had used before he disappeared with the Fates.

Everyone was staring at them. Apparently he had just materialized, or whatever these mages called their arrivals.

He stood, grinned, and doffed an imaginary hat. He looked wonderful. Gallant and handsome and oh so self-possessed.

"Took a wrong turn, didn't I?" he said with a veddy accurate, veddy British accent. "I thought this was Buckingham Palace. My mistake."

And then he vanished.

Vivian smiled in spite of herself. The restaurant burst into conversation, and several people hurried over to the elderly woman, who still looked frightened.

The phone was swinging on its cord, and she could hear Travers yelling.

Vivian picked it up and, without putting it to her ear, said into the receiver, "I'm fine, Trav. I have to go. Something's come up. I'll call you in a few days."

And then she hung up.

The restaurant was in chaos. Even Noah Sturgis looked flustered. But Erika O'Connell had a slight smile on her face, as if she had found everything as amusing as Vivian initially had.

Vivian headed for the back of the restaurant, avoiding the crowd that had gathered at the elderly woman's table, and pushed her way into the kitchen.

Steam rose from several pots on the stove. A young man in a chef's uniform made salads, and a woman in white was rolling pastry dough on the table's steel surface. Ariel was loading full lunch plates on another tray.

Dex was nowhere to be seen. But Blackstone looked like he was ready to rip someone's head off.

"What the hell was that?" he asked Vivian.

"How'm I supposed to know?"

"No wonder the Fates gave him a warning. I would have—"

"Excuse me." Dex stood in the hallway, his face bright red. "I think you meant that question for me."

Vivian's heart leapt. She was relieved to see him, although she wasn't sure why. She hadn't thought he was in danger, but she had been worried about him—and slightly worried that he wouldn't return or, at least, return to her.

Everyone in the kitchen looked at him in surprise. A few patrons poked their heads through the swinging door, apparently thinking that Vivian's entrance gave them permission to come in too.

Dex's sheepish gaze met Vivian's, and she felt his embarrassment as if it were her own. He hadn't checked his location, apparently, before doing the spell. Not that she understood what that meant.

But he was letting her know this as an explanation, a way of telling her why he had screwed up.

It's okay, she sent him, and he gave her a smile so small she wondered if anyone else could see it.

"Into my office, now," Blackstone said, pointing down the hallway where Dex was standing. "You too, Ariel. Marcel, tell Nora to join us when she gets off the phone."

"Oui," said the chef, who had been watching everything from a place near the ovens.

Blackstone put a hand against Vivian's back and actually shoved her forward. She hurried ahead of him to move away from his touch. Dex walked in front of her, then pulled open the last door on the right.

Andrew Vari was inside, going through receipts, adding them up on an old-fashioned adding machine. Without looking up, he said, "Buckingham Palace?"

"Everyone worries about the non sequitur and then forgets the details about the guy who vanished," Dex said, stepping inside.

"If you say so." Vari moved a pile of receipts into a basket and then stood.

The office was small and narrow. Two large desks were crammed into it, bumping up against each other to form an *L*. On one desk, a computer hummed. A screen saver spelled the word *Quixotic* one gothic letter at a time.

A single chair on casters swung between both desks. Above them were flyers and notices, some from the government and the state about inspections and employee notices. A single poster, announcing Quixotic's opening, was framed on the only remaining wall space, and beside it, was a tiny article from the *New York Times*, calling Quixotic the Best of the West.

Vari went all the way to the filing cabinets in the back. Dex followed him, and Vivian remained by his side. Blackstone held the door for Ariel, who mentioned that someone had to take her tables. He told her not to worry. Then he pulled the door closed.

"I don't appreciate careless magic in my restaurant," Blackstone said to Dex.

"I covered," Dex said.

"And repeated the sin," Blackstone said. "The least you could have done was walk into the back."

"And have everyone know where I was?" Dex asked. "Did you see all the reporters out there?"

"I warned you that would happen," Vari said.

"You said all the publicity would be good," Blackstone snapped.

"It probably will be," Ariel said. "Fortunately this happened at the same time as the building fiasco. Everyone'll think this is all related."

"And being caused by me," Blackstone said.

The door opened, and Nora stepped inside. She grinned at Dex. "Quite an entrance."

"Your husband doesn't think so," Dex said.

"Do you know the kind of problems he just caused?" Blackstone asked.

"None," Nora said. "I was talking on my cell when it happened, and people got all excited—"

"We noticed," Ariel said dryly.

"—and by the time I'd hung up, I heard that a man tried to take some lady's purse, that her lunch companion made a pass and she tossed him out of his chair, and that some local actor was taking advantage of the morning's strange events to build himself a career. Nice going. You really confused them with that Buckingham Palace comment—"

"Enough," Blackstone said.

But Vivian felt Dex tense beside her. "No," he said to Blackstone. "Not enough. I told you that ploy worked."

"You only know it because you're careless with your magic in public," Blackstone said.

"At least I don't use mine to improve people's meals or to change the decor. Yes, I've heard all the strange stories about Quixotic. Who hasn't, over the years?"

"Boys," Nora said. "No need to fight."

But Dex wasn't going to stop, even if Vivian asked him to. And she wasn't sure she wanted to.

"Why shouldn't we fight?" Dex asked Nora. "It's clear your husband doesn't like or trust me."

Blackstone made a sputtering sound, but Dex wasn't through. He glared at Blackstone. "You must be happy I have the Fates. That way if something happens to them—and you're not sure that would be a bad thing—then you won't get blamed for it."

Blackstone straightened, as if making himself taller also made him seem more powerful. "I've been trying to help them."

"By talking, dithering, and running your restaurant," Dex said. "Only Vivian and I have taken the risks here."

"That's not fair," Ariel said.

"Fair doesn't matter," Dex said. "Truth does. You people aren't sure how you feel about the Fates, so you haven't been working hard to save them. Well, I bought us a month. And I'm going to do what I can, with or without you."

Vivian had the odd feeling that he was including her in that challenge. She touched his arm. *I'm going to help.*

I know, babe.

The easy communication between them, the telepathic communication, startled her. Especially since she knew she wasn't getting all his thoughts, just most of his emotions and the occasional idea that he sent her way.

"We're going to help you," Blackstone said.

Dex turned toward him as if he'd forgotten Blackstone was there. "By doing what? Feeding every reporter in the Northwest? That's helpful."

"There's no need to be snide," Blackstone said.

"Nor is there a need to be overbearing. If you want to help, fine. Figure out who's after the Fates and let me know. Otherwise, I'm going to take care of this, with Vivian's help."

Vivian nodded so that the others knew she agreed.

"Look," Blackstone said, "we didn't mean to—"

"Let him be, Aethelstan," Nora said. "He's right. We haven't done much. He and Vivian have done it all."

Blackstone looked down at his wife, then his shoulders slumped as he seemed to realize she was right.

"If you're going to take Vivian far away from here," Vari said from his perch beside Dex, "and, I might add, I think that's a good idea, you probably should know she was targeted."

Vivian's hand went involuntarily to her neck. The singed hairs were brittle, and a few of them broke as she touched them.

"Targeted?" Dex asked her softly.

"That's what"—she wasn't sure what to call Vari, since he had so many names—"he said. He did something, and my neck felt better afterward."

"I shorted out the spell," Vari said. "Someone used her signature from the glass jar, traced her, and used her to keep an eye on the Fates."

That wasn't exactly what he said before. Vivian felt her stomach twist. "I was bugged?"

"Essentially, kiddo. But you're all right now."

"You're sure?" Dex sounded breathless, and Vivian could feel his concern for her. "You're sure she's not hurt?"

"Yes, I'm sure." Vari gave him a patient smile. "And no, I couldn't figure out who left the trace. That's one powerful mage we're up against."

Dex's gaze met Vari's. Vivian could feel Dex measuring the other man. "And that's why you think we should continue to work together."

"Didn't say that." Vari leaned against the filing cabinets.

"You didn't have to," Dex said.

Vari shrugged. "We're stronger together."

"If we all have the same goals." Dex gave Blackstone a look.

Blackstone raised his hands, palms extended to Dex as if he were giving up. "I don't understand why I'm the villain here."

"I think Dex is as used to running the show as you are." Ariel had scooted herself on top of one of the desks. She was sitting cross-legged.

Her remark struck something. Vivian felt Dex's irritation rise before he buried it.

"I'm used to working alone," Dex said. "I think it's better if I go back to that. If you find something, great. If you don't, that's all right too. But I'm going to make sure those women are all right."

"Always the hero," Blackstone muttered, and Nora slapped his arm with the back of her hand. He caught her fingers in his. "Well, I'm just calling what I see. It doesn't happen often, but when it does, it's hard to shed."

"Remember Robin Hood?" Vari asked.

"Who could forget?" Blackstone said. "And you had the same trouble with Arthur, right?"

Dex was getting angry. Or maybe Vivian was. She suddenly couldn't separate their emotions at all.

"I may be younger than you are," Dex said, "but I'm old enough to handle this. And I don't appreciate being made fun of."

"We're not making fun of you," Vari said. "It's more like a warning. You can't always ride to the rescue, Kimosabe. Sometimes the forces of evil are more powerful than the forces of good."

Dex stared at all of them, then reached out to Vivian. She took the hand he offered, and that spark rose between them again.

"If I had a team I trusted," Dex said to the others, "then I would work with them. But it's becoming very clear that this group doesn't work well together. Do what you want to. If you want to help the Fates, you'll have to come through me, because I'm not telling any of you where they are."

"This just caught us by surprise," Nora said. "We're not that bad a group—"

"You're probably not," Dex said. "But stuff like this always catches people by surprise, and their initial actions are usually the truest ones. I don't blame any of you for having mixed emotions about the Fates. Hell, I do, and they never punished me. They only threatened to. So I do understand. But because you are uncertain how you feel about them, I'm uncertain about you. I've made my decision. So has Viv, who has no experience with the Fates at all, and who has gotten roped into this whole thing against her will. Right now, she's the only other person I trust."

Blackstone studied both of them. Vivian could feel his emotions suddenly, as if they had grown stronger. He was embarrassed and slightly angry, as if Dex had struck a chord.

"You have a point," Blackstone said.

"We'll do what we can," Vari said, his tone soft.

He seemed contrite and understanding. Vivian was really beginning to like him.

"If you come up with anything," Dex said, "leave a message at my store. Ariel knows where it is."

"I do?" Ariel asked.

"The basset hound puppy, remember?" Dex asked. "How's he working out for your friend?"

"I'm the friend," Vari said. "He's my familiar. And he's great."

Dex nodded, and Vivian suppressed a smile. He had known the answer before he asked the question. He was just using the information to establish his own credentials with the group. He could be as subtle as Blackstone was when he wanted to be.

"Then you know how to find me," Dex said. "And as fun as this has been, it's time for me to leave. You want to come?"

He turned toward Vivian as he asked this last.

She nodded. She wanted to stay with Dex and figure out how to help the Fates. Even if the Fates were all right, Vivian would have wanted to go with Dex.

She was having trouble imagining herself without him in her life.

"I'm ready," she said, and took his hand.

He glared at the group as he swung his arm. Together, he and Vivian disappeared.

Sixteen

Eris sat in the center of Quixotic, nursing a vodka martini. What an interesting hour she'd had. Dexter Grant popping into the middle of the room like a mage newly introduced to his powers, and his startlingly prepossessed statement about Buckingham Palace, proving that he'd made this mistake before. The man could get careless when his mind was on other things.

And Eris had a guess what other things had preoccupied him. Those Fates, of course, and that pretty little psychic who seemed to think she had more power than she did.

Vivian Kineally was prettier in person than she had seemed from Eris's magical glimpses of her. Theoretically, the girl shouldn't have been attractive at all. Her hair was too curly, her features too delicate. But that dark skin and those intelligent eyes made up for a lot. With the right makeup, the right clothes, and the right pair of contact lenses, Vivian Kineally would be a stunner.

Grant had taste.

Eris grabbed the plastic sword that held her olive and swirled it in her glass, pretending to listen to Sturgis, Kronski, and Suzanne discuss the day's news stories. In the back, she could sense the group gathered in Blackstone's office.

Blackstone himself was furious at Grant for taking control of the Fates. Blackstone's little friend, Sancho, who apparently wasn't so little any more, was amused by the turn of events. And Blackstone's wife was trying to placate her husband, her feeble not-yet-developed power glimmering off her like reflected sunlight. The other woman, Sancho's wife, wasn't worth Eris's time or attention.

No, what interested Eris were Grant and Kineally, who had just popped out of the back office on their way to a new adventure. Off to search for Eris, who, unbeknownst to all of them, was sitting front and center in their little restaurant.

She had given Kineally a chance to recognize her. Their gazes had met, and she had felt Kineally's mind probe hers. Of course, Eris wasn't going to open her thoughts to just anyone, particularly not a little not-yet-magical talent whom everyone treated as more important than she was.

That little trick Eris pulled, in fact, proved that Kineally wasn't the talent Eugenia had thought she was. Not that Eugenia had been right about many things.

Eris smiled at the memory, although her smile must have been inappropriate for the conversation. Sturgis glared at her as if she had burped at the table. She let her smile fade, nodded once as if she were paying attention to his prattle, and listened instead to the discussion in the back.

Not that it was much more interesting than the one in the front. The little group of rescuers had no idea she was here. No mage could sense her powers when she used her blocking magic—a series of spells she had devised while undergoing her torture from the Fates. As the blocking spells became more and more successful, she gained some respite from the pain those three harpies had inflicted on her, until, in the end, she felt no pain at all.

They thought their little creative methods of justice worked. All those harpies had really managed to do—at least in Eris's case—was make her even more determined to have her revenge.

And she *would* have her revenge. She was sick of the Powers That Be, and the Fairy Circle, who thought they knew even more than the Powers, had taken self-righteousness to a new art. That didn't even include all the other, tinier groups of magical rulers who thought they had a corner on right, might, and power.

All of them would learn they knew nothing about governing, about control, about the way the world worked. They would learn who was really in charge when Eris's plan hit its final stages.

Getting rid of the Fates and replacing them with those marvelously imbecilic children was simply one of the middle steps along the road to success.

". . . do you, Erika?"

Eris blinked at Sturgis, who was still glaring at her. He knew she hadn't been listening. No sense in pretending she had been.

"I'm sorry," she said, pulling the olive out of her glass and tapping the plastic sword against the rim. "I seem to have lost the thread of the conversation."

Sturgis picked up the tray of spinach-stuffed mushroom caps and scooped the last onto his glass appetizer plate. "Kronski, here, believes we should put some of our science reporters on this, to see if they can figure out what happened to that building this morning. I think this story's run its course, and it's time to leave Oregon for someplace that has real news. Don't you, Erika?"

She set her olive on the bread plate to her right—his bread plate, not hers, but if he challenged her on it, she could lie and say she always got confused by bread plate placement. He was irritating her. It was clear he had repeated his question verbatim after he had given her Kronski's argument.

Kronski had just finished his fourth raw oyster. Who he thought he would bed in the afternoon, of all things, with that scruffy blond hair and poorly shaven face, she had no idea. But his entire meal seemed geared toward aphrodisiacs—oysters, oysters, and more oysters. Too bad she hadn't paid attention to his order for the main course. She had a hunch it had oysters in it as well.

"Science reporters?" she said to Kronski. "You actually believe there's a story here?"

Kronski pushed away his appetizer plate, then grabbed his linen napkin and wiped his hands. "Buildings don't flash in and out, at least not in real life. I wasn't so much thinking about making this story into an evergreen as I was thinking of it as a CYA story."

"Why do we need our asses covered?" Eris asked.

"Because someone could—and I'm sure someone will—accuse us of using CGI to make a slow news day into a real story."

"Nonsense," Sturgis boomed, and half the restaurant looked at him, surreptitiously, of course. He was the famous one at the table—or at least he was the modern famous one. At times in her very long life, Eris had been much more famous than he ever was.

With a slight movement of her left hand, she ordered him to lower his voice.

"Why would anyone think we had to make up a

story?" Sturgis asked. "We're not tabloid television. I have the awards to prove it."

I not *we.* That ego. Eris would have to crush it, and soon.

"The print people love to trip us up," said Suzanne. "They think we wouldn't know real news if it dropped in our laps."

Leave it to Suzanne to state the obvious. But her point was an interesting one. Eris's first inclination had been to send the entire team back to New York and say she'd be meeting with stockholders. But if the team stayed, no one would think twice about her presence.

"You're scheming," Sturgis said.

Yes, idiot, but not about you or your paltry news career. Eris smiled at him and finished her martini. Then she set the glass down. She took a warm slice of bread from the basket in front of her.

"Let her think," Kronski said.

As if they ever interfered. Eris poured some olive oil in the provided dish, then dipped her bread in it and chewed, surprised at the richness and freshness of the oil. Blackstone was living up to his mortal reputation. He had found olive oil that actually tasted like the kinds she had as a girl in what was now Greece.

Kronski, of course, had asked the wrong question—not that, as a limited mortal, he would know the right question to ask. No one cared, in the long term scheme of things, if KAHS was a tabloid news network or a real news network. Hell, the definition of what was real news changed every few decades anyway.

No. The important issue was how she could use their stay in Portland and surrounding environs to further her goal of disseminating the right kind of information to create even more chaos around her.

When she was participating, each story had to

further that goal. Of course, KAHS covered a lot of stories that meant nothing in Eris's scheme of things. But here in the heart of happy mage country, where Blackstone had his friends and his restaurant, where Dexter Grant, that good-hearted do-gooder, had settled, and where the late Eugenia Kineally practiced her particularly offensive brand of niceness . . . well, this would be the best place to dismantle some magical systems that had gotten way out of line.

The fact that the Fates had chosen to hide here, cowards that they were, was simply gravy.

"Erika?" Sturgis asked.

She could tell from his tone of voice that he expected her to agree with him.

"I think we should stay here," she said, setting down the crust of her oil-saturated bread. "We haven't done any live reporting from the Northwest in a while, preferring to rely on our affiliates—and, as we all know, their reporting is beyond wretched. Who cares about trees, anyway—old growth or otherwise? There have to be other stories in this part of the country, right?"

Sturgis was staring at her as if she had grown a new head. Kronski had a grin on his face that he was trying—and failing—to suppress.

"I don't think this is a good idea," Sturgis said. "There's no news here. This is the ass end of nowhere."

His voice carried, like usual, and the patrons of the restaurant looked at him. Half of them seemed offended. Locals, probably. The C-team news crews who had been covering the weird building all morning gave him a sympathetic smile.

"Maybe there's the perception of no news," Eris said, "because no one pays attention to this part of the country. We might break a few stories. Have you thought of that?"

"I've been hoping to check out some of the fringe political movements here," Suzanne said, her voice breathy and timid, as usual.

Fringe political movements. Eris sighed. As if that story hadn't been done to death.

Kronski saw her expression. "I'm sure there are other stories too."

"Like a scientific investigation of the Great Disappearing Building." Sturgis crossed his arms and leaned back in his chair, tilting it on two legs. He nearly collided with the waiter, who was bringing their lunch.

The food was fragrant and simple. Eris had ordered a rabbit stew and found it to be old-fashioned—as in positively medieval—and for a moment she toyed with leaving Blackstone alone to ply his craft. No one made food like this any more and, contrary to what she would have said half an hour earlier, she found she actually missed it.

"Give my compliments to the chef," she said to the waiter, allowing the twinkle in her eye to show.

"Yes, ma'am," he said, bowing to her with a formality she hadn't expected.

Eris smiled and turned to her stew. Staying here wouldn't be as difficult as she thought. She'd even eat most of her meals here, not just to keep her eye on Blackstone but to give herself a treat.

"I think pursuing the science angle might be one small story we could do," Eris said, looking at her small team. "But I'm sure we'll find something else as well. Just give me a little time. I'll come up with a story that will make everyone from ABC to CNN to *Time* to the *New York Times* pay attention."

"You'd better," Sturgis muttered.

Maybe she'd take that deep voice away from him, and make him sound like he was on helium all the time. That would upset him, perhaps permanently.

But not yet. She still needed him.

For now.

However, when that changed . . .

"You're scheming again," Sturgis said.

"Yes." Eris smiled at him. She had a wonderful afternoon planned. Grant and Kineally had gone to Grant's house, where Eris would soon join them, proving to Grant just how meager his powers were and to Kineally how fragile a psychic's mind could be.

Then Eris would go get the Fates and dispose of them. She might even finish her tasks in time to have dinner at Quixotic.

"What are you thinking about?" Kronski asked, which was a much better question than the implied questions in Sturgis's scheming comments.

"I'm thinking that with a few changes, I could grow to like this place," Eris said.

"This restaurant or the Northwest?"

"All of it," Eris said. Her mood was so much better than it been in the morning. Of course, Strife was off on some unimportant mission, so she didn't have him to worry about anymore. "I really think that this little burg will provide the turning point for everyone here."

Everyone, including the mortals surrounding her and the mages who were discussing the "evil mage and his plan" in the kitchen.

Eris smiled again. It felt good to taunt the enemy—even when he had no idea she was doing so. She knew, and that was all that mattered.

Vivian and Dex arrived in his backyard seconds later. His house wasn't a palace by any stretch, and that embarrassed him. He knew the theory, heard it expressed by longer-lived mages than he was:

that any mage who had lived at least a hundred years and hadn't become rich was a failure.

He wasn't rich. He wasn't even close. He'd never been interested in earning money. After the Fates had chewed him out, he had disappeared into public service. Then, when he had enough money saved, he opened his own pet store. Nothing he'd done had been a moneymaking enterprise. In fact, he'd come close a number of times to losing everything.

The fact that his business was marginal and his house had been outdated thirty years ago normally did not bother him. But he wanted to impress Vivian. And even though she professed to know nothing of the magical world, she wasn't shocked by most of the things she'd seen.

Maybe she'd even heard that old chestnut about a mage, his money, and failure.

The backyard was fenced in, with tall trees in the corners, the branches hanging over the fence, the roots pushing up beneath. Fuchsia baskets hung from the top of the fence, and along the sides, hydrangeas grew in a variety of colors. No one could see in, and he couldn't see out. It was his little haven in what had once been the countryside between Tigard and Newberg.

Now the area was all built up. When he'd had enough money to buy his neighbors' lots, he hadn't thought it necessary. By the time he realized it was, he no longer had the funds—at least not without selling one of his hideaways. So he lost his view and some of his privacy. But he didn't care. This little patch of land was his, just like the store was his. Just like the cave was his.

Sadie, his familiar, didn't even raise her head. She was used to Dex popping in and out. She was lying in a patch of sunlight near the back door.

Her eyes flicked open briefly, and he could tell she was angry.

He'd left for the store early that morning—Sadie was not an early riser—and he'd promised her that he'd send for her in time for lunch. Instead he'd been all over the city, using magic, and revealing their special places.

And now he'd brought a woman home with him.

"Where are we?" Vivian asked.

"My place," Dex said. "Technically, we're in Tigard."

"Technically?"

"When I bought the place it was so far out in the country, the real estate agent thought I was nuts."

Vivian looked at his house. It was one of the first ranch houses ever built in Portland. It had even been written up in the *Oregonian*—how the modern new styles were finally coming into the old city. Even though he had a new roof and aluminum siding put on two years ago, the house's age still showed.

"Come on," he said. "Let's go in."

He walked around Sadie and headed toward the back door. Two of his cats popped out of the nearby shrubbery and ran for the front of the building. Another slid through the cat door, off to hide from the newcomer.

Vivian frowned, then focused on Sadie. Sadie raised her head and tilted it to one side. Vivian walked toward her, hand outstretched, and Sadie watched as if she'd never seen a human before.

Then Vivian crouched in front of Sadie. Sadie sat up and put her paw in Vivian's hand, something Dex had never seen before. Vivian smiled at Sadie, shook the paw, and then stood, without petting Sadie's head, which was something Sadie despised.

"Did you hear that?" Vivian asked as she returned to Dex's side.

"Hear what?" he asked.

"I was afraid of that." Vivian shook her head. "I've had a long day."

"Did Sadie say something to you?"

"She talks?"

Dex shrugged. "She's my familiar. She has skills that regular dogs don't have."

"Oh." Vivian gave Sadie another glance. The wolfhound's tail thumped against the grass.

That answered Dex's question. Sadie didn't mind Vivian. Maybe Sadie didn't see her as competition for his affections. After all, Sadie took care of all the strays he constantly brought home. There was no reason Sadie would reject a human just because Dex was attracted to her.

The thought sent a shiver of fear through him. Maybe life would have been easier if Sadie had gone after Vivian. Then Dex could let her slip out of his life like he'd let so many other people do. He always felt that he couldn't share himself, that he couldn't take care of them in the way he wanted, and so he faded away, letting them think he was no longer interested, or he had something better to do.

He pushed open the kitchen door and stepped inside. The kitchen had once been considered huge—a full-sized square room with a window over the sink, a place for the kitchen table, a freestanding stove, and counter space on two walls.

By today's standards, the kitchen was small and dark, its original herringbone wallpaper and green tile ugly and old. The mess didn't help, either. He still had dishes in the sink. Newspapers covered the butcher-block table he'd bought twenty years ago, and rolled-up bags of cat food sat on the counters. The dog food kibbles were spread all over the floor—the cats had been playing with it again.

The house smelled faintly of cat pee, thanks to a late tom he'd saved thirty years ago, and the inevitable litter boxes that he didn't clean as often as he should.

Nurse Ratched, his Siamese, sat on the counter, watching as if she disapproved, which she probably did. When she realized Dex had noticed her, she meowed at him angrily and jumped down, disappearing behind the stove.

Vivian looked around, drinking it all in, seeing his failures and his losses and all the things that he hadn't done in all the years, things people like Blackstone and Vari probably did in their sleep.

She turned toward him and smiled. "I grew up in a house like this. I loved it."

Had she heard his thoughts? He thought he had blocked them, but he wasn't being as cautious now as he had been earlier. Or was she just being polite?

He made himself smile. "I don't know if you're hungry after that soup, but I have stuff here—"

"No," she said. "I'm tired. I just want to sit down."

He'd forgotten how pale she'd been. "Let me check what Vari did to your neck."

She nodded, and turned so that her back was facing him. Her neck was long and slender, the kind that should be highlighted with jewels and open collars. The fine hairs had been singed, many of them broken off, and a line of dried skin ran down her spine, disappearing into her shirt.

His fingers hovered near the base of her skull, not quite touching. "Does it hurt?"

"No," she said. "It did before he took the spell away, but it hasn't hurt since."

"Good." Dex let his fingers brush against the singed hair. It was coarse, although the nearby curls were fine. She smelled faintly of rosewater and soap, a good combination. He wanted to lean in and inhale.

But he didn't. His fingertips brushed the injured area, and he closed his eyes, touching her with his magic as well. No one's power remained except Vivian's. He found Vari's magical signature in the singed hairs, but no one else's. The other spell had been cleaned of its identifying marks. Dex couldn't tell who cast it.

Only its shell remained.

It had been a very subtle and powerful spell. Dex wasn't sure he'd be able to disable it without causing some damage to Vivian's spine. He was glad Vari had done the cleansing.

"Did Vari say who had done this?" Dex asked, opening his eyes.

Vivian had her head bent forward. The dried patch ran up into her scalp. "He said he couldn't tell. There was no—signature?"

Dex nodded. Unless Vari was a more talented mage than he seemed, he didn't have the skill to clean off two spells like that. "Well," Dex said, "looks like he got all of it."

"Good." Vivian started to turn around, but Dex put one hand on her shoulder.

"Let me take care of the damage the spell left," he said.

"Is it burned?" Vivian asked.

"Like a sunburn," he said, and felt thankful that nothing more had happened. There had to have been an explosion to cause this kind of damage. Vari must have absorbed it into himself, or the damage would have been a lot worse.

Dex felt his cheeks heat up. He hadn't really been fair to the Quixotic team. Blackstone had been right: Dex was used to working alone. He hated taking orders, and Blackstone had rubbed him the wrong way. Staying with that group would have meant listening to Blackstone, and Dex wasn't willing to do it.

He also wasn't willing to share Vivian.

He used a light healing spell, sending it through his fingertips. He ran them along the dried skin and the singed hair, restoring it all to its original state.

Vivian's skin was silky, her hair shimmery. He let his fingers linger a moment longer than they needed to before his hand dropped.

"There," he said.

Vivian turned to face him. "Thank you."

He smiled. "My pleasure."

It was his pleasure. She was his pleasure. He ran his forefinger along her cheek and she leaned into his touch. She was enjoying this as much as he was. He could feel her longing mingling with his own.

He cupped her cheek with his hand, and then leaned in, hesitating for a moment in case she wanted to back away. She didn't. Her gaze met his and then her eyes closed as their lips touched.

For a moment, his lips rested against hers, then their mouths opened together and they explored each other. She tasted good. She felt good.

He cupped her other cheek, holding her gently. His eyes were closed too, but he couldn't remember when he closed them. Maybe when she had. They seemed to be in tune on everything else.

He felt himself disappear into her, and knew, for the first time in his life, that he had found the person he had been looking for—even though he hadn't realized he'd been searching.

It felt as if he had come home.

Then, abruptly, Vivian pulled away. She slipped away from his mouth, his hands, backing up until she slammed into the stove. Her mouth was open, her lips swollen from his kiss.

He felt her absence as if he'd lost a limb. He reached for her—and she shook her head, running deeper into the house.

Dex stood completely still, letting his heart rate slow. He thought she had felt the same way he did. He thought they were both enjoying the kiss, enjoying each other.

Had he used her mind to force her to do something he wanted? It hadn't felt that way, but she was such a novice, and he—well, he hadn't thought it through.

Dex bowed his head. Nurse Ratched was weaving through his legs, as if rewarding him for a job well done. He didn't want to pet his crabby, somewhat psychotic cat. He wanted to go to Viv.

And he didn't know if he dared.

Seventeen

Vivian fled blindly into the next room. It was a dining room, filled with an oak table covered with magazines and open books. An archway led into the living room, and she followed the path until she felt like she could have some privacy.

She sank onto a couch so old that its springs no longer worked. It looked like it had been pushed against the wall for decades. The carpet was matted in front of it.

Three cats peered at her from their perches on the coffee table below the picture window. Another cat's tail dipped beneath the closed curtains. A wiry terrier, small and terrified, took one look at Vivian and disappeared beneath an armchair as old as the couch.

She had wanted Dex to kiss her. She had wanted him to touch her. The kiss had been wonderful, and then she realized that her mind had disappeared into his. She didn't know where he began and she ended. They had become one person, moving in unison, just with a touch of the lips.

The thought had frightened her. No—it had terrified her. She was a strong woman, unafraid to be in a strange city alone. She'd handled the murder of her aunt, three odd women coming to her door, a change in her worldview, and an attack by an enemy she didn't even know. But she had done that because she was secure in herself, because she knew who she was and what she wanted from life.

Even when Dex's disappearance had made her uneasy, she had been able to smile at her own reaction, thinking it almost too traditional.

She hadn't expected this, this loss of self. No matter how much she wanted him, no matter how attracted they were, no matter if she fell in love with him, she wouldn't be able to be with him if it cost her herself.

She was shaking. Of all the things that had happened to her this day, from learning about magic to the headache to fainting to being bugged, this was the thing that terrified her the most. She couldn't even trust whether her attraction was real. What if Dex was attracted to her, and all she felt was the echo of his emotions?

Something like that hadn't happened to her since she was a child. And Aunt Eugenia had taught her how to handle those stray emotions.

Aunt Eugenia. Vivian frowned. She'd had a flash memory of Aunt Eugenia earlier. It had lasted only a second, and she hadn't realized that was what the feeling was until just now.

But when had that happened? It felt important.

Vivian stopped shaking and leaned back. It was important. It had something to do with the Fates. Something—

"You all right?"

Vivian jumped, startled, and turned toward the voice. Dex was leaning against the archway, his hands in his pockets. The Siamese that had given

Vivian the evil eye earlier was winding her way around his legs, and Sadie sat beside him, looking at Vivian as if she had betrayed Dex somehow.

Vivian hadn't even heard Dex approach. She hadn't felt him either. She couldn't feel him now. The connection between them, which had been so fine earlier, had been severed.

Had she done that with her reaction? Or had he?

"I'm sorry," she said. "I've never run away from a kiss before. It's just that . . ."

She let her voice trail off. She didn't know how to explain her reaction. She couldn't really, not without sounding accusing. *Were you making me feel like you did? Was the reaction I felt during that kiss yours or mine?*

He was studying her, but she didn't get the sense that he had heard those thoughts. She didn't get any sense of him at all. And she missed it.

That emotion was hers. She knew it. She missed his reaction, missed him. How could she become so dependent on a feeling she hadn't had the day before? She was in love with him—her emotions—and that made this somehow worse.

Because she would want to be with him, and she couldn't. She couldn't because they wouldn't have a relationship of equals. She'd become a nonperson, someone neither of them recognized—and, she would wager, someone neither of them liked.

"It's just that what?" he asked gently. He hadn't moved from the doorway.

Vivian blinked, surprised to find her eyes growing damp. "I got lost," she whispered.

He nodded, just once, and looked down. "I thought that's what happened."

Vivian frowned. He sounded like this was a normal thing—and maybe it was for him. Maybe the women he kissed got so involved in him that they didn't realize what was happening to them. But she did, and she didn't like it.

Dex's head was still down. He wasn't looking at her. But the Siamese was. As soon as she saw Vivian's gaze meet hers, the Siamese jumped onto the couch's arm and stared at her. The stare seemed malevolent.

"I didn't think," he said after a moment. "If I'd considered it, I would've realized that might happen. You and I are so attuned . . ."

The cat's ears flattened, as if she had understood what Dex was saying and didn't like it.

"This has never happened to you before?" Vivian asked, and there was an edge to her voice. Anger. She was blaming him for this. The anger was coming out of her fear, and she knew it, but she couldn't stop it.

Dex looked up. He seemed embarrassed. It felt odd to guess at his emotions. She had known them so intimately from the moment she met him that it almost felt as if part of him were missing.

"No," he said. "It's never happened to me before. Has it ever happened to you?"

She shoved her glasses up her nose with her forefinger, not because they'd been sliding down but because it gave her something to do while she remembered. She hadn't been kissed a lot. In high school, the boys had considered her geeky. In college, she'd dated a few times, but the lack of connection she had felt with the boys there had actually bothered her.

Once she graduated, she'd been more focused on building her psychic hotline than on dating. Or maybe, as Travers said, she focused on her psychic hotline because she wanted to avoid dating.

She had a connection with her family, especially Megan and Aunt Eugenia. She loved Travers and

Kyle, but Dex was the first person to make her feel complete—and the very thought embarrassed her.

"It's never happened to me either," she said. "At least not when I was kissing someone."

That last statement made him raise his eyebrows. "When did it happen?"

"When I was a little girl." Vivian ran her hands over her thighs, looking down. The couch had pilled—probably from generations of cats scratching on it. The Siamese was still glaring at her, but the cats on the coffee table had gone back to sleep. "Sometimes people's emotions were so strong that I thought they were my emotions."

Dex was watching her as intently as the Siamese was, only his expression had none of her malevolence. "How'd you fix that?"

"My Aunt Eugenia." Vivian frowned. Aunt Eugenia again. What was it about her that had been triggered today? And when? Something to do with her death.

"What did your Aunt Eugenia do?" Dex asked.

"After this morning, I would guess she put some kind of spell on me so that my reactions wouldn't be tied into other people's. But at the time, I thought she taught me how to fix it."

"Maybe she did." Dex pulled his hands out of his pockets. He picked up the Siamese. She yowled at him and tried to bite his fingers, but he didn't seem to care, setting her on the floor. "What did she have you do?"

"Pretend there was a wall between me and other people," Vivian said.

"That's the right solution," Dex said, "although if you do it all the time, you don't feel anything. Has it been hard for you to get close to people?"

Vivian started. She had just been thinking about that. Was that because of what Aunt Eugenia had taught her? Had Vivian been distant from everyone around her except her family because there had literally been a wall between her and the rest of the world?

Dex sat on the arm of the couch, where the Siamese had been. "It's kind of like the glass jar you put around the building. It was there. It was real enough that it protected the Fates and real enough for this person who's after them to touch it, and figure out who you are."

Vivian turned toward him.

"It's wrong, Viv, for us to say you won't come into your magic until you're older. You've already got some of it. That's what your mental powers are. Just a hint of the magic to come."

She hadn't moved. There was still no connection between them, but she didn't need it. Not at the moment. He was being sincere and caring all at the same time.

"What we all mean when we say you haven't come into your powers is that they arrive one day, at full strength, and usually out of control, no matter how much training a person has had."

He glanced out the window, clearly lost in a memory. Of the day he had gotten his powers? If what everyone had told her was true, that would have been more than eighty years ago. Would he remember what that trauma was like, then? Would it still bother him?

She wanted to ask, but she knew that she was merely diverting him, that some part of her didn't want to hear what he had to say. She was afraid of this, just like she had been afraid when her Aunt Eugenia had called her over the years, asking her to come to Portland. To explore her future, Eugenia used to say. To see what was possible in the world.

Vivian hadn't wanted to see what was possible. She knew. She had experienced the emotions, the thoughts, the fears of other people. She didn't need to experience any of her own.

"You haven't gotten your full powers yet," Dex said, turning back toward her. He had such compassion in his eyes. She wanted to touch him. But she wouldn't. She wasn't ready. "You won't get those for thirty years or so. But when they come, you'll be one of the most powerful mages ever. You'll probably be more powerful than all of the people you met at Quixotic today. More powerful than the person who's after the Fates. The psychic powers you have—the mental powers—are amazing. What you did earlier today would be difficult for some people who've come into their full powers. You did it on one–one-hundredth of your strength."

Vivian rubbed her hands together. She was shivering again, and she wasn't sure when that started.

"What does that have to do with—what happened in the kitchen?" she asked.

He bit his lower lip, as if he didn't want to say. But he straightened and looked at her. "For whatever reason, there was no wall between us. Maybe because you were using so much of your mental abilities to maintain the protection around your building when we met. Or maybe—the connection between us is strong enough to get past your natural defenses. I don't know. But what happened was so overwhelming because we were—I don't know. Naked with each other. Mentally, I mean."

His cheeks were a faint pink. He seemed as uncomfortable as she felt.

"Then why is the connection gone now?" she asked. "Have I done that?"

He shook his head, stood, and shoved his hands into his pockets again. Then he walked to the window. The cats sleeping on the coffee table raised their heads. One cat rolled over on her back, paws in the air, asking him to pet her stomach.

He didn't. It was as if he didn't see her.

"I did it," he said. "I don't want to hurt you, Viv. Ever. I should have realized what was going on. I just didn't think. I'd been wanting to kiss you all day."

He was staring at the curtains as if he could see through them. She wondered if he could

"What you did," Vivian said. "Can I do it?"

Dex's back became rigid. She wondered if he misunderstood what she was asking. All she wanted to do was control what happened to her mind—to herself. She didn't want to cut him out of her life. In fact, she was feeling better, knowing that what had happened hadn't been intentional, and was something that could be prevented.

Or could be chosen, if they so desired.

Her cheeks grew warm. She put both hands on them, feeling their heat. Sex with him would be spectacular. It would be beyond intimacy. It would be—

"Yeah," he said, so softly she almost didn't hear him. "You can."

She let out a long breath. "How?"

"If your mind can visualize it, you can create it, Viv."

"You mean if I imagine disappearing, I will?"

He shook his head. He still hadn't turned around. "No. What you have is the ability to create things—walls, glass jars—with your thoughts. It will take a lot of energy for you to sustain what you've created, especially if you create a lot of things or very large things like that glass jar. But you can do it, for now. Later, you'll be able to do spells."

She nodded, then realized he couldn't see her. The warmth was receding from her cheeks. "I understand. So I couldn't have made that thing on my neck go away like Andrew Vari did, but I could have prevented it from happening by putting a shield on my neck."

"Exactly," Dex said.

Vivian swallowed. This next was hard. "I have a question—not about you. But it's about defending myself."

"Okay."

"Would you mind turning around so that I can see you?" She missed looking at his face.

Dex turned. His expression was guarded. He apparently couldn't tell what kind of footing they were on.

"If I get attacked again by that person, or if someone I don't like enters my mind, can I protect myself?"

"Their mind is as open to you as yours is to them," Dex said. "If you're strong enough, you can probably use their own powers against them."

"Or they can use mine against me."

"Someone who has that ability," Dex said, "usually has come into their magic. A person like you is rare, Vivian."

She was beginning to understand that. She stood up and extended a hand to him.

He stared at her hand as if he didn't know what to do with it. Then, after a moment, he put his fingers in her palm.

She closed her fingers over his and pulled him close. "Kiss me again, Dex."

"Viv, I—"

"I know what to expect now," she said. "Kiss me again."

He was standing so close to her that she could feel his body's heat. Yet he wasn't touching her. "Without barriers?"

"Without barriers," she said.

He slipped his hands around her waist and pulled

her close. She could feel his hesitation and his
concern, his fear of losing her after he'd found
her.

The walls had disappeared.

She smiled at him, let him feel her reassurance.
He smiled back, then bent down. She tilted her
head upward at the same time and their lips met.

The kiss was everything she had hoped for—and
more. She tasted him, she touched him, she lived
inside his mind, inside his soul. He was part of
her and she was part of him, and yet they were
together—two people who loved each other, becoming one person.

She was dimly aware of him lifting her, holding
her against his chest, just like Superman used to
do with Lois Lane—just like Vivian had dreamed.

Dex had found that dream in her mind, reacted
to it, and was helping her live it.

She found dreams in his mind too, and she
smiled because she knew she could fulfill his fantasies like he was fulfilling hers.

He carried her to the bedroom, still kissing her.
She wrapped her arms around his neck and let the
fantasies begin.

Eighteen

It had taken Eris a few hours, but she had finally managed to lose her A-team. Sturgis was using the facilities at the local affiliate, puffing himself up with importance as he spoke in front of their cameras. Kronski was lining up stories for the following day, and Suzanne was doing the actual grunt work. Eris had no idea what her camera operators were doing, but she really didn't care. They'd been busy enough since they'd arrived in Portland.

Hard to believe they'd only been in the city a few hours. It felt like a few days. She'd used more magic than she had planned, and she was tired.

At least Strife was gone for the time being. He had irritated her too much that morning, and she was afraid he'd cause her team to ask too many questions. She had him searching for traces of the Fates near anyplace that could have a cave.

She would rest, just briefly, and then she'd go after Grant herself. Grant and Kineally, who thought themselves invulnerable.

Eris opened the door to her hotel room and

flicked on the light. The air felt different. Someone had been in here.

She scanned the large living room, with its high ceiling and built-in fireplace. Her briefcase remained on the antique desk, locked, and her Palm Pilot sat on the coffee table next to the half-full pot of coffee she had ordered when she checked in. Even her empty coffee cup, its interior stained and ringed, remained beside it.

The television was off. She never left the television off. She grabbed the remote, which had been resting on the end table beside the upholstered chair, and clicked on CNN. Talking heads pontificated about some unimportant congressional maneuver and, after a few minutes of scanning, she saw nothing about the disappearing building— even though she knew that CNN had covered the story too.

She muted the sound and went into the bedroom. The bed was still made, with the breakfast room service menu carefully placed on the pillow so that she couldn't miss it. She peered into the bathroom. Extra towels sat on the edge of the counter.

Eris had forgotten that she had ordered them, as she always did when she arrived in a new hotel. Hotels had gotten stingy with towels in the past decade, and, whether she needed the towels or not, she asked for more.

Better to let the hotel know what kind of customer she would be up front. That way, they were careful with her requests.

So the maid had been here and meticulously shut off both televisions, cleaning up slightly, before leaving the towels as she had been instructed. Waste not, want not—a phrase that had always driven Eris insane.

Eris opened the cabinet that hid the bedroom's

television, pulled the TV's movable tray out, and clicked on that set with one long red-tipped fingernail. This time, she found KAHS and watched her own talking heads pontificate about the same unimportant congressional hearing.

No wonder cable news station ratings splintered so badly. The stations covered the same stories.

She would have to change that.

After she took care of those Fates.

Eris sat down on the bed and pulled off her high heels, rubbing her nylon-covered feet. Sometimes she thought the torture of proper clothing in this century was worse than the tortures she'd suffered at the hands of the Fates.

Then she would remember those early years and realize nothing could compare. All that organization the Fates had forced upon her had been hideous. Mazes, chess, eventually puzzles—even the music of precision freaks like Bach. Everything in its place and a place for everything. If she moved one small item an iota to the right or left, so that it was just slightly out of place, the Fates would start her punishment all over again.

Eris kicked her shoes, sending them sprawling across the floor. Mess. Glorious mess. It wasn't the same as chaos proper, but it would do.

What the Fates failed to realize was that Eris's plan wouldn't work without their years of torture. She had to learn about order and organization in order to subvert it.

She leaned back on the bed. The meal at Quixotic had been too heavy. She wasn't used to eating so well without walking back to the office. Manhattan was the perfect place for a civilized person to get exercise.

But the meal at Quixotic had given her a chance to watch Blackstone in his native environment. He used his charm to please his customers and kept his magic subverted. No one in Hicksville suspected that they were home to one of the larger magical communities in the United States, and that their most popular restaurant was the one run by a thousand-year-old mage.

Not that it mattered to her. Soon Blackstone would be unimportant. Eris sighed and stood up. She reached into her overnight bag and removed a pair of blue jeans, a summer sweater, and a pair of Nikes. Time to dress like the natives. Then she had to find out where Dexter Grant lived.

She could probably spell herself there, but that would take away her advantage. Instead, she'd find his house on her own, even though no one had told her where it was.

If she had to, she'd use magic. But first, she'd start like all good reporters did. Or, at least, she'd start like all good reporters used to, before the days of high-speed cable Internet access.

She'd start with the phone book.

If someone had told Vivian she would fall completely and utterly in love with a man she'd known less than twenty-four hours, she would have laughed. She would have said it was impossible to get to know someone well in that short a time.

Yet she knew everything about Dex, everything she needed to know, and more. She had been intimate with him in ways that she hadn't believed possible.

She was cuddled against him, her bare skin against his. His hand rubbed her back, while her arm was around his chest. He was muscular and strong, his body as beautiful as she had thought it would be, and she had lingered over it, examining all of it, learning everything she could about it, and this side of Dexter Grant.

Their lovemaking had been as phenomenal as the kiss—more phenomenal in its own way. Overwhelming, completing, and yet so unique that she wasn't sure they would ever be able to achieve this kind of greatness again.

Whenever she felt as if she was about to lose herself, she let Dex know, and then she put up a small barrier inside her mind, just small enough to make her feel safe. It didn't bother him—and she checked in every way she could—his emotions, his thoughts, his actions. He seemed fine with her need to remain separate.

He also seemed to enjoy their togetherness.

One light was on beside the bed. Blackout curtains made it seem as if it were the middle of the night, although the alarm clock on the end table said it was barely four o'clock in the afternoon.

The room was lived in, obviously a single man's space. Clothing covered a chair and a nearby table. A basket of folded laundry bore the marks left by sleeping cats. Tennis shoes covered the floor, as well as books of all types.

His bed was small but comfortable, clearly not a place that he usually shared with anyone but cats. A few of them had crowded on, now that the activity had settled down. The terrier peered into the room, saw Viv, and ran for the door.

"Toto," Dex said, "it's okay."

"Toto?" Vivian asked. That seemed like a mundane name for a terrier, at least from a man who had named his control-freak Siamese after the Big Nurse in Ken Kesey's *One Flew Over the Cuckoo's Nest.*

"It's not my fault," Dex said. Vivian could feel his voice rumble through his chest as he spoke. The vibration was comforting, just like the steady rhythm of his heart was.

"He's a stray?"

"They all are," Dex said. "And he's particularly

sensitive. He's only been here a few months, and he needs a lot of care."

"He doesn't look injured." Vivian pushed her glasses up her nose and studied the dog. He was cute, but wary of her. He had stopped by the door when Dex had said his name, and seemed to be waiting there, uncertain what to do.

"He's not injured anymore." Dex's hand stopped rubbing her back. Instead he held his palm against her spine, as if he were supporting her.

"What happened?"

"His family was in a car accident. He was along, in the pet carrier. He was the only one who survived."

"Oh." Vivian propped herself up on one elbow. Toto sat on the thin gray carpet, watching her warily. "How'd you get him?"

"I went to the vet's on the wrong day. They were patching him up and looking for someone to take him. They'd already called the number on his tag and found out that the extended family had no interest in him. The vet saw me and knew the minute I walked into the place that the sucker had arrived."

Dex kissed her shoulder, then rolled over and extended a hand to Toto. The dog came forward as if he weren't certain he was welcome and licked Dex's fingers. Dex bent over, grabbed Toto, and set him on the bed, petting him.

"I think it's great that you take care of animals," Vivian said.

Dex's long fingers massaged Toto's ears. The dog's tail thumped. Vivian understood the reaction. If she could have, she would have purred with pleasure when those long fingers massaged her.

"I don't think it's great," he said, his head down. Obviously this subject bothered him. "I'm only one person, and there are so many animals in need. And I'm running out of room, not to mention going broke. Besides, animals need personal attention just like people do. I'm going to have to learn how to say no."

"So that's why you were relieved when the Fates took the kittens," Vivian said, reaching across the bed and letting Toto sniff her fingers. His tail continued to wag. He didn't seem so scared of her now.

"I had no idea how I was going to cram an entire family of cats into this place," Dex said.

"You trusted the Fates," Vivian said, "even though they anger you."

"I'm hoping that they'll learn a lesson." Dex sighed, then shook his head. He clearly hadn't meant to say anything about that.

"A lesson?" Vivian asked, gingerly petting Toto's back. She could feel ridges where there shouldn't be any—healing scars. Poor little dog. How traumatic that accident must have been for him.

"Yeah, a lesson." Dex propped himself on an elbow and looked at Vivian. His right hand continued to massage Toto's ears. "I wanted them to learn what it felt like to help someone."

Vivian frowned. "I thought they were your governing body."

"They're the judicial branch," he said. "They mete out punishment, or they did. They had no idea what being a good person is all about."

"Taking care of kittens is part of that?"

"Of course it is," he said. "If you see someone in trouble and you have the power to help them, you should help them, right?"

Vivian felt confused. She didn't understand why that was even an issue. "Yeah."

"That's what I said to the Fates. They called me in front of them for using my powers to help humans. I'd see someone in crisis, so I'd spell the crisis away. The Fates said that wasn't allowed, said I was breaking the law. I argued that I should be able to help people in trouble and they said—oh, forget it."

His voice shook throughout the entire speech. She knew he was still angry at the Fates, but she hadn't realized exactly why. Now it was beginning to make sense.

At least, in his anger, he had taken action to help the Fates, even though he had been worried that they were trying to trick him. He hadn't dithered the way Blackstone and his friends had.

Dex wasn't going to finish the thought. Vivian pushed a strand of black hair off his forehead. Amazing that they could get to know each other as well as they had and yet still know so little.

The intimate contact let them know the core self, but not the details. Learning the details would be the future—if they had a future.

Vivian wasn't going to bring that up. Not yet.

"What did the Fates say?" she asked gently.

"They said if they allowed me to help someone in trouble, then they would have to allow other mages—those with less noble ambitions—to put people in trouble." He wrinkled his nose and raised his voice, obviously imitating the Fates. " 'It is not our duty to take care of mortals. It is their duty. We must take care of ourselves.' "

"That seems pretty selfish to me," Vivian said.

"That's what I thought," Dex said. "So I didn't listen. I continued my work, and they gave me warning after warning, until they swore that if I had one more violation, they'd punish me."

"You quit."

"I had to. Their punishments are—were—are

awful. I'm a big, stupid coward. I couldn't face whatever they were going to throw at me."

"Why does that make you a coward?" Vivian asked.

"Because I didn't stand up for my principles," he said, and his right hand froze on Toto's back. Toto looked up at him in doggy confusion. Dex smiled at him and continued petting him.

"But if they had punished you, you wouldn't have been able to help people either, at least not for the duration of the sentence. At least now—"

"At least now I rescue puppies and kittens and hope that the Fates don't notice," he said. "And I let the Fates use me to give an occasional familiar to a mage. It's small, it's unimportant, and it's all under the table."

"I don't think Nurse Ratched would think it's unimportant," Vivian said. She wasn't fond of the Siamese—not yet—but she sensed a fondness beginning. She rather liked Nurse Ratched's jealous passion for Dex, and the way the cat guarded the household.

Dex gave an eloquent one-shoulder shrug. "If I can save a family from a burning building by putting out the fire and healing any burns, then yeah, saving a few animals is minor. I can do all sorts of things if the Fates only let me."

"But they don't have power anymore."

"For all I know, they left notes with the Powers That Be." He reached across the dog and caressed Vivian's face. "You hungry?"

"I could be," she said.

He smiled lazily. "I could get used to this."

"Me too."

In the distance, the phone rang. Dex continued to touch Vivian, and she got the sense that he was hungry for more than just food. But the phone caught her attention.

"Don't worry," he said softly. "The machine'll get it."

But it wasn't the machine that had her concerned. It was that sense she'd had since Quixotic, that odd feeling of remembering something subconsciously without it hitting her conscious mind. She'd had it first near the bar.

"Viv?" Dex asked.

She frowned, trying to recall what had unnerved her then. "When you popped into Quixotic and made that remark about Buckingham Palace, did you notice Noah Sturgis?"

"The news guy from KAHS?"

"Yeah," Vivian said.

Toto, realizing there wouldn't be more petting, made his way to the foot of the bed. He curled up near a calico cat, who opened one eye, saw who it was, and closed her eye again.

"No, I didn't see him. Why?"

"There was a woman who joined him just before you got there. Middle-aged, really striking. I had the sense that I'd met her before. Have you ever heard of Erika O'Connell?"

Dex grinned. "Hasn't everyone?"

But Vivian wasn't listening any longer. The sensation had finally returned, and this time there were no interruptions.

She had seen Erika O'Connell before, but not in person. And Vivian hadn't confused pictures she'd seen of the famous woman with some other memory.

She'd sensed Erika O'Connell just about a month before—her presence thick and strong, just like it had been in Quixotic. It had been the night her Aunt Eugenia had died.

"Viv, what is it?" Dex was looking concerned now.

"I think I know who's after the Fates," Vivian said.

"Erika O'Connell?" Dex sounded stunned. "Are you sure?"

Vivian nodded. "She's the person who murdered my aunt."

Nineteen

The memory felt as real as the cats pressing against Vivian's ankles. And the ironic thing was that the memory wasn't really her own. It was, in part, Aunt Eugenia's—powerful, strong, and sent across eight hundred miles.

Vivian had been sitting in the kitchen of her Los Angeles apartment. The kitchen had been the best room in that apartment—spacious, well lit, and comfortable, without any horrible sense impressions (Vivian sometimes got them from spaces she lived in, and it wasn't something she enjoyed). She had been drinking hot tea, listening to Bach, and going over the books from her closed psychic hotline.

The money she had made was phenomenal. People wanted to know about their lives—all they really wanted was someone to talk to.

The function she had served was to tell them the truth about how they lived, without any of the tricks the other phone psychics used. The frauds looked at the phone number of the caller (always available to an 800-line, which was why so many people got the first few minutes free before being switched to the 900-line) and then used it to trace the caller's living situation. Once the frauds had the caller's credit card number, they could look up the caller's credit record on the computer and learn all kinds of things—where the person lived, how much they owed on their mortgage, if they were in debt, and what they usually purchased.

It was a brilliant scam, which was why so many people fell for it. Vivian had been trying to run a clean operation, but she hadn't been able to hire a lot of other psychics—certainly none as good as herself—and trying to run the business as well as do most of the work had exhausted her.

She hadn't even realized until she had shut down the business and started going over her bank accounts how much money she had made. It embarrassed her. She felt like she had been making money off other people's dreams. But she wasn't going to give it back—at least not after the first conversation she'd had with Travers.

You earned the money, sis, he'd said. *They called you. You gave them a real service, and you exhausted yourself.*

He had been right, of course, but it bothered her all the same. And she was going to have to go back to him because she hadn't sheltered any of her earnings. Her income was going to have serious tax consequences.

She had been sitting in her favorite chair, the tea steaming in her Wolverine mug—not one from the movie, either, but a real Marvel Comics mug from the 1980s—and letting the numbers swirl in her head along with the precision of Bach, when she saw Aunt Eugenia's face.

Vivian rarely got real visions, and they terrified her. This one came in from the outside. She could feel the invasion. It hit her the way a scream, coming from a neighboring apartment, could hit a person. With shock and sudden fear, and then concern.

Aunt Eugenia's face was pale, her eyes large, and there was blood on the corner of her mouth. *There's nothing you can do tonight, Viv. Don't worry about me. This was foretold. But I failed you. I thought this would happen later—*

And then the face of a stunning middle-aged woman appeared. She seemed to be surrounded by wind and fog. She reached out a hand and light sizzled from it, exploding around Aunt Eugenia.

Vivian felt an echo of the pain so severe that she was surprised that Aunt Eugenia could survive it.

For a moment the connection severed, and Vivian found herself in her kitchen, sprawled on top of the books, her tea knocked over and dripping onto the linoleum.

Then Aunt Eugenia appeared to her again, looking even more battered, near death. *Viv, read everything I sent you. Find a mentor. You'll be strong enough—*

And that was it. Vivian saw nothing more. But she felt it—the horror of Aunt Eugenia's death—and it left Vivian gasping for air. She finally was able to get up, call Travers, and ask him to call Eugenia. Of course no one answered, and it took some explaining—without mention of Viv's psychic ability—to get a cop to go to Eugenia's house, especially since the emergency call was being made in Los Angeles and the emergency was actually in Portland.

Vivian shared her memories—and Aunt Eugenia's—with Dex. He kept his arms close around her, making her feel safer than she should have. She hadn't even told Travers all of it, only saying that she knew Aunt Eugenia was in terrible danger.

No one knew that Vivian had seen the end of her aunt.

"So what did she mail to you?" Dex asked, propped up against the pillows, stroking Vivian's hair.

"Boxes of things, all papers with her writing on them. They arrived the day after she died. They had been sent well before that night."

"Do you think she knew what was going to happen to her?" Dex asked.

"She said she'd known," Vivian said. "As part of that final vision, she'd said so, that she'd been expecting it, only not so soon. I have no idea what that meant. I still don't."

"What were the papers about?"

Vivian sighed. "I couldn't bring myself to read everything. This was just a few weeks ago. It took some convincing to get my family to see the wisdom of me even coming up here."

"What did you read?"

Vivian sat up, looking at Dex. He seemed very serious, and she realized now that he was the one who had sent up one small mental wall. Not from his emotions, but from a few of his thoughts.

"I searched for another copy of her will," Vivian said. "She left everything to me, and I'm not her only family. I don't need her money. I'm the oldest, and the will that her lawyer has was made just after I was born. So I searched for something more recent."

"Did you find anything?"

She shook her head, wondering at his switch in mood. Somewhere, in this entire conversation about Aunt Eugenia, he had become focused again, not on Vivian, but on work, on the Fates.

"I was going to look through the remains of her house, but I just got moved in. In fact yesterday—" And then she paused, feeling stunned. It had been just yesterday. It seemed like a lifetime ago. "Yesterday, my brother and his son left. I was going to go to Aunt Eugenia's today, but obviously I got sidetracked."

"Obviously," Dex said. "So you'd only been alone less than twenty-four hours."

Vivian nodded.

Dex frowned. "All of this happened to you that quickly. No wonder your aunt was worried."

"I don't think she could have predicted the Fates's arrival," Vivian said.

"Don't be so sure." Dex pulled the blanket up around both of them, dislodging two cats. "If her gift was as powerful as yours—and it probably was, since the Fates assigned her as your mentor—then she knew that the Fates were going to arrive soon."

"But the Fates didn't even seem to know."

Dex shook his head. "I'm not sure what the Fates did and didn't know. I get the sense they're not telling us everything either."

"Everyone says that." Vivian felt exasperated, but she wasn't sure if it was at his wall or at the groups' reaction to the Fates. Maybe she wasn't going to be as tolerant as he was of the distances between them.

"You mentioned the remains of your aunt's house," Dex said. "What happened to it?"

"It burned the night after she died." Vivian sighed. Her eyes prickled with tears, but she blinked them back. She had loved that house. It had held so many interesting things—and, of course, the most interesting of all had been Aunt Eugenia herself.

"After?" Dex frowned. "That makes no sense. Why not burn it the night of the murder and hide the body?"

"Because," Vivian said softly, "I don't think the

fire was about Aunt Eugenia's death. I think the fire was an angry response to frustration."

"Someone couldn't find something," Dex said, the realization clearly dawning.

Vivian nodded.

"The somethings you have?"

"I'm not sure," she said.

"Let's bring those boxes here. What do you say?"

"I say my car is still at your shop. I'll bet yours is too." Vivian shook her head. These new modes of transportation were so odd to her. She had been all over the city today, and she'd only driven her car to one place.

"I was thinking of spelling the boxes here. They'll probably be safer with us than at your apartment." He looked at her. "That is where they are, right?"

She nodded.

He clapped his hands together, and a bright light filled the bedroom. When the light faded, the three large U-Haul boxes Aunt Eugenia had used for her papers sat on top of Dex's clutter. One of the boxes tilted dangerously. It rested on two tennis shoes and a brown loafer.

Dex got out of bed and steadied the box. Vivian leaned against the pillows, watching him. He was all sinew and strength, his muscles rippling under his skin. His muscles didn't bulge like a body builder's. He was just so trim that they were visible.

Vivian had never seen a man quite so perfect before.

Dex looked at her over his shoulder and grinned. "I thought physical appearance doesn't matter to women."

Vivian shrugged. "It comes in third."

"After what?"

"Sense of humor and intelligence."

"In that order?" he asked.

She considered for a moment, then nodded. "In that order."

"So you'd prefer me to be funny over smart."

"I'd prefer that you keep me entertained. Didn't you know that a woman always expects a man to entertain her?"

"Hmm." He made it sound as if he was considering her statement, as if she was being really profound. She wasn't even trying. She was just watching him move, enjoying his grace and power.

"Viv," he said, "I can't concentrate when you think about those things."

She smiled. "Maybe you don't have to concentrate."

"Maybe I should." He was moving the boxes so that they all rested on the carpet instead of clothing, books, or shoes. "The fact that you recognized Erika O'Connell changes everything."

And then he stood suddenly. The movement seemed almost involuntary. He put a hand to his forehead, and Vivian felt a thread of panic run through her, followed by an exasperation she knew wasn't her own.

Neither was the panic. It had come from Dex.

"You saw her at Quixotic?"

Vivian nodded.

"With Noah Sturgis?"

Vivian nodded again. Her heart had started beating harder than it had been a moment earlier. She wasn't sure if Dex's panic had infected her or if she was responding to the sense of urgency that suddenly filled the room.

"She owns KAHS," Dex muttered.

"Yes," Vivian said.

"Not K-A-H-S, like we've been saying it," he said. "Like C-N-N. All separate letters. Sound it out. Kay-ah-sss. Chaos."

"Chaos." Vivian felt the uncomfortable urge to

giggle. "It almost sounds like something out of James Bond. What is that? Smurf?"

"You mean Smersh?" Dex asked.

Vivian nodded. One of the cats got up, circled, and laid back down, pressing against Vivian's thigh. "Why would anyone call her company chaos unless she was going for supervillain status?"

"It's a clue, Viv." Dex grabbed his jeans and slipped into them. "We don't use our real names, remember? But sometimes, we use things that are connected to us. A myth we created, or a work of art we've influenced. I'm sure the reason Blackstone called his restaurant Quixotic isn't because he liked the adjective. I'm sure it has something to do with Vari. Didn't you hear everyone call him Sancho?"

Vivian nodded.

"Erika O'Connell was in Quixotic," Dex said. "I didn't notice, but I wasn't there long. I'm not sure I would have sensed her, since there were so many other magical people around."

He picked up his shirt and slipped it on without buttoning it. Then he handed Vivian her clothes. His mood definitely had changed. He even seemed to have forgotten his real hunger—for food, not for Viv.

"I'm sorry," he said. Apparently she was broadcasting, and he knew what she was thinking, each and every word of it. "It's just that this situation is even more dire than I thought, Viv. If she was in Quixotic, then Blackstone and Vari had to know who she was."

Vivian shook her head. She had no sense that Blackstone or Vari had lied to her about knowing who was going after the Fates.

"Viv, they should have sensed her. They would have recognized her."

"Unless she was a regular customer."

"Why would she be?" Dex asked. "She's from

New York—or so all the gossip rags say. She wouldn't be a regular in Portland."

"Maybe they know her from the past." Vivian still couldn't make herself say *a few hundred years ago.*

"Maybe." But Dex didn't believe it. She could tell from his tone as well as his mood. "I'm so glad I didn't tell them where my cave is. They would have gone right there."

"I don't understand," Vivian said, slipping into her clothes. "If they were helping Erika O'Connell get the Fates, then why would they let the Fates out of their sight?"

"I didn't give them much of a choice," Dex said.

"Yeah, but they had a lot of chances to take the Fates away before you did, and no one took advantage of it." Vivian finger combed her curls. She adjusted her glasses, feeling somewhat put together, although not at all the same as she had been before. Her entire body tingled. Even her mind tingled, and all that tingling was wonderful.

"You have a point." Dex smiled. "And another one about the Fates."

Vivian grinned.

"But I'm not sure what to make of it. We recognize each other's magic. It's part of our abilities. We even recognize those who haven't come into their powers yet. They should have known she was there." Dex had his hands on his hips. He was staring at the boxes.

"You and Vari said that the magic she was using was advanced stuff," Vivian said.

Dex nodded.

"Couldn't this be advanced too?"

He looked up at her. "You're saying she's hiding who and what she is from us?"

Vivian nodded.

"I don't think that's possible."

"I saw her," Vivian said. "And I almost didn't remember it. I even had trouble remembering it here. When I saw her in the restaurant, it was like we knew each other, like we were past enemies or something."

"Future enemies," Dex said. "Given what your aunt said."

"Why would Erika O'Connell kill Aunt Eugenia?"

"I don't know," Dex said, "but the answer's in those boxes."

Vivian sighed. Toto had sat down near the door. He was watching her. Sadie was in the room too, near the pile of clothes. Vivian hadn't noticed that before.

"You're going to have to look through the boxes sometime," Dex said. "Let's do it now, when it might make a difference."

Vivian nodded. "Here? Or in the living room?"

"Neither," Dex said. "I'm taking you somewhere new."

"New?" Vivian asked.

"Yeah," he said. "Don't argue with me about it. We're in big trouble here and we need a lot of protection."

"You have another cave?" Vivian asked.

"Not like the ones the Fates are in, but I—" He stopped, put a finger to his lips, and then frowned. "Forget it. Let's just take them to the basement."

Vivian felt an odd disconnection, as if Dex weren't even speaking to her. Then she realized what he was doing. He was lying in case Erika O'Connell was monitoring them somehow. "Basement?"

"Yeah," he said. "I have a family room down there. We can spread out."

"All right," Vivian said, hoping she sounded convincing.

But Dex didn't pick up any of the boxes as he walked out of the bedroom. Vivian followed, knowing they weren't going to any family room, though she was uncertain where he was taking her.

How many hideaways did this man have? And how many did he need?

Just two, he sent back to her. *I made a few enemies who are long-lived and probably won't forget.*

Vivian's heart was still pounding too hard. She wondered if Erika O'Connell ever forgot.

Then Vivian remembered the look on O'Connell's face as she used her magic to attack Aunt Eugenia. Somehow, Vivian sensed, O'Connell never forgot.

And that was part of the problem.

Twenty

It wasn't the hidden panel in Dex's linen closet that unnerved Vivian. It wasn't even the fact that the hidden panel opened to reveal a state-of-the-art elevator. What unnerved her was the way all Dex's animals responded when he yelled, "Basement!"

Pets ran toward the linen closet from all corners of the house. Sadie stayed beside Dex, as if waiting for the others to show up. Even Toto, who had been lumbering along behind Vivian, waited beside Dex as if he were afraid of losing his only family.

Nurse Ratched scurried past both dogs and stopped in the back of the elevator. The other cats followed, until a dozen of them covered the elevator's floor.

More cats waited outside, along with a rabbit Vivian hadn't known was in the house and a ferret that only had three legs. One more dog showed up, its head bandaged and its back covered with scars. It was the last creature to arrive.

Vivian had never seen animals behave like this.

They weren't fighting, and yet they were in close quarters. If they weren't on the elevator, they were waiting to get on.

Dex reached inside, pressed the button marked BASEMENT, and slipped his hand out as the door closed. The group of cats disappeared, and after a moment, the elevator whirred.

"This house doesn't look big enough—" Vivian started, but Dex put a finger to her lips.

"Wait here," he said. "I'm going to get a couple of boxes."

He slipped past her and headed back to the bedroom. Her stomach growled. She wondered if there was food in this second hideaway, and then decided it wouldn't be a problem. Dex could probably conjure up food whenever they needed it.

She sighed. She wondered what it would be like to have that kind of power. To make anything appear when you wanted it to, and to make it disappear if you didn't want it there. To make yourself vanish.

Someday she would know what it was like. Someday she would be able to do what Dex did and more.

She wasn't sure how she felt about that. Her psychic gifts had been difficult enough. Adding real magic on top of them wouldn't be the free ride a lot of people seemed to want. She knew that much.

The animals were still waiting patiently in line. Sadie and Toto remained in front of the elevator door, as if they were guarding it, although Toto kept peering down the hall, looking for Dex.

Finally, Dex reappeared in the hallway, carrying two of the boxes. Together, they were taller than he was. He staggered beneath their weight.

He arrived at the elevator door just as it opened a second time. He set the boxes inside first. Then most of the remaining pets got on. All of the cats squished toward the back, not seeming to mind the close quarters. The ferret joined them. But the rabbit hung back, and so did the injured dog.

Dex reached inside and pressed the basement button again.

Of all the strange things that had happened that day, this had to be the strangest of all. But Vivian didn't say that.

"Who's this guy?" She nodded toward the injured dog. She didn't pet it because she was afraid she'd hurt it.

"Mmm." Dex peered down. His look was fond. "That's Portia. She's another one the vet gave me. Just last week. She's doing a lot better."

"What happened to her?"

"Don't ask." He crouched, held out a hand, and let Portia sniff it. "Good girl," he crooned. "I know how hard this is for you. I'll make sure you have an extra-comfortable bed downstairs."

The dog licked his fingers. Even that seemed like an effort.

Sadie watched, and Toto trembled. The rabbit continued to stare at the elevator, as if willing it to arrive.

"How many pets are here?" Vivian asked.

"I don't honestly know," Dex said. "I'm afraid of the number."

"Then how do you know you have all of them?"

He scratched under Portia's chin. The dog's tail wagged. "Magic. I know I use too much, but—"

"But it's for the right cause," Vivian said.

Dex nodded, but it was an absent gesture. "Let me get that last box."

He hurried down the hall. Toto watched him go, still trembling. Portia sighed and laid down.

Dex saw his magic as a burden, a gift he couldn't properly use. Vivian hadn't really understood that completely until she saw Portia. There was a lot of suffering in the world, and Dex didn't like any of it. If he had his way, this place would be perfect, with no one hurting and nothing evil around them.

But because he wanted things that way, he had two hideouts and trouble with his own judiciary. He had to hide his good deeds.

Maybe Vivian would talk to the Fates about that. Maybe Dex's ploy would work. Maybe after taking care of the kittens, the Fates would understand what Dex was struggling with.

The elevator clanged. Sadie whined, as if she were urging Dex to hurry up. Toto trembled again, and his trembling seemed to strike fear into the rabbit. The creature was completely immobile, only its nose twitching.

Dex came out of the bedroom carrying the last box. Vivian wondered why he wasn't spelling them to the basement, as he called it. It would certainly be easier.

He arrived just as the elevator opened. He set the last box inside, then helped Portia. Sadie nudged the rabbit forward, and Toto followed.

"Go on," Dex said to Vivian. She nodded and stepped inside. She felt like she was stepping off a cliff. This was harder than the sudden appearance/disappearance thing. This was a conscious choice to get on an elevator that probably shouldn't exist, to go to a place she didn't know, with a group of animals that behaved like—well, like drugged people.

Sadie waited outside until Dex stepped in. Once he crossed the elevator's threshold, Sadie entered too.

The door closed as Dex pushed the basement button for the final time. The elevator lurched once, then plummeted, almost as if it were out of control.

Vivian grabbed onto the railing behind her. Toto whined and leaned on Vivian's leg. Vivian found the trust oddly touching. Sadie didn't move. The rabbit stayed in the middle of the floor, its nose twitching. Dex braced Portia so that she wouldn't fall.

Vivian made herself breathe. "How come you didn't just magic us down below?"

"Magic leaves a trail that can be followed," Dex said. "Or it should. Somehow O'Connell has figured out how to defeat that too."

"The signature you were talking about with my neck?"

"That's part of it," he said.

Portia sighed. The dog was in a lot of pain, but she was healing. Vivian wanted to touch her but knew better.

"Why bring the animals?"

Dex kept one foot braced on the box, so it wouldn't slide into the frightened dogs and rabbit. "Think about it, Viv. If someone wanted information from me, what would be the best way to get it?"

"They'd hurt these creatures?"

"I don't know for sure," Dex said. "But I can't risk it."

The elevator lurched again. It seemed to be picking up speed instead of losing it.

"Do you run drills to get them to do this?" she asked.

"You mean like grade school fire drills?" he asked.

She nodded, imagining Dex with a whistle, herding animals toward the linen closet. *Now, class. No pushing and shoving. No fighting. One at a time through the doors. The quicker you do this, the safer you'll be . . . .*

"I wish it were that easy," he said. "I tried a whole bunch of things. First I used food, but that only got the healthy or the hungry pets. Then I tried having Sadie herd them, but that made some of them hide."

Sadie looked up at Dex at the sound of her name. Her tail thumped once, as if acknowledging his mention; then she turned her attention to the elevator again.

"In the end, I had to use a bit of magic to explain to them the importance of going into the basement. Once the animals know that this is for their own safety, they cooperate."

Vivian smiled at him. She had never met anyone like him. "You could have spelled them down there the first time, right? Then they wouldn't have been so frightened."

"Actually, no. The basement is—" He stopped and shrugged. "Well, you'll see."

The elevator stopped suddenly, bouncing on its cables. Vivian was very glad she was still holding the interior railing.

The door opened, revealing a herd of animals on the floor outside. Vivian couldn't see beyond the cats and the ferret. Toto was still leaning on her leg, and the rabbit was blocking their exit by refusing to move.

Dex picked it up. "Everyone, into the kitchen."

The cats dispersed, and none of them went in the same direction. The ferret took its time. Once it was gone, Dex set the rabbit on the floor outside the elevator. He turned around, picked up the box, and set it outside, next to the other two boxes. Then he picked up Portia and carried her out.

"I have to feed them now," he said. "Their reward for being good. When I'm done, I'll show you around."

He and Portia turned left, disappearing down a long hallway. Sadie gave Vivian a worried look, as if she was preventing Sadie from doing her duty.

"It's all right," Vivian said. "I'm coming."

Sadie woofed softly, then hurried after the others, with Toto at her heels. Vivian left the elevator slowly.

The room she stepped into was huge. It wasn't a room so much as a great hall or an antechamber. The ceiling—several stories above her—glittered with its own light, as if a hundred stars had been captured against its darkness.

A large corridor opened to her left. The wall, black and shiny, curved away from her on the right, widening as she stepped into the great hall. A series of lamps, designed to resemble torches, flickered against the blackness, their fake flame reflected in the surface.

More lights illuminated five steps that led into the hall proper. Vivian walked toward them.

The great hall wasn't really a hall. It curved, the walls protecting it on all sides. More stairs led down to another level. A car was parked there. Vivian saw its rounded hood and oddly shaped headlights, and found herself thinking of the Batmobile.

She supposed it wasn't unlikely for Dex to have a tricked-up car á là James Bond. After all, Dex had said he had a lot of enemies, and he had taken a lot of his ideas from comic books. Clearly this place was based on the Bat Cave, and Professor X's secret rooms, and all those hidden chambers that showed up in various superhero myths.

It just startled her. The house above—way above, if that elevator ride had been any indication—had seemed so normal. So single-guy chic.

This wasn't normal at all.

A desk, also made of the same shiny black material, protruded from the far right wall. A black leather chair, pushed up against it, was nearly invisible until she came upon it.

Computer screens receded into the wall, all of

them dark. She saw no keyboards, so she touched one of the screens. It instantly turned white.

"Unauthorized access," said an androgynous voice. It echoed throughout the entire chamber, and probably down the corridor. "Security breach. Security breach. Securi—"

And then, as quickly as it started, the voice stopped. Vivian heard a clunk, and then Dex's voice, sounding small, said, "I'll show you around, Viv. Just give me a minute. Don't touch anything else."

The screen before her was still white. Gradually it faded to black again. Vivian clutched her hands behind her back, resisting the urge to touch the other screens. She didn't even know how to answer Dex.

Instead, she walked toward the steps leading to the car. She passed a cabinet, its front covered in smoky glass. She thought she saw clothing inside, but she couldn't be sure. She wanted to cup her hand against the glass, block out the ambient light so that she could see inside, but after that last encounter with the screen, she knew better.

Vivian shivered. The temperature down here left a lot to be desired. She wasn't wearing warm clothing, and she had nothing else with her. She hoped that somewhere down that long, mysterious corridor, Dex had a blanket. Or a sweater. Or a thermostat.

Then she reached the stairs and looked down. The car wasn't some cartoonish contraption, with rocket jets instead of a combustion engine and wings that made it soar across canyons. It was a 1930s Packard convertible, an old-fashioned, stylish car, the kind people thought of—or at least the kind she thought of—when she thought of elegant vehicles.

The Packard was black too, and just as shiny as

the walls around it. The roof was down, and the leather seats looked new. But the interior, right down to the wood radio in the dash, all dated from the period. As she peered inside, she realized that the gearshift was slightly worn, and the leather padding on the driver's door had a small rip in it.

"Like it?" Dex's voice sounded loud, and it echoed, overlapping itself before fading away.

Vivian turned guiltily, clasping her hands even tighter behind her back. "It's beautiful. What's it doing down here?"

Dex was standing at the top of the second flight of stairs, near the cabinet. He looked sad, and smaller than he had in his house. "It draws too much attention these days, and it doesn't really like the rainy weather. I don't have the money to detail it every time a bit of rust shows up."

Sadie walked up behind him, then sat down. She looked tired and wary, as if just being down here made her nervous.

"Animals fed?" Vivian asked.

"And shown to their rooms," Dex said.

He wasn't smiling and she couldn't tell if he'd made a joke. She wouldn't put it past him to have a bedroom for each creature he brought down.

"Let me show you around," he said. "Come on."

He led the way up the stairs. When Vivian reached the top, Sadie stood too, as if Vivian were one of the dog's charges. Nurse Ratched had come down the hallway, tail switching. She looked like she was hunting for trouble.

"No, Ratchey," Dex said. "You know this area is off-limits."

The cat sat down as if she had understood him and proceeded to clean her face with her right paw. She looked regal amid the shiny black stone, as if the entire place had been built for her.

Sadie walked to the edge of the great hall,

blocking Nurse Ratched's ability to come any farther inside. Dex led Vivian past the cabinet and the computer system as if they weren't even there.

"This is security, as you already know." He grinned at her. She shrugged. She hadn't meant to set it off.

"Regular security?" she asked. "Not magical security?"

"No, there's magical too," he said. "No magic spells—at least spells that I know can be done—can reach down here. This place is fortified with rock that prevents magical conductivity, and it's got some magical shielding. The normal security is for regular people. There are a few outside entrances. I did manage to do this inside a neighborhood."

"With all the zoning clear, and the permits?" She couldn't restrain the grin, but he didn't smile back at her.

"I did the first version of this around the time everyone was building bomb shelters. No one thought it was strange."

She nodded, then thought of something. "How come no one thinks it's strange that you haven't gotten older?"

"You know," he said in a conversational tone, as if he was speaking to someone he didn't know well, "the men in my family look a lot alike. Everyone always said I look like Uncle Dexter. I was named for him too."

Vivian laughed. He slipped his arm around her and led her to the corridor.

Sadie stepped aside to let them pass, yet she still managed to block Nurse Ratched. The cat glared at the dog, then turned away from the great room, as if she'd been interested in Dex all along. Nurse Ratched led him down the corridor, her tail high.

Sadie followed Vivian, toenails clicking on the

black floor. Vivian didn't see any of the other animals. She had no idea where they could have gotten to.

The corridor went on for a long distance with no visible doors on either side. The ceiling was not as high as the great chamber's, but it was higher than any ceiling Vivian had ever seen in a corridor before.

"How come you didn't bring the Fates here?" she asked Dex.

"I thought about it," Dex said. "I didn't want them that close."

"And you were afraid they'd blow this place's cover." The phrase was not one that Vivian normally used. She had to have plucked it, word for word, from Dex's brain.

He looked at her, startled. "There are a lot of ways out of here. Even if I disabled the elevator, the Fates would have found the other exits. And probably at the wrong moment, if I know those women."

"This place is very important to you," Vivian said.

Not as much as it used to be. The sentence came to her, as clearly as if he'd spoken. If he hadn't been right beside her, and if she hadn't been watching his lips, she would have thought that he had spoken.

"It's my safe place," he said as the corridor dead-ended into a *T*. The wall in front of Vivian was the same shiny black material, but to her right, the black had been replaced by normal white walls. To her left, the corridor continued, the same black color, the same monotonous walls.

He led her into the white-painted corridor. Or rather, Nurse Ratched led all of them. The cat picked up her pace, trotting forward as if she'd seen a bird.

The ceiling here was at normal height, and Vivian felt relieved. She had no idea that high ceilings made her nervous, but apparently they did. Or maybe it was the way she expected spaces to be—and this place did not conform to those expectations.

Doors opened off this corridor. The first room nearest the black corridor was filled with ancient computer equipment. She recognized the remains of a Mac Plus, an Apple //e, and several IBM clones. A Kaypro sat on top of a heap of wires and discarded disk drives as if it had won a game of king of the hill. Old CDs, manuals, and floppy disks were scattered on a desktop, and in the middle of them, two cats slept as if it were the most comfortable place on Earth.

The next room held the remains of an even older computer system. Vivian recognized this one—which filled the entire room—from 1960s Disney movies and the documentaries she'd seen on the space program. She had no idea what that computer—which had component parts taller than she was—was called, but she could see the slots where the punch cards went.

In fact, there was a stack of punch cards holding the door open.

No cats were in that room, but the ferret was sniffing its way toward the back as if it hadn't seen the area before.

The third door was open, and the light was on. The room held cushioned beds and medical equipment, including a refrigerator. Portia was the only occupant. She was asleep on one of the beds, her breathing labored.

"Is she going to be all right?" Vivian asked.

"It took her a lot to get down here," Dex said. "But she's got a fighter's spirit."

It wasn't quite a yes, but it was better than an

absolute no. Vivian wondered how he could open his heart to all these creatures, knowing the odds. But the odds didn't seem to bother Dex. What bothered him was how the animals got treated in the first place.

Dex didn't let Vivian linger anywhere. Each room seemed to have its own purpose. One of them held filing cabinets. Another held more cabinets—smaller than the one out front. Each cabinet seemed to hold a variety of bizarre weapons, from a Buck Rogeresque ray gun to a giant plastic green hammer.

She was about to ask what the weapons were for when the corridor turned a final time. This time it opened onto a sunken living room, complete with big-screen TV, two couches, several love seats, and a dozen upholstered chairs.

Each piece of furniture, including the large television set, had its own animal—or two or three. The older cats had claimed the most comfortable chairs, leaving the younger ones to glare at each other on the couches and love seats. Toto had curled up on an ottoman. His tail wagged when he heard Dex's voice, but his eyes remained closed.

All the animals had the contented look of the recently fed. Vivian's stomach growled. She'd been hungry for a while now.

The kitchen was up three steps, to the left of the living room. The kitchen floor was littered with pet dishes. Only the rabbit remained inside, crouching against one of the cabinets.

"I have a pizza in," Dex said. "It's frozen. I hope that's all right."

Vivian was a pizza snob, but at the moment, she was so hungry she would eat paper slathered with tomato sauce and covered with mozzarella cheese.

"In the meantime," Dex said, "let's start going through these boxes. I'll put them on the table."

Vivian felt her stomach tighten. She didn't want to look at Aunt Eugenia's papers. She hadn't wanted to look from the beginning. If she looked at them, then Eugenia—who had seemed so wonderful, so powerful, so strong—was gone forever.

"Viv," Dex said, his expression gentle, "she wanted you to see these."

"I know," Vivian said.

"Then the best thing you can do for her is to honor her wishes. From the way you described her and the things I've felt through you, she cared about you very much. She wanted you to have these things right away."

"I know." Vivian sounded like a three-year-old. She felt like one too; she wanted to stamp her feet and refuse to help Dex.

He slipped his hand in hers and led her to the dining room table. Unlike the house upstairs, the hideaway was neat. Either it meant he didn't use it often, or that there was yet another side to Dex— an organized one, the one who was in charge when he was working.

"I have a really good sound system down here," he said. "Care to hear anything while we're working?"

"Got any Mozart?" Vivian asked. "I'm in the mood for precision."

He looked at her, frowning just a bit. "Bach's more precise."

"I know," Vivian said. "But I want a bit of emotion too."

Dex smiled. He went to the wall, pressed a few buttons, and a Mozart rondo filled the room.

"How'd you do that?"

"Science," he said. "A five-hundred-disk CD player hooked up to the internal system."

She shook her head. And here she'd been expecting more magic. She would have to learn that

Dex didn't use his powers idly. She wondered how someone could avoid using his powers when they made things so much easier than doing actual work.

"I'm going to get the boxes," Dex said. "Would you mind pouring me a Sprite? There's other stuff in the fridge too. Whatever you want."

Vivian pulled the refrigerator open as Dex headed off down the hall. She had never seen such a full refrigerator before. Everything she could think of seemed to be inside—from different kinds of soda to fresh milk and cheese to yogurt and lunch meats. Cans of Sprite, obviously Dex's favorite, lined the door.

Chill air seeped out, making her shiver again. She was really cold down here. She'd have to mention it when Dex got back.

She took out two cans, closed the door, and set the cans on the table. Then the oven timer beeped. She shut it off, checked the pizza—which didn't look half bad—and decided to let it cook for a few more minutes.

Dex staggered in with two of the boxes. He dumped them on the dining room table. "I'll get the other one when we're ready."

Vivian nodded. She found some dishes, put them on the table as well, and added napkins. Then the timer beeped again.

This time Dex took the pizza out, set it on top of the stove, and used a pizza cutter to make wedges. Vivian took two and went to the table.

Aunt Eugenia's handwriting was all over the outside of the boxes. The florid style made Vivian's eyes fill with tears. She blinked them back, sat down, and stared at her pizza, no longer hungry.

Dex put a hand on the back of her neck. "Eat, sweetheart. You'll feel better."

Vivian's feminist friends in L.A. would hate it if

they heard him call her sweetheart, but on his lips, the endearment sounded natural. She smiled at him and took a bite of pizza to satisfy both of them, and her stomach growled in response.

She would be able to eat after all.

Dex took his place across from her, and while he ate, dug into the first box. Vivian decided to wait to examine hers until she'd finished her dinner. She had a hunch she'd need her strength as the days went on, and eating regularly was part of that.

"Wow," Dex said, studying Aunt Eugenia's notes on a series of yellow legal pads. "She had a vision of her own death shortly after you were born."

Vivian sighed. She wouldn't get to wait after all.

"It says here that she knew her magic would fail her."

Vivian made herself eat both pieces of pizza before talking to Dex. She ate quickly, the pepperoni burning her tongue.

"Do the notes say who was going to kill her?" Vivian asked.

Dex shook his head. "Someone stronger. That was all she knew. And it worried her, because there weren't many mages stronger than she was."

Vivian sighed. She pulled open her box. More yellow legal pads filled with Eugenia's handwriting. And, below them, some mythology books specializing in the "lesser gods." She had noticed them while searching for the will but hadn't thought much about them.

But now that she knew about magic, magic systems, and the way that people's actions turned into myths and legends, she realized how important these books were.

Vivian took one out. It had the dry look of a fifty-year-old college textbook. The brown cover showed

Michelangelo's painting of the three Fates. Vivian stared at it for a moment.

Michelangelo had depicted them as elderly peasant women, heavyset and sad-faced, carrying the burden of their office. They looked nothing like the women Vivian knew. Obviously Michelangelo hadn't met them.

Aunt Eugenia had marked several pages in the text with Post-It notes. The notes were yellow, and stuck on the sides of the pages. She hadn't written anything on them. Instead, they all rested below a name in bold-face.

Vivian read the entries. The first said:

All the gods came to the marriage feast of Peleus and Thetis. But one deity had not been invited. Eris or Ate, the goddess of discord, was angered at the oversight.

The second was a quote from Spenser:

Her name was Ate, the mother of debate
And all destruction.

The third was a definition:

Eris: Sister of Ares, mother of Strife. The Goddess of Discord, sometimes called the Goddess of Chaos.

Vivian shuddered, and this time the movement had nothing to do with the cold. "Dex," she said, staring at the page.

"Hmm?" He didn't look up from the legal pad he was reading.

"I think you should look at this one." She slid the book over to him, leaving it open to the definition.

Dex frowned, reading it. Then he grabbed one

of the other books off the pile and looked at the marked pages.

"Eris, Erika," Vivian said. "Chaos, K-A-H-S. It could be her."

"Chaos," Dex said. "Not Discord. They're not the same thing. I think the Greeks even had a God of Chaos."

"They had two Gods of War too, if these books are to be believed," Vivian said. "Ares, the God of War, and Enyo, the Goddess of War."

Dex grabbed yet another book. He thumbed through it. "All of these sticky notes underline her name."

"You think it's her, don't you?" Vivian said.

"If it's her, Viv, we're in a load of trouble." He set the book down and looked at her.

"Why?"

"Because the people who are that long-lived, who've gone on to become well-known mythic figures, are usually extremely powerful. Some of them have become Powers That Be. The Fates were part of that group. They've held power for a long time."

"But Andrew Vari's that old. He isn't that well known," Vivian said.

"He was punished by the Fates."

"Maybe this Eris was too."

"I'd ask them," Dex said, "but I don't want to go see them. I might be leading her to them."

"What about the Interim Fates?"

"They didn't know who I was," Dex said. "They barely know who they are."

Vivian sighed. "Then how will we know?"

"We keep reading," Dex said, "and hope our guess is wrong."

Twenty-one

It had been years since she had driven a car herself, and even then the car hadn't been a stick shift. But Eris had decided to drive to Dexter Grant's. She didn't want to pop in on him, and surprise him in his own home. For all she knew, he might have the place booby-trapped.

She'd heard such rumors about him. He'd taken out some of the more powerful mages in Canada, the ones who had actually used their magic to start crime syndicates in the 1920s and 1930s—back when such things were lucrative. Dexter Grant had kept Canada clean, so to speak, until he saved a friend of two teenage boys and saw his exploits written up in a comic book.

That had been the beginning of the end for him—except when those mages' friends had tried to get revenge. A number of them had died in mysterious circumstances, circumstances Grant never got into trouble for.

The Fates, apparently, didn't punish attacks on mages they considered evil. The Fates only punished people who attacked mages considered good. Yet another thing to hold against those three women.

Eris drove Portland's network of freeways, following the map she had pasted to the inside of the driver's side window. The car bucked and lurched every now and then, and it had died at two separate stop lights before she remembered to use the clutch when applying the brake.

But it didn't take her too long to get to Grant's neighborhood, considering all the driving she'd had to do. He was in one of the suburbs—Tualatin, King City, Tigard—she couldn't tell the difference. The western suburbs seemed to be exactly the same: modern houses (much too big at 3000 square feet for any normal family) usually painted white, scattered on the hillsides, near shopping malls and shopping malls and, in case there weren't enough, more shopping malls.

Oh, and traffic lights to match the malls.

She had to turn at one of those traffic lights—and, fortunately, the light had been green, so she hadn't had to stop—and head down a windy road, past brown office complexes that all looked the same. For a moment she thought she had doubled back somehow, and then she realized that this set of brown buildings that disappeared into the young trees was a slightly darker brown than the ones she had seen earlier. Later construction, because the doors were wider, proclaiming their politically correct handicapped access.

The first thing she would do when she ruled the world was make anyone who uttered a politically correct phrase bathe in boiling lava for a week. In Los Angeles the week before, one man had had the audacity to tell her that the problem she was having with one of her male CEOs was because she was gender-challenged.

It took her a moment to realize that he meant it was because she was a woman.

She had him on her list. When she had a free moment she'd turn him into a rat—a gender-challenged rat who was involved in some university's breeding experiments.

The brown buildings became country stores, which then became large lots—acres, actually, with older trees. The buildings on these lots looked like farmhouses or modified ranches, with big back-yards and garages twice the size of the houses.

The neighborhood seemed very old—for the West Coast, anyway—and somewhat rundown. She wouldn't have expected Dexter Grant's home to be here.

But it was, if the address she had was correct. His house was at the end of a long gravel driveway that ran between two large oak trees, the roots sticking up into the road itself. She could barely see the house. It appeared to be another ranch—and one not kept up since it was built.

The door's paint was peeling and the garage was missing a few slats. But the fence around the backyard looked new, and Eris thought she saw, in the fading light, evidence of a well-tended garden.

So young Mr. Grant understood the importance of appearances as well. That shouldn't have surprised her.

Eris parked the car in a neighbor's driveway, several yards down. No one appeared to be home at that house—and hadn't been for some time, if the knee-high grass and empty windows were any indication.

She doubted anyone would notice her here.

She walked down the street as if she had done so every day of her life, looking at the large oaks on several of the properties, and the for-sale signs on many of them as well. All of the houses had acreage. She supposed Grant's did too.

If it did, it probably hid his real home, perhaps disguised as that masterful garden in the back and defined by the fence. And if Dexter Grant went to that kind of trouble to hide a house, he probably figured he could keep the Fates there safely as well.

Eris stopped on the edge of the gravel road. Even though it was nearly sundown and shadows had fallen across the grass, she knew that Grant would be able to see her if she wasn't careful.

First she had to scope this place out, and then she would make her move. She wanted to surprise Grant and his pretty little girlfriend as much as possible. Grant wasn't as powerful as Eris—not by a long way—but he seemed to use his magic creatively, and sometimes that gave the mage an extra few seconds of surprise.

Kineally herself wasn't much of a worry. Now that Eris knew Kineally had psychic abilities, Eris knew what to expect from her.

In fact, all Eris wanted from Kineally was her ability to scream.

It was clear that Dexter Grant was already infatuated with the woman—why else would he help the Fates who had forced him away from his life's goal? Not to mention the fact that he looked at her like he wanted to take her right then and there.

Grant was notoriously softhearted. He saved people he didn't know. He would do anything for the woman he had fallen in love with.

He would even give up the Fates to save her life.

The remains of the pizza were scattered around them. Dex was on his third Sprite. Vivian had switched to coffee an hour earlier, even though her stomach wasn't happy about it. Or maybe her stomach was responding to what she was reading.

A stack of notebooks sat before her. The mythology books were off to the side. Dex had looked through them and decided they weren't useful— at least not at the moment.

All of the legal pads were filled with letters, written to Vivian, from Eugenia. A stack that Dex had put back in one of the boxes explained the magic system that Vivian had learned about earlier that day. Eugenia had started writing the letters when Vivian was a little girl, apparently planning to use them to explain the system to her once her training began.

But the training had never happened. In the later notebooks, Eugenia was quite apologetic about that. She had a sense that time was running out. She had conveyed that sense in her e-mails to Vivian and in several phone calls, but Vivian had pooh-poohed them, apparently thinking Aunt Eugenia would live forever.

At the top of one of the boxes, Dex found a sheet of fax paper, with an airline reservation on it. Aunt Eugenia had planned to spend this very week in Los Angeles. With Vivian.

Apparently, Eugenia felt that since she couldn't bring the mage-in-training to the Pacific Northwest, she would bring a bit of the Northwest to the mage-in-training. Or something like that.

As Vivian delved into her aunt's things, her good mood disappeared. Dex didn't say anything about her mood change, but one of the cats—a white and gold calico—crawled on her lap about fifteen minutes ago.

"Cat therapy," Dex had said with a smile. "Cats believe if you pet them, you'll feel better."

"The added benefit being that they'll feel better too," Vivian said, not looking up.

"Exactly."

She did pet the cat and she did feel better, but the mood didn't last. Because the documents she and Dex were going through now bothered her the most.

They were about Eris, who was, in fact, Erika O'Connell. Eris had had a number of names over the years. One of them had been Esme Pompedeau, a piano teacher who lived in the same women's boardinghouse as Eugenia at the turn of the century. They had become good friends—not because Eugenia had sought Eris out, but because Eris had sought her.

Eugenia thought they had a shared secret and friendship based on dedication to the same principles. It wasn't until Eugenia caught Eris going through her things that she realized something was wrong.

"I think I found it," Dex said.

Vivian looked up from the notebook she'd been reading. Her eyes were muzzy. She'd been looking at blue ink on yellow paper for hours. "Found what?"

"The reason Eris killed your aunt."

Vivian's breath caught. She put her hand on the calico's back, and the cat started to purr. It didn't bring Vivian the advertised comfort. "What?"

"Eris thought that your aunt was the Fates' defender."

Defender of the Fates. Vivian frowned. Where had she heard that before? Then the hair on the back of her neck rose. That had been the title of Kyle's comic book. And the superhero in it, the man, had looked just like Dex.

That had to be more than coincidence. Obviously, Kyle had the family curse. He had powers too. She had just thought he had a lot of good hunches. But that comic book had been eerily accurate.

Dex set the notebook down. "Eris thought that if anyone wanted to take out the Fates, they had to go through Eugenia first."

"Why would she think Eugenia was the defender of the Fates?" Vivian asked. She couldn't think about Kyle, not now. She would worry about him later. Right now she had to focus on herself, Dex, and the Fates.

"Because of the prophecies." Dex folded his hands over the notebook. "Has anyone told you about the prophecies?"

Vivian shook her head. "Not really. They were mentioned, but no one really explained them."

He brushed a strand of hair from his forehead. He really was a handsome man. She wished—

"Focus, Viv," he said with a grin. "Prophecies."

She had been broadcasting. She flushed. His grin widened. "Prophecies," she repeated.

"One of the duties of the Fates—of our Fates— is to give each mage a prophecy. These prophecies are always about love."

"What does love have to do with Eris?" Vivian couldn't think of two more disparate concepts.

"Nothing," Dex said. "It's what your family has to do with the Fates."

"My family?" Vivian reached for the notebook. Dex didn't move his hands. He wasn't allowing her to take it. Apparently, he wanted to give her the information.

"Your Aunt Eugenia shared your prophecy and hers with you. She knew others as well, but she didn't write them down. She says the whole family is tied into the Fates."

"But I'm the only one with powers," Vivian said, and then bit her lower lip. That obviously wasn't true. Kyle had them.

Dex shrugged. "You and your aunt, and maybe someone else. She didn't say."

He slid the notebook to Vivian. "Hers is first."

Vivian studied her aunt's flowing handwriting. The prophecies were the only things on the page. Her aunt's was:

Your defense of the Fates will lead to a great love.

And Vivian's was:

You shall have a great love should you survive Fate's darkest day.

"She had it wrong," Vivian said, then she looked up at Dex. "It's not Fate's darkest day. It's Fates'—as in all three Fates—darkest day."

Dex nodded. "I think Eris had the same understanding that she did. I think everyone thought Eugenia would be the Fates' defender. I think your aunt thought she was your defender too. If your prophecy is misread, like you say, then your future would be bright if Eugenia managed to save the Fates."

Vivian stared at the words, shaking her head and feeling very sad.

"That's why the Fates were so shocked she was dead," Dex said. "And Eris thought she had a victory when she killed Eugenia."

"How did Eris know the prophecies?"

"They're written down," Dex said. "Anyone can find them if they look hard enough."

Vivian sighed. "So the prophecies are wrong sometimes?"

"Never." Dex sounded shocked.

"But Aunt Eugenia's was." Vivian frowned. "She never had a great love."

Dex reached out and took Vivian's hand. "Interpreting prophecies is very difficult. Even the Fates get the interpretations wrong sometimes."

"I thought they came up with the prophecies."

"They do," Dex said, "but the prophecies come

from some force outside themselves. Some people say the force is the Powers That Be, but others don't agree."

"Don't the Fates know?"

"No one knows for sure," Dex said.

"I guess it really doesn't matter," Vivian said. "Aunt Eugenia's prophecy was still wrong."

"Read it again, Viv," Dex said softly.

"It says, 'Your defense of the Fates will lead to a great love.' " Vivian shrugged. "So?"

"It didn't say *her* great love." Dex's hand tightened on hers. "Now read yours."

Vivian did. *You shall have a great love should you survive Fate's darkest day.*

She felt cold. "You think Aunt Eugenia's prophecy refers to us?"

"Yes," Dex said.

Vivian tightened her hold on his hand. A great love. It felt like a great love. And he believed the prophecy pointed to it.

She looked at him, feeling warm and loved and upset all at the same time. His gaze met hers, and it was full of compassion.

"That's so sad," she said. "It means her whole life was pointing toward mine."

"I doubt she looked at it that way," Dex said. "Maybe she spent all that time waiting for her great love."

Until the end. Vivian got his thought as clearly as if he had spoken. *She knew in the end.*

"Because she sent me all the materials," Vivian said.

Dex started. He must have thought she hadn't heard that thought. "Yes."

"That makes sense," she said. "But if the Fates knew they were going to face trouble, why did they come here? Why did they let their magic go?"

"There's no figuring those women," Dex said.

"You don't even have an idea?"

He gave her a wry grin. "They do believe in fate."

Vivian rolled her eyes. "I still don't get it. Even if the Fates are determined to believe in the prophecy, why would anyone else? I mean, if the Fates are the all-powerful judges, jury, and executioners, where would Eris get enough magic to fight them?"

"I don't know," Dex said. "And why wouldn't Eris have taken Eugenia out when they first met?"

Vivian shivered. Her life would have been so different if she hadn't had her Aunt Eugenia to rely on. So different that she really didn't want to think about it.

The hair rose on the back of Vivian's neck. "Is there a draft in here?"

Dex shook his head, obviously not expecting the question. "From where? We're really deep underground."

"Maybe the heating system?"

"I can get you another sweater, Viv," he said.

She wrapped her arms around the one she was wearing. It was too big and smelled of Dex. "This one's fine. It just felt like a goose had walked on my grave."

Dex's expression turned sharp. "Are you sensing something?"

Vivian wasn't sure. She concentrated for a moment, tried to judge the sensation she had just had. Had it come from all her reading—which was disturbing her? Or the conversation? Or the fact that she had been cold since she arrived in this hideaway?

Or was it something more?

"Did it feel like that spell Vari took out of you?" Dex asked.

Vivian shook her head. "That was a lot more powerful. This was just—a draft."

She didn't want to tell him that sometimes she

couldn't tell a premonition from a sneeze, particularly if the response was mild. She had been concentrating on her reading, not on her various psychic abilities.

"I thought you said a spell can't get us down here," she said.

"I said we're defended against all types of magic I know about."

"There are types you don't know?" Vivian asked.

"By our people's standards, Viv, I'm a baby. I'm always astonished by how much I don't know."

That didn't reassure her. Of course, it wasn't meant to. But she had been feeling safe until that moment. She thought of the other part of the prophecy.

"The Fates' darkest day," she said to him. "Is this the Fates' darkest day?"

He shrugged. "I'd like to hope so, because we saved them this morning. But I doubt it. I think their darkest day is ahead."

"So we have this . . ." She paused, not sure she wanted to say it before he did.

"This great love," he said.

"And we might lose it?"

"Might," he said. "Only might. We might get to enjoy it as well."

Vivian bit her lower lip. "But there are no guarantees."

"No."

Then she frowned. "What's your prophecy?"

He blushed and blocked his thoughts.

"Dex, please."

He shook his head, but the block lifted. Still, Vivian couldn't read much more than embarrassment.

"My prophecy," he said, "is 'Only through foolish heroics will you find a great love.' "

"Foolish heroics," Vivian repeated.

He nodded.

"Like rescuing animals?"

"Or people, when it's not approved."

"Or the Fates when they might punish you for it."

He nodded.

"Foolish heroics." Vivian smiled. "I like that."

"I never have," Dex said.

"But you've lived up to it."

"I guess."

Vivian took a deep breath. "So there's no comfort in your prophecy either. You've found the love."

"Yes," he said.

"And mine says we might lose it."

"That's one interpretation," Dex said.

"It seemed to be Aunt Eugenia's," Vivian said. And then Dex opened to her as all of his blocks left him. He was worried, and beneath that worry was a subtle fear. "And yours."

He took her hand. "Vivian, you'll be all right."

"It's not me I'm worried about," she said.

"My foolish heroics only lead me to love," he said.

The implication was that she might not survive, and he would. He must have heard the thought.

"I'll do everything in my power to keep any harm from coming to you," he said.

She knew that. She trusted him beyond all measure, beyond all logic. But she also knew that his resources were limited, just like hers were.

And now that they'd found each other, they both had something precious to lose.

Twenty-two

Eris waited until the sun had set. Her magic was stronger in the dark. But this street wasn't entirely dark. Street lamps cast large pools of light on the road and the surrounding yards.

Eris pointed her right hand at the first streetlight and pinched her thumb and forefinger together. The light went out. She continued the process until all the other lights were out as well.

The change was silent. No big explosions, no cascade of sparks. The neighbors—the handful who lived on the block—probably hadn't even noticed.

Eris smiled and walked farther up Dexter Grant's driveway. While she had been waiting for the twilight to end, she had been sending out thin feelers, searching for magic. She made sure the feelers didn't touch the magic; if they did, they might alert Grant.

The feelers found a deep sense of magic all around the house. Grant had used standard protect spells and had updated them just that afternoon, probably when he arrived home with Kineally. Two bits of magic still floated in the air above the house—one a large relocation spell, bringing two people into the area (it took little work on her part to realize those people were Grant and Kineally) and the second a small relocation spell, which brought three boxes into one of the bedrooms.

The boxes carried the faint odor of Eugenia Kineally.

Eris had finally found where Eugenia's spell recipes had gone. They had gone to her niece Vivian, who in return gave them to her new sweetheart, Dexter Grant.

The recipes were a bonus. Eris could hold the Fates without them. But the recipes would show her the protection spells that surrounded the Fates, the way Eugenia Kineally had shown them how to protect themselves even though they had given up their magic.

Eugenia's spells had to have been very powerful, given the success the Fates had had so far. Eris was certain the spells had been designed to protect magical Fates. The fact that the spells protected nonmagical Fates showed just how powerful Eugenia Kineally had been.

The night had become pitch black. The moon wouldn't rise for another two hours, and then it would be a pitiful sliver—certainly not enough for some inept souls to pull magic from. Eris never pulled her powers from anywhere else. She stole magic from rivals—although she hadn't been able to get Eugenia Kineally's, dammit—and she absorbed glimmers from the marginally magical, but she never used an object outside of herself as a source for her power.

It simply wasn't practical. Other people, other *things*, couldn't be relied upon. One had to learn to rely upon oneself.

Eris extended a hand and cast a shimmering red light forward. The light was almost invisible to the untrained eye. She loved this spell; it detected hidden magic.

She sent the light toward that fence in the backyard, where she was certain Grant had built a second house, this one shielded and magical. The light floated around his ugly ranch, caught on the weak shielding, and shimmered for a moment.

Then it disappeared.

Eris followed it, careful to avoid the edges of the shield. The light had not gathered in the backyard, as she had expected. Instead it was seeping into the earth.

She had never seen anything like it before, and she wasn't certain what it meant. The light didn't sit on top of the ground and shimmer; the ground had apparently absorbed it.

A spell she didn't recognize? A protection she wasn't certain of? She hadn't encountered one of those in more than four generations. She had to give Grant credit for resourcefulness. For such a young man, he had a wide repertoire.

She tried to call the light back to her, but it wouldn't come. It felt stuck, and now she recognized the spell. If she tugged on her own magic, urging it to return to her body, it would instead pull her into the trap, holding her there until someone—probably the mage who laid the trap—set her free.

Clever, clever Grant. Her respect for him grew even more. Too bad she had to rely on her careless son Strife when a talent like Grant was in the world. Too bad she couldn't bring him over to her side.

She put her hands on her hips and studied the aluminum windows of the horrible little ranch house. She couldn't sense any life in there at all—

not even the animals Grant was famous for rescuing.

He had them hidden somewhere. Just like he had the Fates hidden. And he had them hidden very well.

But no one thought of everything—at least, no one as young as Grant. He would have made a mistake, left an access point somewhere, or allowed a weakness in one of his shieldings.

She just had to find it.

A klaxon sounded overhead.

Vivian jumped, her heart pounding. The calico cat scampered off her lap, leaving deep claw marks in Vivian's thighs. Out of the corner of her eye, she saw other animals scurrying for cover.

The klaxon continued, and over it, a digitized female voice repeated, "Security breach, south lawn. Security breach, south lawn. Security breach, south lawn."

Vivian wasn't sure if she had transported to the bridge of the Starship *Enterprise* —that klaxon was damned familiar—or if the elevator had taken her to the White House. She wondered what the president would think if he heard "Security breach, south lawn," and then decided he probably wouldn't have felt a lot different than she did now.

Adrenaline rushed through her system, and her heart was pounding. She looked over at Dex, hoping he would tell her what to do. She was in his world now, and it was about as alien as a world could get.

"Audio system off!" he shouted, and the noise ended in mid-klax and halfway through the eighth round of "Securi—."

Vivian's ears rang. The noise had given her an

instant headache. "Well, let me guess," she said. "You got that klaxon from *Star Trek*."

"Original *Trek*." Dex was standing. "I tend to prefer prototypes."

Even though he was speaking lightly, he wasn't smiling, and his mind didn't seem to be on his words.

"What's going on?" Vivian asked.

"Probably nothing." But he wasn't acting like there was nothing. He was acting like there was something. And, she realized, he had cut himself off from her. She couldn't reach his thoughts or his emotions.

"Dex, you can't lie to me."

"I'm not," Dex said. "When the system's on, it's very delicate."

"This was a magic warning?"

This time he did grin. "No magic at all. You can buy all this stuff and program it yourself from half a dozen Web sites."

"So what was breached?"

"The backyard. Might have been anything. A deer. A neighbor. I'll just go to the cameras and see."

"Okay." Vivian stood.

"I'm going to go alone, Viv. I work better alone."

"I thought you were just going out front," she said.

"I am, but there's an entrance into this place from the south lawn. If someone found it, they could conceivably be heading into the main area now."

His explanation sounded true, but he was still cut off from her.

"What am I supposed to do?" she asked.

"Keep researching, so that we know what we're up against."

"What if it's Eris out there?"

"I'm not leaving the building, Viv." Dex sounded impatient. "Now let me go."

She realized then that she'd been forcing him to stay by quizzing him. She nodded once, reluctant to let him leave, but not willing to cross him either. This was his place. He understood it better than she did, and he knew how to respond to it.

She would have to trust him.

"What if you don't come back, Dex?" she whispered.

He was already halfway through the kitchen. "I'll come back, Viv," he said. "I always do."

Twenty-three

He lied to her.

Dex was astounded at his own behavior. He had just lied to Vivian.

He'd had to hurry out of the dining room because he couldn't hide his thoughts or his emotions from her any longer. Both were threatening to spiral out of control.

At the moment the klaxon had gone off, his own magical system sent a shiver through him. A very delicate spell—some kind of light, done to suss out his own magic—had been absorbed by his backyard trap. He'd set up that trap so that he would be alerted whenever something magical touched it.

And this time, the magic was subtle and ever-so-faint.

Then the alarms had gone off, warning of an intrusion. Even though the breach had been in the backyard, Dex had a hunch that whomever had done that was long gone. Either that or it was a way to use his own system to snare him.

He wouldn't be trapped. And to prevent that, he had to keep Vivian protected.

As long as she stayed down here, she would be all right.

He hurried toward the main room. Sadie joined him halfway there, looking concerned. He wondered where she had been when the alarms went off. He hadn't seen her in the dining room.

All the lights were on in the main area, making the black walls seem even shinier. The computer screens were up. Words scrawled along the center of one: Security breach, south lawn, Quadrant A. The other screens showed the lawn—all of it, including the north, east, and west portions. Floodlights had turned on, making it seem like daylight outside.

Other screens showed the interior of the house. The lighting hadn't changed there. It remained the way he and Vivian had left it—a few lights on in some of the rooms, off in others.

The rumpled bed caught his attention, the pillows propped against the wall, the sheets tangled. That bed—that room—probably still carried the faint scent of their lovemaking. It had been the best experience of his long life.

He hoped it wouldn't be one of the last.

The reading he had done worried him. Eris was, by far, the strongest mage he had ever encountered. If Vivian's Aunt Eugenia was right—and he had no reason to doubt her—then Eris had been stealing magic for years. She would be even more powerful than the woman whose impetuous actions had started the Trojan War.

If this were a normal situation, he would have gone to the Fates and begged for their help. He would have told them he would be able to prove that Eris was abusing some of their magical laws, and he would have demanded—and probably got—justice.

That was how he had caught his first few mages, the ones who were so much stronger than he had been. At first the Fates had thought Dex was doing a good thing. Then, in a blink of an eye to them, two decades to him, he'd been outed, in a comic book of all things, and the Fates' attitude had changed.

Their biggest problem was their hatred of mortals. Or it had been their biggest problem, until they decided to venture into the real world with no power at all.

He reached the computer screens, Sadie beside him. He was still angry at the Fates. Even though they had enabled him to find Vivian, whom, he knew, was the woman he'd been waiting for.

He had always wanted to be loved as freely as he loved. And, because he could touch Vivian's mind—or, more accurately, she could touch his— he knew that she loved him as much as he loved her.

Ironic, because until now, he had not believed in love at first sight.

Perhaps his feelings for her had grown so quickly because they only had twenty-four hours in which to live a lifetime.

He tamped down that thought. Negative thoughts destroyed confidence in times of crisis. He'd learned that one the hard way.

This was the reason he hadn't wanted Vivian beside him. He would worry about her, and wouldn't be able to concentrate on the mission at hand.

He couldn't see Eris, but he'd felt her in that delicate magic. Not that she'd left a signature. Somehow she'd managed to filter out her signature from all her spells.

No. He recognized the spell as being as elegant as the one threaded into the rope, the one that caused the puppet to kidnap the Fates. The texture of the magic was the same.

As they figured out who their enemy was, she had found them. And he knew she wouldn't leave until she had what she wanted.

Somehow he had to protect the Fates from her. The Fates and Vivian.

He sat in his chair and used the cameras to scan the lawn again. He couldn't see anything. He closed his eyes and used his own magic, feeling for a strange presence.

Nothing.

Except the odd sensation that they weren't alone.

He opened his eyes. He had lied to Vivian about two things. There was an entrance into the hideaway from above ground, but it wasn't on the south lawn, and no one could crawl down it without being zapped by both his state-of-the-art security system (the kind designed for survivalists, paranoiacs, and other wackos) or by the handful of spells he'd left there to trip up the magical.

Every way down here was protected, but that wouldn't stop Eris. Her magic was so powerful, her mind so strong, that she'd figure out how to break in. Dex was under no illusions about his own powers. He was no match for a woman who had been practicing magic for around four thousand years.

He couldn't even call for help. He wasn't sure if the Quixotic gang was involved with Eris, since they'd let her in the restaurant, and his old magical friends were too far away. Besides, if he sent out a magical signal, Eris would feel it.

Instead, he would have to take a chance that had worked in the past. Eris would expect him to stay hidden, to play defense, protecting Vivian and the Fates.

Eris would never expect him—the weaker of the two of them by a considerable amount—to take the initiative.

The problem was, he'd only have one shot at this. But one shot was all he needed.

Twenty-four

Eris had tried everything. She had used tiny spells and large ones, important spells and half-forgotten spells, trying to reveal where the magic lived on Grant's property. She found nothing.

She stood just outside the ring of protection he had put around that dilapidated ranch house, her arms crossed. By now, Grant would know she was there. She'd tripped at least two traps, although she hadn't been caught in them, and she'd used enough magic to alert even the most inept mage.

She only had two more things to try before she could conclude that the house was just a house, with no magical hiding place anywhere nearby.

Eris had made an assumption, something she used to warn Strife about when he was a young mage-in-training. Assumptions could be false. She had assumed, because Grant's property was so large, that he had placed his real living quarters somewhere else. She had also assumed they were large and spectacular and well protected.

But she based that assumption on the way she

lived, not on the way he did. She had been around for a very long time and comfort was important to her, particularly after all those years of torture in the name of justice.

Dexter Grant was just a pup, and a male pup at that. Perhaps he had no interest in comfortable living or, like many male pups of the mortal persuasion, no idea how to take care of himself.

Eris wouldn't live in such a tiny home—her apartment on Central Park West had five bedrooms and three floors, and it was the smallest place she owned—but that didn't mean Grant wouldn't.

And if that was the case, then he had only added one or two spells to his protect spell. He'd put some kind of block on the house so that Eris couldn't sense any living creatures inside, and he had erected some kind of magical shield spell so that most magic performed inside the house would be impossible to detect outside.

She doubted this last because she could trace the relocation spells. But he was weak enough that his abilities might not allow him to block magic that originated from the outside.

If these spells didn't work, she would have to see if he owned property elsewhere in the city, and had set this place up as a dodge.

Either way, she would have to dismantle his protect spell and go inside the house. She might be lucky and find Grant and Kineally inside, or she might have to do some searching through his personal papers or his computer to find out what else he owned.

Dismantling a protect spell wasn't something to be done lightly. And with as many traps as Grant had established outside the house, he was certain to have many more inside.

Eris would have to proceed with caution.

After all, she wouldn't put it past Grant to use

the weak protect spell, the leftover relocation traces, and Eugenia's papers to lure Eris inside the house. The house itself might be a trap.

And it was up to her to disarm it.

Dex had left the basement. Vivian knew the moment he had stepped out of the area. That sense she'd had of him, like the hum of a computer screen or background music played so softly that it only registered on the subconscious, had disappeared.

She felt alone again, like she had felt in Quixotic when he had taken the Fates to his so-called cave. Only this time, she didn't feel abandoned. There was a connection between them now, an understanding of each other that was so strong, Vivian could feel it even though Dex had physically moved away from her. She knew him now, almost as well as she knew herself, and he would do everything in his power to return.

He would also do everything he could to protect her. That was the part of this whole thing that worried her. She didn't know the details of his history, but she knew enough. Dex was the kind of man—or he had been until the Fates finally got through to him—who acted first and accepted the consequences later.

She sighed and continued sorting Aunt Eugenia's papers. Vivian didn't know what she was looking for, but she would know it when she found it. Maybe Aunt Eugenia had some insight into how to defeat Eris.

But if Aunt Eugenia had known that, why hadn't she used it? Why had she allowed Eris to kill her?

Something wasn't making sense, and that something centered around Aunt Eugenia. If only Vivian had listened to her. If only she had come up north for the training sooner, maybe none of this would have happened.

And then maybe she might not have met Dexter Grant.

Somehow she knew that, if they survived this, they would be a great team. One of those legendary teams, a couple who, while powerful as individuals, were stronger together than they were when they were apart.

Vivian glanced into the kitchen, where she had last seen him. She sent him all the warmth and love she had, even though she knew he probably couldn't feel it from this distance. That rock he had put in this basement had probably blocked any chance of psychic communication, just like it blocked magic.

She resisted the urge to beg him to hurry back, just in case broadcast thoughts were getting through. She didn't want to distract him.

She had a hunch he would need all his concentration to make it through the night.

Dex wished he had made the elevator run silently. He had never planned for this contingency—that he would leave the safety of the basement hideaway and return to the house to check out what he had seen. He'd always figured that whatever came through the elevator would attack him, not the other way around.

He could spell it silent once he rose above the protective rocks, but magic might draw more attention than the click-click-click of the gears as they moved.

He leaned against the handrailing, holding it tightly. He had his plan. Once he found Eris, he would use a binding spell, then immediately transport her to the Interim Fates. Not that those children would know what to do with her, but at least she'd be far away from him.

And the Interim Fates would have to do something with Eris, even if they had to consult the Powers That Be first.

Dex shifted from foot to foot. He was nervous. He hadn't been nervous in years. Of course, he hadn't done anything like this in years. He'd been a kitten superhero, not a real one. The only times he ever got a chance to use his skills had been when his old enemies sought him out.

But he was primed and ready now. The magic hovered on his fingertips, and the spell was in the forefront of his mind. One chance. One chance only, and he had to be careful. He couldn't set off the spell too early, couldn't jump at shadows. He had to be very precise.

Finally the elevator lurched to a stop. He took a deep breath and calmed himself. If he found her, he had a plan. If he didn't find her, he would at least reassure himself—and Vivian—that they were safe for the time being.

The elevator doors opened. Dex stepped into the darkened linen closet. He thought certain he had left the light on, but maybe force of habit had made him shut it off.

After all, he didn't want to point someone to his secret elevator. He opened the linen closet door and found the lights on in the hallway. His heart pounded. He had remembered this backward—light on in the linen closet, off in the hallway. Funny how the mind played tricks.

The house was unusually silent without the animals in it. He didn't step into the hallway until he checked his shield, traps, and protect spells that surrounded the house. All were intact.

He started for the kitchen when the linen closet door slammed behind him. He whirled, expecting to see an animal he had somehow missed in the mad dash for the basement.

Instead he saw a tall black-haired woman, neatly dressed in a summer sweater and blue jeans. Even in such casual attire, she looked elegant and expensive.

Eris.

Even before Dex could send off the spell that hovered on his fingertips, his entire body went rigid. He tried to move but couldn't. He couldn't even move his lips to recite the spell.

She had captured him without saying a word, without moving a finger.

She had trapped him, and worse, she had seen him come out of the linen closet. He hadn't even closed the secret panel to the elevator.

Eris could get to his secret hiding place. She could get to Vivian.

And he wouldn't be able to stop her.

Twenty-five

Eris chuckled as she walked toward Dexter Grant. He was so much better looking in person than he had been in any of the photographs she'd seen. Hair so black it looked almost blue—and that dimple in his chin; how adorable was that?

If she'd known it was this easy to catch a superhero, she would have done so sooner.

"Lookee what I did," she said as she reached his side. "And I didn't even have any Kryptonite."

His lips twitched, and she knew what he wanted to say. He wasn't Superman. He had never been Superman, and there was no such thing as Kryptonite. Amazing the things people focused on. Amazing the things the mythmakers got wrong.

Eris understood because she had never been that interested in discord. *Discord* was such a wimpy word. She thought it only one step up from *disagreement,* an even wimpier word. She and Dexter Grant were having a disagreement. There was discord between her and Dexter Grant.

Minor, minor words for minor, minor leaders.

She wasn't the Goddess of Discord. She was the Master of Chaos. And she'd prove it just as soon as she made sure those pesky Fates were out of the way forever.

"You don't seem that formidable." Eris flicked Grant with her forefinger and he fell backward, a straight shot, as if he'd been attached to a board. His head narrowly missed the corner of the wall.

He landed with a whump and a whoosh. The whoosh was the one that pleased Eris most. She'd knocked his breath away. Literally.

"I at least expected a fight from you," Eris said. "One of those large good-versus-evil things you like so much, with plenty of fireballs and lightning and wild magic. Of course, I have you pinned now, and eventually I will have to kill you."

His eyes had caught the light. They were the only things on him that proved he was alive. Such fire in them. Such passion. They were quite eloquent. She could feel their defiance.

She sat down beside him, crossing her legs. "I will have to kill you, unless you tell me where your pretty little Miss Kineally is. Or we can skip over the nasty parts where I torture the powerless little psychic who hasn't come into her magic yet, showing her what the Fates did to me for two thousand years—as if starting a war was a crime! They were just angry at the way I exposed the pettiness of Hera, Athena, and Aphrodite. Who's the fairest of them all? And the hapless Paris picks Helen, of course. Foolish man. It was his fault, after all, for picking a mortal woman over a mage. Not mine."

Dex was still glaring at her. She wished she could let him speak, but if he spoke, he could cast spells, and if he could cast spells, he might, just might, be able to hurt her. Better not to take that chance at all.

"Ah, yes. I was talking about skipping the nasty

parts. Because you could just tell me where the Fates are and let me get underway."

Eris tapped her lips with a fingertip.

"That won't work, though, will it? Because you'll use that ploy done in a thousand movies. You'll lie to me and tell me whatever you think I want to know so that I'll unbind your mouth, and then you'll use that feeble magic on me. If you can. Looks like I'll just have to torture Ms. Kineally myself."

Dex's eyes narrowed. She could feel his anger. It made his body vibrate, and the vibrations were harming the integrity of the spell. Stubborn and strong. She wondered if he realized that he was messing with the harmonics of the binding spell.

Probably. Add smart to the equation. She strengthened the binding spell to accommodate his little temper tantrum and smoothed that pretty hair off his forehead.

"The real question, then, is do I go after Ms. Kineally while leaving you up here? I do like that elevator of yours. Your bunker must be buried deep, because I never would have found it from the outside. Or do I wait here with you until she comes up on her own, just to investigate?"

Eris leaned against the wall. Grant watched her, and she could tell he was hoping she'd wait, hoping that someone else would find them and rescue them, or that he'd figure out a way to escape in the hours that it took little Ms. Kineally to realize her big, strong man had deserted her.

"Hmmm," Eris said, dragging out the moment. "I think I *will* wait. Much as I would like to see what you've done with your underground hideaway, I think it would be better if Ms. Kineally came to me. That way I don't have to disable any more spells and traps—good thinking, by the way, but you did forget to reinforce the point of origin for those spells. Or did no one ever tell you that the point of origin is always the weakest point, and can be entered by anyone if found?"

His eyes widened slightly. Fascinating. His mentor was as bad as they said he had been. Grant had learned much of this stuff on his own.

"Anyway, if I wait here," she said, "I can rest up and be at full force so that I can really make that little girl suffer. She did love her Aunt Eugenia, didn't she? Maybe I'll make your Vivian relive that death over and over again."

Eris held out her hand, studying her fingernails.

"Such choices facing me tonight. Psychological torture or physical torture? Or perhaps a mixture of both? I'll just have to see what my mood is when little Ms. Kineally comes through that linen closet door, crying, 'Dex, oh, Dex! Are you all right?'"

Grant started. Apparently Eris's imitation of Kineally was as good as she had hoped it would be.

"Let's just sit here together you and I. I can tell you about my exploits, and you can tell me about yours. Oops! You can't, can you? My mistake. I'll just have to make them up myself. Just think: your legacy in my hands. Maybe I'll even make your death a news story on KAHS. It is time the world learns of magic, don't you think? Imagine the problems that will bring. The *discord* between the haves and have-nots."

Eris chuckled. "I'm having such fun." She continued to stroke his hair. "I hope you are too."

Vivian didn't like the feeling of unease that was building in her stomach. Her emotions had received so much exercise that day that she wasn't certain if her discomfort was coming from her own anxieties or from a true psychic sense that something was wrong.

She had repacked all Aunt Eugenia's boxes, leaving out only the notebooks that mentioned Eris. Vivian put the mythology books on top of the nearest box in case Dex wanted to look at them again.

But Dex hadn't returned. She had thought he would be back by now.

Part of the problem was that she wasn't staying busy. If she stayed busy, she wouldn't obsess about Dex.

She'd finished Dex's Sprite. She needed something else to drink. She turned toward the kitchen and stopped.

Sadie was sitting by the door, a frown on her doggy face. For the first time since Vivian had met her, Sadie seemed uncertain, as if she couldn't decide what to do next.

The dog's appearance startled Vivian. She had thought Sadie was with Dex.

How long had she been sitting there?

"What's going on?" Vivian asked.

Sadie whined and looked over her shoulder, as if she saw something down the corridor. Vivian went to the dog, her thirst forgotten.

"Show me," she said.

Sadie led her down the corridor. Everything seemed the same as it had when Vivian arrived. Animals were scattered in various rooms. The ferret had made its way around the room with the giant computer and was asleep on top of the punch cards. Portia was curled on her side in her hospital room, her paws twitching with a dream.

Vivian didn't linger at any of those places. Instead, she hurried with Sadie toward the main room. Vivian knew Dex wasn't here—because she could sense his absence—but the fact that he had left Sadie behind disturbed her.

The computer screens were all on, but the sound appeared to be off. SECURITY BREACH, SOUTH LAWN still scrolled across the center screen. Hadn't Dex fixed that breach? Had he even made it there?

The other screens acted like closed-circuit televisions, showing various parts of the house and yard. Sadie went to a side screen and pawed it.

Vivian had to come close to see what was going on.

Dex was lying on the floor in the hallway, his arms at his side, his feet pointed. He almost looked as if he was preparing to go down a water slide, except that his arms weren't crossed over his stomach.

Beside him sat the woman Vivian had seen in Quixotic, the woman she'd seen murder her Aunt Eugenia. The woman appeared to be waiting—and Dex was clearly helpless.

They had to be waiting for Vivian. The scenario Dex most feared had happened. He would be forced to tell Eris where the Fates were to protect Vivian's life.

Vivian touched the screen, wishing she could touch Dex without Eris knowing. Only once before had Vivian felt so helpless—and that had been Eris's fault too—the night Aunt Eugenia had died. Vivian had had to watch that, through the filter sent by Eugenia's mind.

She wouldn't watch again. She would rescue Dex.

And then she slipped into his chair. The impulse was noble but misguided. He had more magical powers than she could dream of. And Eris appeared to have defeated him in a moment.

There was nothing Vivian could do—except watch and hope that someone else would ride to the rescue and save them all.

Twenty-six

The one thing evil bad guys all seemed to have in common was their tendency to yammer. As if someone cared about their horrid little plots to take over the world.

If you'd heard one megalomaniacal speech, you'd heard them all. At least that was the conclusion Dex was coming to. Eris was telling him—apparently trying to impress him with her brilliance—about the skills she'd acquired since the Fates let her go, and how she had used those skills to create KAHS and her own Erika O'Connell personality.

Pretty soon, he was sure, she was going to explain to him how she would conquer the world, and why it was necessary for her to be the one to do so. She'd probably follow that with an evil laugh—something that would sound like *Bwa-ha-ha-ha,* since evil people rarely had normal and pleasing laughs—and then she'd find a new way to torture him.

He could practically write her dialogue for her.

He'd heard it in enough bad movies, read it in a thousand comic books, seen it on a million television programs. She thought she was original, but she wasn't.

That was the problem with these supervillains; they all wanted the same thing. One day he'd like to run into a megalomaniacal nut with the dream of taking over all the newspaper recycling businesses worldwide, or conquering the ice cream industry. Or wait—that plot had already been done in a delightful little Scottish film called *Comfort and Joy*.

Dex had stopped trying to move. Moving only seemed to make the binding spell tighter. He didn't have real telepathy—not with anyone except Vivian, or so it seemed—and that was his own fault. He could have worked on his telepathic skills, but he never saw the point. He liked keeping his thoughts private—or he had until he met Viv.

There was no way to contact her. The rock and protection spells guarding the basement made that impossible. And he couldn't send out a warning to anyone else. He didn't know any spells that could be cast with the mind alone.

Until he could get Eris to release his mouth or his hands, he was doomed to lie here like a two-man luger whose partner had fallen off the sled.

And this, to Dex, was complete torture. Eris probably knew that, just like she knew the droning of her voice was torture. She was delighting in his pain, waiting for Vivian.

At least Vivian hadn't come up—not yet. Maybe she wouldn't. Maybe she would wait long enough for Eris to become restless and make a mistake.

That was their only hope now. It was up to Eris. She had to make one of those colossal supervillain blunders or Dex and Vivian were doomed.

Because Dex wasn't about to turn the Fates over to Eris, not even to save Vivian's life. He wasn't dumb. He knew there was no bargaining with people like Eris. She might promise to let Vivian go if Dex gave up the Fates, but in the end, Eris would kill them all.

At least with the Fates still around—and their cell phone in hand—they might eventually contact someone else to help them. They might solve this Eris problem long after Dex and Vivian were dead.

He hated being so pessimistic. It wasn't his usual style. But he'd never been out of options before. Or, more accurately, his options had never been this bad.

And he'd only had to worry about himself. Never before had he had to protect someone he loved.

That made his job a thousand times harder. It made his job impossible.

Vivian was on her feet, investigating the Packard, before she'd even realized she had stood up. The problem with waiting and hoping, she'd discovered, was that she had never been very good at either. And she didn't like the idea of being rescued.

She just didn't make a convincing damsel in distress.

The Packard was in lovely condition. If Dex hadn't spelled it down here, then there had to be a way to drive out. Vivian figured it would take some exploring, but she would find that way—or maybe Sadie would show her.

The problem was that the Packard had no gasoline in it. Dex had followed the rules. He hadn't stored a vehicle filled with a flammable chemical in his basement. Normally Vivian would have applauded such good sense, but right now it irritated her.

Why did he have to be so squeaky clean? A few

rough edges would have been good at the moment. Some kind of bad guy image—something she could use.

Next she checked out the weapons closet, and nearly put her fist through the wall. The weapons weren't weapons at all, but collectibles. *Star Trek* phasers (who'd've thought he was a Trek geek?), high-end light sabers, and every comic book villain's weapon ever drawn. The only thing that was close to a real weapon—which probably was a real weapon, come to think of it—was a kitana that had come from the *Highlander* website. Apparently Dex was a Duncan McCleod fan as well.

Nice that they had so much in common. Now if Dex would only live so that they could enjoy each other.

Sadie had followed Vivian everywhere, and Vivian could feel the dog's urgency. Or maybe it was her own urgency mingling with Sadie's.

There wasn't a phone down here, and there seemed to be no radio equipment either. Nothing that connected this little bomb shelter prototype to the surface.

Except the elevator—which led directly to Dex and Eris.

Vivian walked to the elevator, put her hands on her hips, and stared at it. Sadie whined, as if she disapproved of this train of thought.

But Vivian felt like she was getting somewhere. After all, who was the expendable one here? Certainly not Dex, who was the only person who knew where the Fates were. It was Vivian, and she might be able to use that to her advantage.

She'd been hearing it all day. In fact, Dex had said it not a few hours before. Vivian could do anything she put her mind to. Anything.

The Fates had shown her that by making her envision that glass jar. She'd encased an entire building, cutting the spell that threatened it off at the knees—or the feelers, to be more accurate.

Her heart started pounding, hard. If she could get high enough in that elevator to get past Dex's magical prohibitions, then maybe she could use her mind to give Dex a few moments of freedom, just enough to get away, or to hurt Eris, or to find help.

Vivian would have to trust him to do the right thing. Somehow she would have to convey to him that she was the expendable one without having him realize that she truly meant to sacrifice herself if that was what was needed.

All of that would take a lot of mind control for a neophyte. But she could do it.

After all, she could do anything she put her mind to.

She just had to believe anything was possible.

And, after the day she'd had, believing was the easy part.

Twenty-seven

Sadie insisted on accompanying Vivian into the elevator. In fact, Vivian doubted she would have been able to get the elevator doors closed if she hadn't permitted Sadie to join her.

Sadie gave Vivian comfort, even though the dog was pacing and looking panicked. Vivian had the sense that Sadie might actually bolt from the elevator and chew Eris into teeny, tiny pieces.

It was a great image, but not a realistic one. Eris would probably do something to Sadie long before the dog got near her.

Dex was going to be really angry that Vivian had brought Sadie along.

Oh, well. That was the least of her worries.

Vivian clutched the handrailing and closed her eyes. Timing was critical. She had to wait until she felt the barest hint of Dex's presence. That meant she was out of the magical protection zone and into the main part of the house.

The elevator moved slower on the way up than it had on the way down. Or maybe it just seemed that way. Vivian wanted it to zoom to the top, and she wanted to spring out, do her battling, and hurry away—or suffer the consequences, depending on what faced her.

Timing. It was all about timing.

And luck—although she refused to believe in luck. If she believed in luck, she'd have to believe in bad luck, and if she believed in bad luck, she might fail.

So she would believe in timing and—

—she felt him, just a hint of him, like elevator music imposing itself on her conscious mind (only much more pleasant). And that was enough.

She envisioned a solid stone box made of the same shiny black rock Dex had used to line his basement hideaway; the rock he said wouldn't allow magic to penetrate through.

She made the box two feet thick on all sides and shaped it so that it would fit around Eris. She had to leave the bottom open for just a moment, and she hoped that moment wouldn't be too long.

Then Vivian pushed the box away from her, just like the Fates had taught her, and visualized it scurrying down the hall—like a Borg ship in deep space—and slamming down on top of Eris.

The box left Vivian with the force of a sneeze. At least she had done part of this right.

The elevator still hadn't stopped. Vivian kept concentrating—and hoping that her vision would work.

Dex sensed Vivian very faintly, like perfume left behind as a beautiful woman walked past. She was on the elevator, a third of the way from the top.

She was coming to rescue him.

No, Viv! No, he sent. *That's what she wants! Stay away!*

But he didn't get any answer. He didn't get any
answer at all.

The elevator finally lurched to a stop, and as
the door opened, Vivian pushed her way out. The
secret panel was open, and so was the linen closet
door.

She hurried through it, trying not to visualize
all that could have gone wrong (Eris and Dex,
squashed by the cube: Vivian arriving to see their
toes curling under like the Wicked Witch of the
West's curled under the house in *The Wizard of Oz;*
Dex smashed; Eris cackling, her hands reaching
out . . .). Vivian made herself concentrate on holding that cube down.

When she reached the hallway, she turned and
saw Dex sitting up in surprise. The floor was crum-
bling away from him, and the stone box Vivian had
created around Eris was sinking into the wood.

Immediately, Vivian visualized a bottom on that
box.

The wall was buckling and the ceiling was starting
to come down around them. Chunks of plaster and
something that looked suspiciously like asbestos
were raining down on Dex.

"Is she inside?" Vivian asked.

"She must be," Dex said. "The spell she put on
me is broken."

Vivian's head was aching, just like it had with the
glass jar. She was feeling dizzy, and she knew she
would pass out a lot sooner this time.

"She's fighting back. You have to do something,
Dex."

Sadie joined them, running to Dex and licking
his face. He put his arm around the dog but looked
at Vivian. "I've only got one idea," he said. "You'll

have to concentrate like you've never concentrated in your life.''

Tears were running down her cheeks. Her head hurt so bad that she could barely think. It was taking all of her strength to hang on to this vision.

"Okay," she said.

Dex waved his free arm in a circle and said into the air, "Take Eris, me, Vivian, and Sadie to the Fates!"

And, for the second time in her life—the second time that day—Vivian fainted.

She woke up sprawled on the floor of a huge library. The tile hadn't been cleaned in generations and the dirt was all over her clothes. Dex was standing near a sorting table, talking to three teenage girls who sat on top of it.

Eris sat in a chair in the corner, ropes holding her in place. Duct tape covered her mouth, and a hat made of that same shiny black rock covered her head—apparently to prevent her from sending spells the way Vivian sent images. Eris's eyes were narrowed in fury. If she ever got loose, they'd all be in big trouble.

Shards of black rock littered the entire room. Sadie was cowering underneath the checkout desk.

"I don't care that you don't know what to do with Eris," Dex was saying. "She's your responsibility now."

"No one told us we'd be responsible for adults," said the blond teenager. She was twirling a long strand of bubble gum around her right index finger.

"She's really old. What could she have done that's bad?" said the next girl. She shook her corn-rows as if the very idea of a bad adult frightened her.

"Yeah, like we can discipline anyone," said the redhead, tugging on her nose ring.

Dex sighed. Vivian could feel his exasperation. "Well, can you at least keep her tied up until we figure out what to do with her?"

"Why can't you?" the blonde asked.

"Because," Dex said, in that tone people used with particularly dumb children, "she's stronger than I am."

"Isn't that just like a guy?" the middle girl said. "He can't control a woman, so he wants the law to do it."

"That's right," Dex said. "You are the law, and she's breaking it. It's your job to punish her."

"We don't know what our job is yet," the redhead said. "We haven't finished all the reading."

Vivian sat up. Her headache was gone, but she was still slightly dizzy. Sadie saw her, and her tail thumped.

Eris was examining the ropes as if they held some kind of secret.

"Why don't you just ask the real Fates," Vivian said. "They'll know what to do with her."

"Who're you?" the blonde asked.

"Who're you?" Vivian asked in the exact same tone.

"I'm Brittany. I'm a real Fate."

"Oh, really?" Vivian stood. She'd had arguments like this with Kyle. This was a world she was used to. "If you're so real, then how come you can't handle one measly criminal?"

"He says she's not measly," the middle girl said.

Vivian arched an eyebrow at her. "I don't believe I was talking to you."

"If you talk to one of us, you talk to all of us," the redhead said.

"Really?" Vivian raised both eyebrows. "Just like real Fates?"

"We are real Fates!" the girls wailed.

"Then prove it," Vivian said. "Do something with her."

She pointed at Eris. The girls all looked at Eris, who glared at them. The girls looked away quickly. The redhead started thumbing through a book. The middle girl looked like she was about to burst into tears. The blonde—Brittany—whispered, "We don't know what to do."

As if Vivian knew.

"If you don't know, you ask someone for help," Vivian said. "Dex, bring Clotho, Lachesis, and Atropos here."

"No!" the Interim Fates wailed in unison.

"If we ask them what to do, then they'll know we failed," the middle girl said.

"Who're you again?" Vivian asked the middle girl.

"Tiffany."

"Well, Tiffany, you have failed. You don't know how to handle a simple problem."

"Neither does he." The redhead pointed at Dex.

Dex was watching all this with great consternation.

"Yes, he does," Vivian said. "He captured the bad guy and brought her to you for trial, just like he was supposed to."

"He said you captured the bad guy," Brittany said.

"Whatever," Vivian said, using the phrase with as much emphasis as Kyle always did. "The point is that you have to deal with her."

"We're not getting anywhere," Dex said. "I'll get the real Fates."

He raised his arm. Vivian felt her stomach clench. What if Eris broke free and did something to all of them—the Fates, the Interim Fates, and Dex, Viv, and Sadie?

But Vivian wasn't going to stop Dex, because this was their last hope.

Dex started to swing his arm down in completion of the spell when a voice boomed, "Belay that!"

Dex's arm froze in place, and for one horrible moment, Vivian thought Eris had done something to him again.

Instead, a man appeared beside him. He was short and squat and had a square face that reminded Vivian of a bull. Yet there was something oddly appealing about him.

"Daddy!" the Interim Fates cried.

"Oh, Daddy," said Brittany. "I'm so glad you're—"

"Shut up," the man said.

Dex had a look of sheer horror on his face. For a moment he didn't move, and then he bowed.

Bow, he sent to Vivian. *Now.*

I've never bowed before anyone in my life, she sent back. *Why should I bow now?*

Because he's one of the Powers That Be.

Vivian looked at the man, who was grinning at her. Except that it really wasn't a grin. It was a leer.

"Yep," he said. "A Power That Is, that's me. Better than a Power That Was, I always say. You really should bow, young lady. It's protocol."

Vivian gave him a hesitant bow, which made her dizziness worse.

The man came over, put a finger under her chin, and helped her stand. The dizziness fled, but she shivered just the same.

"This is a pretty one, Henri Barou. Where'd you find her?"

Dex was standing. "Leave her alone." Then he blanched and added, "Sir."

"I hate *sir,* don't you? Makes me sound old." The man turned his back on Dex and nodded toward Vivian. "I usually go by Jupiter, but I suppose in this place you can call me Zeus with no harm at all."

"Ze-Ze-Zeus?" Vivian said, wishing her mouth would obey her. "The real Zeus?"

"Nope, the fake one," he said with incredible cheer. "Yes, the real one. Who else would you expect?"

Vivian shrugged.

"Pretty but slow," Zeus said over his shoulder to Dex. "No wonder you like her. The dumb ones really have the benefits."

Dex's neck was turning red. Vivian could feel his anger. "She's not—"

"It's all right," Vivian said. They couldn't be distracted. Eris was still staring at her ropes, which looked thinner to Vivian. "Can you do something about Eris? She murdered my aunt, and she's been after the real Fates—"

"They're not the real Fates anymore," Zeus said. "My daughters are the real Fates now, or they will be once I convince the rest of the Powers to forgo this stupid application process."

Vivian made herself take a deep breath and try again. "Well, then, would you show them what to do with her? Because she's been trying to—"

"Eris, you say?" Zeus turned toward Eris and peered at her. "Ate? Mars's sister? Strife's mother?"

"One and the same," Dex said.

Zeus let go of Vivian's chin. She resisted the urge to rub the place where his finger had touched. She couldn't stop another shudder, though. He was one of those exceptionally virile men who thought all women found him attractive—even the ones who didn't.

He stalked over to Eris and peered into her face. "It is you. I have a bone to pick with you, missy. You made Hera mad. And when Hera gets mad, she takes it out on me. That apple thing really pissed her off. I was in the doghouse for at least three hundred years. Had to hide among the nymphs, which isn't as bad as it sounds, but still the bawling out I got when I got home was not worth it. Not at all."

Eris looked up at him. She was so frightened that Vivian could feel her fear—and Vivian doubted it had anything to do with psychic powers. Everyone else seemed to notice Eris's fear too.

"Clotho, Lachesis, and Atropos were too light on you, sweetheart," Zeus said. "They blamed you for getting in the way of some lover or other, but that's not the issue. The issue is that Hera still hasn't gotten over the entire Trojan War—in fact, if I go home and mention it, I'll be in the doghouse again—and you're the one who started it."

Vivian edged closer to Dex. He shook his head slightly. Zeus probably wouldn't appreciate any sign of closeness.

"And that little brat Strife. Clotho, Lachesis, and Atropos never did deal with him, did they?"

Eris's eyes got even wider.

"He interfered with my life more than any other mage's kid ever created. It's like Strife is my middle name. Whatever happens to you, happens to him." Then Zeus nodded, as if he were agreeing with himself. "Yeah. I like all that. Now I just have to figure out what exactly to do with you. I think you should be punished for—oh, heck, why should I decide how long?"

He grinned, and it was a real grin this time, one that made him seem a lot more pleasant.

"I'll punish you until my daughters know every detail of this job. Then, when they finally know what they're doing, they'll punish you. Begone!"

And Eris vanished, leaving behind the rope, the duct tape, and the stone hat. Vivian thought she heard a scream echo through the library, but she couldn't be sure.

"There we go." Zeus came back to Vivian. "Answered your prayers, sweetheart. Got a reward for old Zeusy?"

Vivian glanced at Dex, who looked worried.

"No, of course you don't. You're in love with the cowboy over there." Zeus turned to Dex. "Listen, kid, hasn't anyone told you love is overrated? Find yourself a few concubines. Have some affairs. Women are for enjoying, not for living with."

Dex started to speak, but Zeus silenced him with the wave of a hand.

"Don't argue with me. I've heard all the arguments. I'm sick of all the arguments. Hell, I even made the arguments when I met Hera, which was probably my biggest mistake." Zeus nodded. "But things are changing, boyo. My girls, here, they'll make sure this love and romance stuff will be taken out of the equation. Save the world for satyrs, that's what I say. Provided I can convince the rest of the Powers. Aphrodite's being a pill, but that's because she thinks she'll be out of a job."

Zeus clapped Dex on the back, and Dex staggered forward, as if he were trying to prevent himself from falling.

"About the time you'll be sick of this little filly— and you will, guaranteed—things'll be just the way you'll want them to be. I can promise you that." Zeus walked over to his daughters and kissed them all on the top of the head. "Get back to work, girls."

"But Daddy," Tiffany said, "you know I hate homework."

"You're not at home, baby girl," Zeus said.

"But it's the same concept—"

"Listen, child." His voice boomed the way it had when he arrived. "This is a modern world. Girls'll enjoy the changes you make, same as boys. I was just talking to the cowboy because he should be old enough to understand. But he's not. He thinks he's in love. And he's friends with the old Fates.''

"Daddy, please. Can we just go home?" Crystal asked.

"Honey, we all do things we don't like. You girls thought this would be fun. Now live with it." Then Zeus's expression looked horrified. "Crap. The Old Ones are right. You always end up sounding just like your own parents."

And then he vanished.

Vivian glanced at Dex, who looked as startled as she felt. Sadie walked to his side and leaned against him as if the entire thing had tired her out.

The Interim Fates burst into tears.

Let's get out of here, Dex sent. *What do you say?*

The sooner the better, Vivian sent back. Ear-splitting wails echoed around her. *The sooner the better.*

Twenty-eight

It was dawn when Vivian and Dex arrived in the backyard. The sun was a big red ball on the horizon, and the light, a gorgeous mixture of orange and yellow, made Dex's garden glow. Vivian was never so happy to see anyplace in her entire life.

"Are we safe now?" she asked.

He nodded. "Eris can't touch us anymore. If Zeus's punishment stands, I doubt she'll ever go free again."

Vivian sighed with relief. She was tired. Dex slipped his arm around her and she leaned against him. Together they walked to the back door.

Sadie was already there, wagging her tail, waiting to get in.

"What about the Fates?" Vivian asked.

"What about them?" Dex said.

"They can go about their business now."

Dex shook his head. "I think we should leave them exactly where they are. I told them this would take a month. Let's make sure it does."

Vivian looked at him, frowning. "Why?" And

then she knew the answer without him saying a word. "Oh, yeah. The kittens."

Dex pulled the back door open. "It's more than that, Viv. They wanted to know what it was like to be helpless. They're safer being helpless in my cave than they are out on the streets of Portland."

"Good point," Vivian said, stepping inside.

"And," Dex said, "maybe by then they'll give up the whole idea of going out into the world and they'll fight to get their job back."

"Especially after we tell them about the Interim Fates."

"Exactly," Dex said.

They stepped into the kitchen. The light filtering inside was as beautiful as it had been in the garden, but here it illuminated dirty dishes and clutter.

"Why don't you clean up your house?" Vivian asked.

"Expectations. It keeps the neighbors thinking I'm a young single man."

"You are," Vivian said.

"But not for much longer." Then Dex looked at her in surprise. "I hope."

Vivian laughed. "That was a proposal?"

"Oh, god," Dex said.

"It didn't sound like a proposal," Vivian said, teasing him. It felt great to have the luxury to tease him. They had survived. Fate's darkest day was over, and they had survived.

Now they could enjoy their great love.

The thought made her smile, so she continued the tease. "That comment sounded like an expectation. Was it an expectation?"

"I didn't mean it to come out that way," Dex said. He was appalled. She could feel it. "I mean, I know how you feel. It's how I feel."

Vivian was having trouble suppressing a smile. Dex was so wrapped up in his own propriety, he